Praise for Pa~~~

Cut By Cut is yet anothe~ ~~~ ~~ ~~~ novels by the prolific and talented Patricia Vaccarino. It draws the reader into a single November day in Seattle: pounding rain, wind, and the things Seattleites think about to get through the dark: money, sex, power, and evolving relationships. Organized the way a film is cut, this is a superbly written, fast-paced story of betrayal and murder, and if you figure out who the murderer is before the ending, you will be the first. This is, literally and figuratively, a "cut" above other thrillers. Vaccarino never disappoints with her fine eye for characters, ear for language and attention to the little details that make it all work!

–John de Graaf, filmmaker and author

Four words describe noted film director Harry Hill – talented, charismatic, powerful, and dead. Brutally murdered alongside his next leading lady, the beautiful, blonde Jewell Cleary, whose hair is now caked in blood around an unrecognizable half-face. **Cut By Cut** is a love letter to author Patricia Vaccarino's adopted home town of Seattle, paired with her insider knowledge of the art and business of filmmaking to conjure up a modern noir crime thriller that grabs you by the throat and won't let go.

–Manny Frishberg, Author of "The Emerald City"

An intricately-plotted mystery where no one's motives are pure. It will keep you guessing right up to the very end.

–Susan Alice Bickford
Edgar Award Nominee: *Dread of Winter*
Left Coast Crime Debut Author Nominee: *A Short Time to Die*

"Cut By Cut is a relentless thriller that demands to be read in a single sitting!"

–Jordan Riefe, Critic and Author

"As a writer of thrillers, I love the action and have a keen eye for that sense of guessing the final twists. I very much enjoyed **Cut By Cut** with its unexpected and intricate plot. A really good novel."

–**Marcella Nardi**, author of the *Marcella Randi mystery series and Joshua and The Brotherhood of the Ark* (Italian: *Joshua e la Confraternita dell'Arca*

The relentless rain on this dark November day in Seattle will leave you chilled to the bone. Superb plot. Masterful storytelling. Vaccarino once again proves that she is an exceptional writer, a cut above the rest.

–**David L. Laing, Author and Artist**

Patricia Vaccarino cuts no slack in Cut By Cut. Is it a whodunit or a who's gonna? A mind-bending film industry murder mystery. Behind the scenes in Seattle, the movie production sequence of events unravels. The scenes are time-stamped in keeping with film industry standards – and to keep readers on their toes. Get the buttered popcorn ready as you sit down to enjoy this book! –

–**Dean Landsman, Author, Digital Strategist**

CUT BY CUT

by Patricia Vaccarino

Modus Operandi Books

Modus Operandi Books • New York

Cover design by Josue Mora

Published 2021 by Modus Operandi Books
www.modusoperandibooks.com

ISBN: 978-1-7365462-2-2
Library of Congress Control Number: 2021919430
Printed in the U.S.

"SMPTE Time Code identifies each frame of videotape because scenes are shot out of sequence. Videotape is made up of scans and there are two scans to every frame. Thirty frames to every second, then it goes up in minutes and hours after that. Time code is just a sort system like a digital file cabinet. It's not real time. It's cutting time."

- **Kenny Kix, Master Film Editor**

ONE

SMPTE TIME CODE 00:02:00:01 Two minutes after midnight on the Thursday one week before Thanksgiving, a haze of grey-blue smoke clings to all four corners of the soundproof editing room. Kenny Kix shakes his head like a shaggy dog to loosen his hair from sticking against his neck. He wears his brown hair down to his waist. His full beard and moustache are unkempt. The collar on his shirt is damp from rain. This is the ideal way for Kenny to work, lots of smoke with two young ladies learning the routine.

Kenny stands, deliberately homing in on two young women who cower like ducks on a frozen pond. At five feet four inches, he's not tall but his energy is scary. Thumping his chest, he yells, "Why are you here?"

He has already interviewed them—he knows what they told him during the interview, and he knows what they said is bullshit.

"Why are you here? I'm asking both of you the same question!" His head trembles with manic energy. "Do I have to ask it again? Why are you here?"

Andy Andrisevic, the blond Russian girl, has a moon-shaped face and is sloe-eyed. Obviously trying to impress him, she slowly nods her head. "Someday, I want to direct."

The other girl, the big one, with cocoa-colored skin, stretches and yawns. Ensley Sharp is beautiful, but she wears too much bright red lipstick and the back of her mouth is crowded with silver.

"Cat got your tongue, missy! You," he says, pointing his finger. "You have not answered me!"

Ensley shrugs. "I'm not sure what I want to do. Direct, probably."

Kenny snaps at her, "Everyone in the world and their mother wants to direct!"

He sits on a stool between the two girls. Andy sits on his left and Ensley is on his right. He swivels on the stool from side to side to make sure he can see their eyes. He repeatedly turns his head, looking at each girl and leers. "Neither one of you is fit to direct. You don't even know how to cut film. And you're just barely competent enough to work with me! Now pay attention to what I say and what I do!"

He extends his arms and waves his hands in front of two video monitors as if he's about to perform a magic trick. Both screens show the same image. Close shot of a hot guy wearing a smile as wide as the Columbia River. Close up, the dude has flawless skin and prize-fetching dimples, messy long blond hair and clear blue eyes.

"The footage sucks," Kenny says. "The director thinks he's good, but he's not!"

Kenny turns away from the monitor and points in Ensley Sharp's face as if he means to poke out her eye. The girl quickly snaps her head back. "The director that made this spot shouldn't be working, but you know what he's got going for himself?!"

Both girls seem to be holding their breath. They do not look at each other, and they do not say anything.

"He's got charm!" Kenny yells. "Mr. fucking charm!"

Kenny reaches for the console and turns a dial. Scenes of the blond guy and a dark-haired woman are zooming forward so fast that their images are spinning, melding together, making one indistinguishable from the other. Everything is a blur. The machine whirs the sound of a nest of rats chewing on utility lines.

"Mr. fucking charm," Kenny says again. "I am so tired of saving his ass in this editing room!"

But fortunately," he says, raising his hand, pointing to himself. "A great editor can make anything work."

He looks at both girls and smiles.

The bar running across the bottom of the screen ticks off Hours: Minutes: Seconds: Frames. SMPTE Time Code.

Swiveling backward away from the monitors, the balled wheels of Kenny's chair squeal along the floor in fits and stops, leaving skid marks.

"Editing suites rarely have windows," Kenny says. "The rooms are kept in the dark. Like gamblers in casinos, people working in editing suites do not have a concept of real time."

"Editing takes intense focus. Life in real time is put on hold," Andy offers enthusiastically.

Ensley looks at Andy and smirks at the way she is sucking up to Kenny Kix. The room buzzes with electrical energy and reeks of plastic-coated wire and metal, the bitter burn from overheating equipment.

Kenny scrunches his head turtle-like and looks up at the girls with intensity. "Now listen..." His voice is megawatt hot, charged and trembling with urgency. "SMPTE Time Code identifies each frame of videotape because scenes are shot out of sequence. Time code isn't put on the tape until the film is actually transferred to videotape. Videotape is made up of scans and there are two scans to every frame. Thirty frames to every second, then it goes up in minutes and hours after that. Time Code is just a sort system, like a digital file cabinet. It's not real time! It's cutting time!"

Banging his hand on the console, Kenny is hyper. "Got that?"

Andy Andrisevic writes a memo to herself on her phone. Her dark eyes can't be seen in the absence of light. Only monochromatic glow emanates from the two monitors.

Kenny yells at her. "You're not texting anybody I hope because when you're with me, you give me your undivided attention!"

Andy blanches but catches her breath. "I'm taking notes. Every little thing you say, so I can study it."

Kenny nods his approval. "Always remember we think in time code."

Ensley looks to Andy then back to Kenny. Talking for the both of them, Andy says. "We know. We've cut on both film and tape."

"In school! You've never made a real film in your life! Don't talk shit to me! Talk shit to me and I'll show your ass to the door and kick it all the way out of here!"

Ensley rolls her eyes as if she wants to say, *Give me a break.*

"What's that for?" Kenny yells. "Don't you know how lucky you are to be here?"

Andy emits a peep, the short circuit of a nervous giggle but catches herself in time so she doesn't appear to be disrespectful. She wants the job.

Kenny swivels in his chair, turning the seat round, but not traveling on the floor. "You wouldn't know 35mm film if it bit you on the ass!" He rocks in his seat like an autistic child, bent on behaving badly.

"Hardly anyone shoots in film anymore," Ensley says. "Who cares about it?"

"Who cares about it?" He yells. He stands and talks right in her face. "Do you even know the difference between an upright Motorola and a flatbed?"

He is close; Ensley can feel his spittle that throws off the scent of bitter tobacco. She rolls her eyes and turns her head away from him. "Honestly, what difference does it make?"

Andy Andrisevic zooms in to score brownie points. "A Motorola is an outdated upright film editing machine. It was replaced by flatbed editing machines, and later by video tape editing processes. Hardly anyone uses an upright or a flatbed anymore."

Kenny looks disgusted. "You're both digital dummies! Digital nightmares!"

He is thinking it isn't likely either lady would ever cut real film for a real movie. "Forget it," he tells them, mumbling to himself. "Just forget it. You're both hopeless."

Ensley's eyes enlarge as though she's spooked. "I can't believe he's talking to us this way."

Kenny scoffs and laughs at her. "You know what you are? You're a waste of life! You should probably get the fuck out of here now while you have a chance."

The lack of expression on Ensley's face tells Kenny she is either scared to death or unimpressed, but she does not move to leave.

Her attitude is pissing Kenny off. "You need to be excited about working in the film business," he yells at her.

"I am," she mumbles, giving him big eyes and blinking—her way of saying she wouldn't put up with his tirades if she didn't want the job.

Kenny couldn't see the Russian girl's eyes because she lowers her head, deliberately looking at the parquet floor. Kenny's own eyes are rolling to the back of his head. He takes a long meditational pause and looks up at the curdled cheesecake texture of the ceiling that helps to make the room soundproof. Then he shakes his head as if he is coming to after suffering from a bad concussion.

"Consider this. I've had hundreds of assistants," he brags. "They're as plentiful as sheep. If I lose one, believe me, I'm not gonna go looking and I'm not gonna be grieving. There's always a hundred more to take their place. Everyone wants to work in the film business."

Kenny turns away from the monitor and charges toward Ensley Sharp's face. The girl flinches away from him. He keeps reaching forward and gently tosses a wad of her coarse black hair behind her shoulder. He is trying to get close to her ear. He speaks confidentially—to Ensley but intentionally loud enough so the Russian girl can hear every word. "Are you sure you want to work for me? I mean are you sure? Really sure?"

Kenny searches each girl's face and laughs. He loves it when he is about to drop a dirty bomb. "I always hire two interns, but only one of you will make the cut."

The girls are so quiet that it is as if they have both stopped breathing. Their faces are blank, totally devoid of emotion. They are waiting for his next wild rant.

"You should probably know that I will only hire one of you." He yells, "One of you!"

He holds one finger in the air. "One job. One assistant. Just one." He picks up his phone and holds it. "Your phone is your lifeline. Check your messages, every five minutes. No one knows the day or the time when the break will come. It will come like a thief in the night and you better be ready. No one gets a second chance." He stops and looks at Ensley. "No matter how pretty they are." Then looking at Andy, he says, "or hot."

He decides to let them sit on that for a while.

TWO

SMPTE TIME CODE 08:01:16:02 One week before Thanksgiving at 8:01 a.m., Mia Hill bolts awake in a state of panic. Something tells her today her husband is going to die. She shivers under a four-inch-ply goose-down quilt. A measure of chills runs the course of her face and body in a sweep of electrical energy. The surge of terror is powerful. Dampness settles in between her breasts and small beads of sweat begin to trickle down her chest. It occurs to her that she could be suffering from fever, but she has previously experienced these same symptoms due to the dream. It is the fifth time she has had this dream and it is beginning to make her crazy.

Opening and shutting her eyes, she sits up in her bed, forcing herself to blink back tears. She can't shake off the violence that is oozing from every pore of her body and seeping from her half-shut eyes that she keeps opening and closing, blinking, wishing everything away, hoping she will see something other than the images in her dream.

Leg to leg, her flesh next to his, she knows he is in bed with her. She is too afraid to look at him—the great film director Harry Hill. The bed reeks of his sweat burning off alcohol with the faint residual odor of beer and stale cigarettes. She feels the warmth of his body coming from his side of their bed. Harry Hill snores the slow uninterrupted wheeze of deep sleep. He is feeling no pain.

In Mia's dream, a blond woman takes shears from the kind of flat, grey box that holds expensive knives. Harry is getting his hair cut. The woman's scissors have shiny silver blades. Mia hates the woman who is cutting her husband's hair. She resembles Harry, tall, a blonde who could easily pass for his twin, unlike Mia with her long limbs, wiry black hair and bronze skin.

Mia knows if she does not pay attention to the passage of time and waits patiently, the dream will fade and go away until she falls asleep and experiences it again. The hazy details of the dream will shear off and float onto the floor like snips of his golden hair.

In the bed, Harry's blond hair, still long, falls across his face like a fan made from old straw. His hair has not been cut. His mouth opens wide, exaggerating his breathing, hard and throaty like an old internal combustion engine.

She slides under the covers and tries to hug his back but stops herself. He told her he had come home late after a long film shoot. She knows he is lying. The film shoot did not happen. During the gap in time between when he went out early in the evening and much later when he crawled into bed, never touching her, he had been with another woman.

Harry had come home close to dawn. She pretended to be asleep when he slid under the covers. Now he stirs in the bed, opening and closing his mouth as if he is trying to rid himself of the bad taste left by the woman with sharp scissors.

"Mia, will you shut the curtains? I need to sleep." He rolls around the bed, turning the quilt into a jumbled heap. "I don't know what's wrong with you," he says. "But if I can't help you, no one can." He groans, pulling the pillow over his head. "You're just insane."

His barbs and tirades occur with such frequency, she expects nothing else of him. She leans in, squirming her body closer to his back. She wants to make this marriage work, and will do anything, even tolerate the humiliation of the strong scent of another woman on his naked body.

He heaves himself away from her in irritation. "Come on, Mia, let me sleep."

She catches the scent of his breath burning off more than alcohol and it's disgusting. She wants to kill him and wants to love him too, and it is such a desperate place for her to be. She still yearns for those short sweet bursts when he is good to her. She wants him to shower her with his love. Maybe he'll change. Maybe he will be the way he once was and fall in love with her all over again. Maybe he was never the way she thought he was, and he was just a pretender to win her love. Some men are like that—they will do anything to make a conquest.

This is what love is, she tells herself. Why do I want him? Back and forth. I don't want him. She cannot control her thoughts. But what about the children? She is a mess and does not know how to fix it.

Mia gets out of bed carefully, crosses the room to the nearest window and partially rolls up the shade. The light outside is murky and hisses of indifference.

November is Seattle's darkest month. The days are short and intensely grey. The temperature stays the same, sustaining, always several notches above freezing at a perfect forty-four degrees with barometric pressure low and sinking. She regards the rain and wind as a curtain of doom that does not possess the temerity to burst from the sky in a sudden squall. Instead, the rain is unrelenting, a permanent and cruel force of nature. For days this city, her city, is suited-up in a steady and persistent steel-grey-drizzle, violently marauding all things from inside and out, living or not, blocking any hope of warmth or light.

She sits on the side of the bed, holding her head in her hands. She wonders why she cannot feel anything. Death would be far better. She wants to cry but tears will not come. It is as if the rain must cry for her.

She turns to see Harry in the bed. He is not dead. She is coming to know something she should not have to know. She is fully awake and yet a separate layer of consciousness

is percolating in the space of her psyche usually reserved
for the passage of dreams.

Even inwardly, she cannot quantify or articulate her
feelings with words. Something is happening to her and she
feels as though she is slowly slipping, losing her mind. What
she is experiencing seems to be unreal, a movie or a dream.

She eyes a small Delft blue pitcher set on a nightstand
that is full of water. For a split second, she considers
dumping it onto his head, a payback for his cruelty. There
are so many times when she wants him to die.

She hears him breathing. It's the shallow breath of
someone who is restless and cannot sleep. The certainty of
his impending death comes back to haunt her.

In the dream she sees Harry's head, or what's left of
his head, which is gone. The floor floods with pools of
blood, rivulets and streams explode into an overflowing
river of blood. There is no gulch waiting for tears or rain.
Harry's head is gone. Mia's hands are covered with blood.
She looks for his head so she can put it back onto his body.
She looks everywhere but the blood has hidden everything,
and she cannot find his head. She rushes to find a fragment
or two, maybe a hunk of flesh, raw sinew and bone. She
refuses to struggle with what cannot be explained. She
fights hard to resist the power of the dream. She feels like
she is falling off the edge of her bed and almost does.

A loud crash against the front door makes her jump.
She does not cry out but feels a fusillade discharging in her
heart.

"What the fuck was that?" Harry yells.

Mia has been on edge for too long and cannot stand
one more shock. She listens intently, waiting for another

crash but it does not come. Harry writhes in the bed, throwing off the quilt. She feels the sheets, damp with his sweat and detects the strength of his sweet odor, growing pungent too, the morning after his all-night binge.

Mia hears a pickup truck outside, speeding away. "It's the newspaper," she says. "He throws it onto the porch and it always hits the screen door. He does that because we never tip him."

Harry doesn't say anything. She knows he doesn't believe in tipping service people. She always thought it was kind and considerate to tip people; it is how she was raised—to show gratitude. It makes people care about doing a better job.

She does not see him looking at her, then she realizes he is, but it is not a look of love or desire. His pupils are enlarged, darkening eyes. It's not that he does not love her. He hates her. His hatred scares her and makes her shrink so small inwardly that the only sensation she feels is a lump in her throat obstructing her ability to swallow. She is a prisoner of both him and the dream.

Wearing the thigh-high black tights she had slept in, she eases into her flip flops and walks along wide planks of the fir floor down the long, skinny hall. She feels older than this house, over a hundred years. Harry used to like to look at her in black tights, but he no longer notices. She thinks she cuts a sexy image to someone—anyone who is not her husband. She has a feeling that someone is looking at her from outside.

Every time she turns her back, she feels the presence of someone watching her. The feeling creeps up on her slowly, a touch as soft as a bug creeping up her back until she shudders, suddenly jerking her body to brush it away. Drawing her arms closer to her body, her shoulders sag and her head drops. She looks out the window, but no one is there. No one is ever there. And it always ends up feeling like a dream. She knows the tension with Harry is so awful that she has become paranoid—of everything, even of her two children who she wants to protect from harm, especially from their father.

She moves quickly past her son Maxie's room, slips into the bathroom and closes the door behind her. She turns on the water full force in the sink and washes her face. She wants to scrub her skin hard to rid herself of the nightmare. She is rubbing her face with a cocoa butter paste as thick as oatmeal to smooth her skin. She dampens a clean white cotton washcloth with water as hot as she can get it and rubs her face hard.

In the dream she has blood on her face. She tells herself it is only a bad dream and she is doing everything to wash away the blood. In the mirror, she sees her face more brown than red, glowing, with a shine coming on. She imagines her face to be too painful to touch. She just craves pain. She needs to feel something. In an odd way, being brutal with herself gives her a modicum of comfort.

She opens the medicine cabinet, pulls out perfunctory toiletries and dabs deodorant under each arm. She sees the single edge razor blade she had once used to scrape old dry paint from around the rim of glass in the bathroom window. The razor blade has been washed many times to remove the blackness left from sterilizing its edge in a flame lit from a match. She takes a dab of alcohol to clean the blade. She makes the edge as shiny as the scissors in her dream. She eyes the blade as if it is an exit strategy.

If she cuts herself, maybe she will be able to feel something. She wants to feel again. She wants to have a range of emotion greater than the large egg of a knot that sits permanently lodged in the back of her throat. The notion of cutting herself takes the edge off of feeling so numb.

She takes the blade and cuts into the skin on her left wrist, just inches away from her radial artery. She knows cutting the artery means bleeding to death and stays away from there.

Her left forearm is her cutting companion and is covered with thin scars, a tan striated pattern, like stripes on the jacket of an old military uniform. Her skin is puffy and ashy but she decides against softening her flesh in the bath. There is no need to open old scars. She's after a fresh cut. She makes a delicate new incision on her wrist that oozes a slender line of blood. All she wants is to show the outward sign of her pain, something real, immediate and tangible, not terrible and faraway, like a movie or the dream.

THREE

SMPTE TIME CODE 15:08:06:03 Exactly one week before Thanksgiving, at precisely eight minutes past three, on a rain-soaked Thursday afternoon, Steve Olin momentarily forgets why he has returned to Jewell Cleary's house. He knows why he is there has something to do with his producer Wendy Wachter, but she has left the scene, shrieking like a banshee. He changes into a dry parka, throwing his sodden coat into the back of the pickup. The lack of light in the sky shares the same dark grey cast as ten in the morning. The rain is coming down so hard he does not want to get out of his pickup truck. As he opens his door, the wind slams it shut. He uses his strength to power the door back open.

Puyallup, Enumclaw, Cle Elum, Wenatchee and Yakima, Steve Olin grew up in the small Washington towns bearing Native American names. A local boy who has broken out, Steve Olin works in the film business as a Grip from New York to L.A. Since landing back in his home state, Steve is on the A list as a Key Grip—first to be called, everyone's favorite. But all he really wants to do is to become a director.

Harry Hill is the only barrier to his ambition.

The image Steve cuts for himself is the kind of guy women like to have around because they find him attractive and vulnerable; they can confide in him. Men like him too, and although he courts the favors of women, he never does anything too uncool about it on the set. Crew dynamics is in all ways a man's game, the last great bastion of traditional comradery, backslapping, wisecracking and roughhousing, akin to construction workers working high in the air on the beams.

He picks up his phone, scanning for texts. The last text is from Harry's producer Wendy Wachter—a single question mark.

Steve finds the whole scene confusing and he isn't thinking clearly. There are too many bizarre schemes to track. He did not know why Harry Hill texted him again after the way he had treated him. Harry Hill is not a nice guy. He is being summoned to bring Harry to the airport. The guy has plenty of money to call for a car. Steve resents being treated like a Production Assistant, a P.A. grunt.

He runs from his car, sloshing through water that is rushing downhill from the driveway. He pulls his hood across his face, rubs his hands together and hops on one foot at a time, trying to stave off the raw chill that is beginning to penetrate beneath his heavy parka. He looks up and feels rain washing over his lashes making his eyesight blurry. Jewell Cleary's ranch style rambler is decidedly respectable—neat, clean and middle-class, totally uncharacteristic for a bohemian film slut. Steve grins at the thought of Jewell the slut and walks into a large metal recycling bin, catching his sleeve on its handle.

Yanking his arm free, he yells out, "No, fuck," as he tears open the Gore-Tex skin of his coat, spewing feathers in the air that are immediately made heavy by the rain and pelt the wet earth. Yelling and cursing, "shit," he stomps over rain-sodden winter cabbage and pansies that edge the waterlogged trim green lawn. Pissed at the hole on his sleeve, he kicks over a planter and spies two brown slugs clinging to rotting wood. He tells himself the damage to his sleeve can be sewn and patched. Maybe he could even convince Jewell to do it for him. She used to be a wardrobe girl and could be pretty darn handy with a sewing machine. But who is he kidding? Jewell Cleary is into directors, not grips.

Between the cowl bulk of his hood and the steady welt of rain, he can hardly see the numbers on the mailbox. He sees Harry Hill's fully-loaded bronze BMW parked behind Jewell's round bubble of a Karmann Ghia.

The eaves protruding from the roof of the rambler are short and do little to shield him from the wind-charged rain. He is getting drenched and can detect the vague scent of wet down drifting up from the gash in his sleeve.

It isn't until he actually reaches the front door that he notices something out of the ordinary. The heavy oak door is open about six inches. He does not want to go inside, but if he doesn't then he will have to deal with Wendy Wachter. Steve prides himself on being brash, but he isn't a total fool. The only thing worse than Harry Hill's anger is the hysterical shriek of his producer, Wendy Wachter. He doesn't bother ringing the doorbell and walks in.

The moment he steps into the hall he hears the steady drum of rain on the roof, cars swashing by on the road and the thrumming hiss of electronics. He thinks it is too quiet for comfort and he wonders if they are *off fucking again.*

Despite the fact Harry Hill is married, he and Jewell have become an item unto themselves. In the halls, on the set, on location, in the editing suites, they'd graze an arm, bump a leg, brush a hip or hand and smile apologetically, as if a grappled touch was merely accidental. They embarrassed everyone, reveling in a sort of high school ecstasy deemed secretive, excessive and thought to be noticed by no one other than themselves.

He raps the wood-paneled wall of the hall with his knuckles. "Hello, anybody home?"

Steve shouts, "Jewell! Harry!"

A puddle of water is on the floor in front of a large copper urn holding two umbrellas. The puddle signals the beginning of a trail of clothing running the length of the hall, growing increasingly lightweight, and more intimate toward the end of the line, which is ultimately marked by a single black snakeskin cowboy boot.

"Jewell," he yells. He listens for the sounds of erotic coupling. He does not find comfort in the sound of his own breath, a pant really, that has grown choppy and irregular from the moment he walked through the front door. His heart is beating hard, not because he is fearful for his safety; he is scared because he knows he is going to piss off Harry Hill by showing up at the worst possible time.

"Hello," he calls. It is a feeble greeting. He is running at a low ebb and leans against the door frame opening into the living room where he sees two large, overstuffed floor pillows, a couple of Starbucks cups, a director's chair frame sans canvas, a gumball machine, a bonsai tree shedding leaves, and a complete set of tough rawhide Ghurka luggage that looks packed and ready to go.

"Hello."

He drives his heavy work boots hard into the floor, making noise on purpose to warn them that he is in the house. "Harry," he yells. "Is anybody here?"

The dining room didn't have furniture except for four chrome clothing racks on wheels. A panoply of clothing and accessories hang from the rods like clutter found in a thrift store: male, female, character and caricature, tossed like liquid over hangers; furs, crowns, sequins, satin, some torn, some stained, some sashed; hats, coverlets and lace; Victorian, contemporary, western, antique, Hollywood, gold and silver metallic dresses shimmer, mounds of fabric are thrown onto the floor, or heaped into boxes; some things reek of mothballs; all of this mess is the byproduct of Jewell Cleary's occupation as a stylist.

"Hey Jewell," Steve yells. He grows bolder and shouts toward the steps leading upstairs. "I ripped my coat on your goddamn dumpster! Would you fix it for me?"

He picks up a generous blond wig from the top of a box and puts it on. "No shit," he says. He is certain Harry and Jewell have done something real dumb, the thing people-in-lust do all the time, like take a long walk in the freezing rain. He has no idea why Wendy Wachter had become hysterical. Everything seems to look the same as the last time he was here.

He begins to dance, warming up and hip grinding the ode to sex he had fantasized about from the moment he spied signs of the clothes shed and dropped on the floor. Unzipping his parka, he sticks out his butt and whirls around the room under the fake mane of blond hair. With femme exaggeration, he juts out his hips, rotating and rocking, pretending to be Jewell Cleary.

Then a funny feeling hits him. He thinks he hears the sound of wind whipping down the hall. His parka is unzipped and his ass feels cold. There is no doubt he is feeling a strong gust of cold air. Cross currents are breezing through the house. Steve listens carefully and is sure the wind is making a slight whistle. Wind, blasts of cold air, the combined effect makes Steve think two doors are open instead of one. And if a second door is open, it has to be located toward the back of the house.

He feels cold and very alert. Opening and closing his fists, his whole body tenses as he considers the possibility of violence, his second favorite topic after sex. The rise and peak of Steve's emotional register always rally together and meets at the same point. He thinks sex, even sex cradled in love, is ultimately a violent act and the adrenaline pump of feel-no-pain violence, no matter how heinous or wrong, is seductive. But if Jewell Cleary's back door is open, now that is really weird and definite cause for alarm.

He flings the blond wig onto the floor and zips up his parka. He looks around, over his shoulder for shadows and movement. An intruder could be present. A routine burglar might be equipped with nothing more dangerous than a crowbar. *And that's okay*, he tells himself. *I can handle that.*

Steve could not bring himself to believe a more significant weapon could render him powerless. He thinks about what he will do and braces himself for impact. He moves lightly, taking a succession of soft steps. His eyes squint, struggling to clear his vision of the shapeless clot of grey permeating the interior of the house.

As he walks, the air is colder and numbing. He hears a noise, distinctly like electronic equipment. A TV is on, set on pause or stop, tuned into nothing. White noise freaks him out. He can't wait to find the source so he can turn it off. He follows the static and a trail of silver-thin shadows. The shadows remain stable, never moving, and simply provide evidence of walls and furniture, rebounding from a monitor emitting a steady rush of white light.

There is no other form of light, not from windows or from the coved ceiling. Arriving at the back room of the house, he finds the source of extreme cold. The double-pane, sliding glass door is wide open, sucking up wallowing folds of drapery into the steel-driven-rain with the force of a vacuum. A whorl of paper flies around the room, making strange flapping sounds. Steve runs to the door and pulls it shut. At that instant, the paper loses the inertia of wind and floats to the floor, startling Steve with the overwhelming viscosity of blood.

He quickly reviews a rough cut of very shocking images. He sees bone fragments, a hunk of flesh, a piece of skull clinging to blond hair and a blood-soaked body slumped on a chair. The lifeless torso is missing a large chunk of his head and most definitely a man who had been nude at the time of impact given the frontal exposure of his genitalia. Steve emits a chilling sob, piercing his own ears.

He is running, clumsily twisting one way, then another. Jutting forth all of his limbs does not stop his feet from sticking to the floor. Skidding in puddles of red liquid, he feels warmth splash upward onto his ankles. He wretches violently, trying to expel the sick horror. He is wading through blood still warm from life. The blood on the floor is slowing him down. Using his arms as leverage, moving in a mock swim to keep from slipping, he scrambles past a wide screen TV monitor, headsets and electronic gear. He can only see the sharp contrast between the white screen in a grey-lit room and red splatter everywhere.

His mouth and nose are flooded with the overpowering scent that reeks like rust shaved from metal. Reeling and gagging from the smell of fresh blood, he feels like vomiting. His skid loses footing and becomes a clumsy grind. Shimmying along the blood-laden floor, he lands in a slide precisely between the horrible room and the kitchen floor where a second pool of blood and gore, completely recharges his horror. The naked body of Jewell Cleary is lying on the floor. Half of her head is blown away. Her face is an unrecognizable pulp. She is only identifiable to Steve by her remarkably long blond hair, which is presently clotted off to one side of her shoulder.

Steve screams repeatedly, "Oh my God." He wrenches himself up from the floor and continues his frenzied rearrangement of the chaotic pattern of blood.

In his optimum moment of horror, Steve does not consider checking to see if Jewell Cleary and Harry Hill are dead. It is hard to describe them as resembling human beings anyone would recognize. Even in his extreme disorientation, he knows there is no hope. "Blood, the blood." These are the only words Steve could bring himself to say for a long time.

It is not a good time for heroics. Not thinking clearly, he runs in chaotic circles in and out of the kitchen. Only a few paces away from Jewell Cleary, he notices her one arm is outstretched away from her body as if she meant to hail a cab. Her hand is clutching silver scissors.

He did not pull out his phone to call anyone or to take a photo. He flees from the house through the same front door that had first provided him with an inkling of sex or violence—his two favorite subjects. He runs into the street, screaming for help. He sees his bloody feet, and the blood beginning to mix with the rain, dissolving to the color of water tainted by rust. He does not know what to say to the police when they arrive. More importantly, he does not

know who should be told of Harry Hill's death first: his
wife or his producer.

FOUR

SMPTE TIME CODE 16:30:09:<u>04</u> At 4:30 on Thursday
afternoon, Harry Hill's producer is stuck in traffic. The
wind and rain smash with equal force against the
windshield of Wendy Wachter's light gold Mercedes sports
coupe. Although the car stands temporarily stalled, Wendy
does not beep her horn. More than anything, she is intent
on keeping her cool. If she loses control, even for the brief
duration of a 10-second lift from the average 30-second
spot, she will lose it all. Her whole life has been dedicated
to the behind-the-scenes orchestration of television
commercials.

Never the person in front of the camera, Wendy is the
person people clamor to see behind closed doors in the
protective nest of her office, where her casual smile
extinguishes the need for a contract. GASP Productions
has won sixty-three Clio Awards during her time as
executive producer and manager of the company. Three of
the company's commercials have aired during the Super
Bowl. But making Harry Hill a star has been her greatest
triumph.

She slips down in the leather seat of her car, trying to
appear invisible. If this scene was being framed by a
director's finder—the eyepiece often used by directors on

the set to frame a scene—no one would find her. She feels that small and powerless.

Her one hand is on the steering wheel, the other pins her cell phone to her left ear. She knows she should not be talking on a phone unless it is hands-free, but technology makes her crazy, and she does not know how to set it up! Despite her inner hysteria, the tone of her voice is deliberately well modulated.

"Why hasn't Sollie come back yet?" she asks Yolanda.

Yolanda staffs the front desk at GASP, the hottest and busiest commercial production house north of Los Angeles. Although the girl is off-camera, her response on the phone is the beginning of a long whining apology. "Sorry, Wendy, I can't seem to get through to Sollie. The only person who seems to have seen him is Mia Hill..."

Then the call drops.

"Fucking Sollie," she sobs repeatedly, calling out his name.

She wants Sollie Berg much more than she wants any other man, including her current husband. Both she and Sollie have been previously married to so many people that it is as if—between the two of them—they had married the entire world.

She does not know where she is going and pulls to the side of the road, where she puts the car in park and leaves the windshield wipers on in a brutal drone. She lowers her head to the steering wheel and starts to cry. She has to get through to Sollie. She has to make him understand that she is capable of building a stable of bankable directors. She is no longer at the mercy of Harry Hill.

Without looking, she moves back into the traffic. Another car swerves around her, narrowly escaping collision. She hears a metal crunch, a bang and a dull thud. Then she sees a blur of blue. The vehicle is larger than her car. She is sure she has been sideswiped and hears the other car's horn, a startling and terrible long wail. But the vehicle does not stop. Through her fogged-up windshield, she sees a blue pickup truck driving fast to get away. Whoever is in the truck could care less about getting a ding or a dent. She's the one with the expensive car.

She is terrified of losing everything she has gained. She toys with the opera-length strand of pink pearls around her neck. Worry beads. Her husband, Ray, had given her the pearls. With a glint in his eye, Ray had said the pearls were as translucent and as pure as tears. Then he kissed her. His mouth was as open and as expectant as a largemouth bass. But that was months ago. Now his lips stay closed tight like a sealed drum.

After twelve years of running GASP, she's jinxed. She is the racehorse Seattle Slew. Even after she jumps through hoops and wins the triple crown, no one says she deserves it. They call her a conniving bitch. They say she doesn't have any talent. They say her success is due to the benevolence of Harry Hill. They—everyone in the film business—are wrong. It is Wendy Wachter who has made Harry Hill a star.

Fallen star, she snickers, not knowing whether to laugh or cry.

She tries calling Sollie Berg again, but the call does not go through. Dead air throbs in her ear like the deafening silence that comes after a shotgun blast.

She is adept at putting things together—deals and phone calls. She thinks she stands a chance with Sollie Berg. No matter how many women Sollie has taken into his life, there is always room for one more.

Wendy remembers feeling his breath traveling along her neck. "Oh, that neck," he had told her on two separate occasions. He fingered the curve along the nape of her neck and whispered into her ear, *My little girl*.

She has to convince Sollie that GASP Productions will not only survive without Harry Hill but flourish.

Even if Harry Hill hadn't... She chills at the thought because "it didn't happen" she whispers. Her hands hold the steering wheel in a death grip. She knows she is in shock, yet she also knows the truth. Harry Hill is dead.

She throws her phone on the passenger seat and rubs her ear because it feels sore and hot. Looking in the rearview mirror, she sees the red mark on her ear that resembles a mosquito bite. In contrast to her reddened ear, her face is starchy white, taking on the claylike-pinched appearance of a death mask.

She needs to wash her hands to preclude the possibility of the faintest trace of blood. Two people are dead. She suddenly realizes not only did she not know where she is going, but she could not recall exactly where she had been.

She has lost all concept of time.

Driving recklessly in the rain, changing lanes and wedging in between other cars, she brakes, then speeds up, darting into a narrow space between two other cars moving cautiously on the slick road. A black SUV cuts her off, causing her to slam on the brakes. Lurching her car forward, she speeds into an oncoming lane of traffic quickly enough to go around the BMW. Horns blare. She is neither fazed by the horns nor dazed by the blare of oncoming headlights.

Her hands are sweaty and shaking. She holds onto the steering wheel so hard that her knuckles hurt. The lump in her throat is like a tumor large enough to obstruct her breath. Her heart is pounding loudly and she imagines that her heart has been cut from her chest and is stashed on the seat beside her. The life-blood of her long career as a producer is draining away with as much trauma as a mortal skull blown away by a shell from a twelve-gauge shotgun.

"He deserved to die," she yells.

She knows no one can hear her.

FIVE

SMPTE TIME CODE 08:28:16:05 Mia has been awake for less than thirty minutes and has already made her first cut of the day. She feels compelled to cut her wrist twice, but she remembers she has not checked in on Chloe. The little girl struggles to fall asleep at night and always sleeps best in the morning. Mia yearns for her touch and wants to rub her face in her hair. Maybe that will quell her demons. She does not want to infect her little girl with her madness.

She looks out the window and sees a dark blue pickup truck, the same one she has seen before and thinks it belongs to the newspaper delivery man, who is making

another stop. She expects to hear a distant crash or a thud
hitting the ground. She should run away with the
newspaper man. She imagines going to her front lawn,
waving him down and jumping into his blue pickup truck.
Riding in the passenger seat, she rolls down the truck's
window and tosses rolled-up newspapers onto front
porches. He will take her out of here, away from this mess.

Leaning her head against the bathroom door, she
listens to the sounds of the house. The clock radio goes off
in the bedroom, blaring static, local news and hard rock, all
at once. The dial was obviously set in between stations.
One of the kids must have played with the radio and tuned
away from NPR.

"What the fuck!" Harry yells. "I've had enough!"

Mia hears the news on the radio: *A magnitude 3.2
earthquake struck near the town of Snoqualmie at 3:38 a.m. The
earthquake was 4.46 miles away from Fall City, Washington, and
24.61 miles from Seattle, according to the Pacific Northwest Seismic
Network.*

Mia remembers the mirrored bedroom doors
trembling in their metal tracks and perfume bottles rattling
in a glass tray on her dresser. It had only lasted a few
seconds. She had felt the small quake, not knowing for sure
if it was real or part of her dream. She did know Harry still
had not come home.

The news report ends abruptly with a crash, much
louder than the newspaper hitting the screen door. Mia
does not know for sure but suspects Harry has thrown the
clock radio onto their bedroom floor. She presses her
hands up to her mouth and stifles a small sob, but it only
lasts for a moment. She is used to Harry. A crazy little part

of herself wants to cry, but crying is not possible. There is never any relief from him. He could have hit the snooze button. Instead, he breaks the radio.

Maxie's bedroom shares a wall with the bathroom. Even with the bathroom door shut, Mia can hear her son's laughter, but his laughter is not coming from his bedroom. She hears the low, almost inaudible hum of the TV drifting upward from the first floor of the house. Max is watching TV, babysitting himself until Viv has finished making breakfast. It is how he entertains himself when his mother is gone, which is all of the time. Mia is never there even when she is physically present.

She has lost her mind.

Thinking about Maxie makes Mia cross her arms across her breasts to hold them up and to shield them from his prying eyes. After nursing two babies she is not as proud of them as she once was, but that is not the reason why she covers them. She is hiding her breasts from her son. Maxie is six, the age when little boys are in love with their mothers. Mia's nudity makes him uncomfortable and he giggles. He says the sight of her breasts makes him feel funny.

Maxie is okay, Mia tells herself. She wants to believe he is watching an older rerun of Mr. Rogers but given the frequency and pitch of cranked-up voices, she thinks he is watching a jarring succession of weirdly disturbing images. While she brushes her teeth, she looks out the small bathroom window again and notices the blue pickup truck is gone. She has lost her chance to make a clean getaway with the newspaper delivery man.

She slumps down to the floor. Leaning her head
against the door, she is no longer listening to the sounds of
the house. She is quite still, paralyzed by some unbidden
part of herself. Despair is too light a word to describe what
she is feeling. To an outsider, she could appear to be
depressed, but depression is a clinical condition that does
not describe the depth of how badly she feels. She does not
know if her paralysis is a form of self-protection, or if she is
totally broken as a human being.

Max bangs on the door, wanting to know when Mia is
going to come downstairs for breakfast. Mia is still stuck on
the notion of the relief she finds in a single razor blade and
calls to Max without bothering to open the door. "Do me a
favor, Maxie, go back downstairs and turn off the TV. Start
getting your clothes on for school."

"Can't fool me, Mom. I saw your boobs." Maxie
shouts to her through the bathroom door.

She puts on her robe, opens the bathroom door and
looks at her son. "Breasts," she corrects him.

Max's skin is as white and as unblemished as Harry's,
but his coarse hair is tightly cropped and glistens like a
black helmet. She forgets about the razor blade and speaks
softly, almost whispering, "Not so loud, Maxie, your dad's
sleeping."

"I saw your boobs," Max shrieks, laughing. "They
look stupid and big."

"Please keep it down," Mia says. "You'll wake your
dad. Please go downstairs and turn off the TV."

The little boy answers her with a mischievous knock-
knock against the bathroom door.

"I'm going to count to ten. Ready or not, here I go," Mia says firmly. "One, two, three..."

"Okay!" Max shouts. "You're the meanest Mom in the whole wide world!"

"Never mind about that," Mia says. "Are you going to do what I asked?"

"Okay, already," Max yells. "I'm going!"

Mia congratulates herself. The counting routine always works. She has never gotten to ten. There are some things you can always trust, she tells herself, and the thought of that brings tears to her eyes.

Viv calls up to Mia from the bottom of the staircase. "I'll have coffee for you when you're ready." Viv's hands are on her hips. Her hair is prim and as unapologetically grey as the mid-November Seattle sky. Viv wears a navy canvas apron, which is too small for her. Covered with white cut-out stars, the apron belongs to Mia, but she had always used it to paint watercolors, not to cook.

The two women make sharp eye contact that lingers long enough to be an unspoken conversation. Mia sees concern in Viv's eyes, and can't be sure if it is compassion or if the woman pities her. As the old woman smiles, Mia detects her sincerity. Viv Reinking doesn't have a cruel streak or an ulterior motive; she's not out to get her. Mia might have lost her mind, but she can still spot genuine kindness.

Eventually, Viv's smile slips away. Mia can't be sure of what the woman is thinking and decides it is best to leave. She walks back into the bathroom and catches herself smiling in the mirror above the sink. One minute, she's scared to death, another moment she's thinking about cutting her flesh. *Now I'm smiling.* She nods in the mirror as if she is seeing a mirage of her former self—a beautiful dark woman with gleaming white teeth.

"You can't trust dreams," she tells the mirror. "If I look happy will that mean I didn't have the dream?"

She knows what she's saying is crazy. She looks back at her reflection in the mirror and sees her eyes, red and rimmed with old mascara. She dips a Q-tip into a small vial of hemp seed oil and dabs under her eyes. She knows she's a mess and is trying to pull herself together. She vows to be strong for the kids.

Mia thinks Harry is oblivious to her whereabouts and the shouts of their son until she swings open the bathroom door. Harry stands at the other end of the hall. His hands are hidden in the pockets of his plush white terry cloth robe. "Are you going to get the kids to school or do I have to?"

She is not sure why she suddenly thinks of him as Harold Cobb Hill instead of just Harry, the man she fell in love with. Harold Cobb Hill is the rich white boy with a trust fund, who could have had any woman he wanted. He picked Mia, making her the luckiest woman alive. Now he rides her like a horse he wants to break.

He could have done anything in life that he wanted to do. He wanted to become a film director. Everyone calls him *Harry Hill.* And his chosen path has been made easy for him. Money always makes a difference, opening doors that are otherwise shut.

Mia does not understand why he looks angry, very much a wild man. His long blond hair has fallen out of its elastic band. His voice rasps from too many cigarettes.

"You never let me sleep," he tells her. "You always say you'll let me sleep in, then you never do. Thanks a lot!"

He stomps back into the bedroom and slams the door hard enough to crack wood. The sound makes Mia wince.

She picks up Chloe's *bah bah bear* from the hall floor and walks into her daughter's room. The little girl is up, looking unusually alert, and smiles at her mother. Mia presses the bear into her hands.

"*Bah bah*, how are you?" the child asks.

Cradling the worn bear, the child moves to the edge of her bed. Her right thumb is stuck in her mouth. Her large eyes are aimed at her mother so intensely it is as if she cannot see anything else. Mia reaches down and strokes the top of her daughter's head. Her hair is a mass of blond corkscrew curls. Chloe does not move. She continues to suck her thumb as if she is deep in thought. Mia touches her tawny cheeks, first one then the other. She swoops the child into her arms and hugs her. The warmth of the child's body heals her and restores her sanity but only for the duration of time that she holds her.

"I love you," she tells the little girl.

Chloe pulls her thumb out of her mouth, making the distinctive sound of a wet pop. "Preschool, Mommy?"

"Yes, darling," Mia tells her. "I'm going to take you to preschool."

"Are you and Daddy getting *a 'vorce*?" Chloe asks her. "Maxie says it's a *'vorce*."

"Don't worry," Mia whispers to the little girl. "Everything will be okay. Remember what's in your heart."

Chloe shakes her head and leans her face into Mia's shoulder. "Love you, love you forever," she says in a voice muffled by the fabric of Mia's bathrobe.

Harry walks by them with the heaviness and pace of a cantering horse, tensing his shoulders, hunkering his head low, looking away from Mia and Chloe and toward his feet. His long legs are exposed in the robe and his feet are bare.

"Daddy," Chloe says brightly.

Harry gives Chloe a quick stab of a smile. Grabbing onto the handrail, he continues to look at his feet while he stomps down the steps. Mia presses her hand to her mouth as if she means to say something but decides not to. Any words will invite his cruelty.

"What's wrong with Daddy?" Chloe asks. "He looks mad. I don't like that."

Nothing," Mia says. She smooths the hair on her daughter's head. "It's nothing. Everything is okay," she says. She knows her voice is unsteady.

She hears Viv talking to Harry. His voice is growing louder, but Viv sounds calm. Mia is afraid that if Harry does not leave Viv alone, the woman will leave.

Then Mia will have no one.

Mia tries to suppress the vivid imagery of scissors and blood in her chilling dream, but reality slips away and settles like a hard knot turning to stone in her stomach. Her skin feels burned and she cringes at the thought of being touched. She owns a heart that bleeds too much. She swears everything happening in the last ten minutes is part of the dream too. The dream is plaguing her. She stops herself from believing. She cannot deal with what is happening. She throws her face into her daughter's blond curls. The dream is too disturbing, violent, and irrational. Dreams don't mean a thing and rarely come true.

SIX

SMPTE TIME CODE 11:06:18:<u>06</u> Before noon on Thursday, one week before Thanksgiving, Wendy Wachter's husband Ray saunters into the lobby of his Advertising Agency. The grand old brick building in Seattle's historic Pioneer Square district has large leaded glass windows looking out to downtown and the Puget Sound. Each inner office has French doors opening onto a terrace. In the six dry-hot weeks of summer, from August to mid-September, business meetings are often held outdoors. But now the long rainy season has set in. Ray stares out the window and mourns for a sun that no longer seems to exist.

He immediately zeros in on Christy. Leaning against the reception desk, he mumbles, "Hello Beautiful," and cocks his cell phone to his ear even though there is no one on the other end.

Without looking up, Christy knows it is Ray Wachter. He calls all women beautiful even if they are not. He knows it makes them feel good because they always seem grateful and smile.

"You're looking particularly fetching today," he tells Christy. She is wearing a bone-colored cable knit sweater that accentuates her thick waist and large breasts. Her super-straight long brown hair stretches halfway down her back and parts too far on the left side of her head.

Ray doesn't like the look of her hair, which is plastered to her head, making it look like a comb-over covering baldness. He swears she only washes her hair once a week and does nothing to style it. His own hair feels slick from gel, wet from the rain, and he hopes it doesn't look as greasy as Christy's.

Christy gives him a pleasant nod and checks her watch. Ray has known her long enough to detect that she is being polite. She knows she is not beautiful, but she is grateful to have a job managing the lives of some very cool people. Not bad for a girl who grew up on a small llama ranch in Kalispell, Montana. She came to Seattle seeking fame and fortune, opportunity.

For Christy, the cool factor has worn off. Most of her work is dull and no one has given her ample opportunity to learn new skills so she can grow. She knows she can get a better job somewhere else.

"I'd like to talk to you privately when you have a chance," she tells Ray.

Ray nods absentmindedly and says, "uh-huh," acting as if he is distracted by his cell phone. He knows what's coming. She has been here for eighteen months—the cutoff for doing the same old work for low pay. Sometimes it takes two years. Once he had a front desk girl who lasted for four years, but she was exceptionally lacking in ambition and loved it when Ray called her beautiful.

Christy wants more money, but he does not have it, and even if he did, he would just as soon get rid of her and hire someone new.

The girl looks at him like she thinks he is being lazy. "Harry Hill's already here with Jewell," she tells him. She is letting her boss know in a nice way that he is late for his meeting. Leaning forward, she whispers, "Harry Hill keeps bugging me, wanting to know where you are. I think he's in a bad mood."

"Didn't you tell them that I was on my way?"

Christy blushes and nods her head. "Of course, I did. That's my job."

Ray searches the girl's face. He sees that her forehead is pinched into a tight row of wrinkles well beyond her age. Ray gives her a quick smile that means *thanks, but no thanks and I guess you needed to tell me that but so what?*

The girl immediately busies herself with her cell phone. Ray thinks she is mildly put off, but he could care less about her feelings. Soon she would be out of here, like everyone else who had ever sat at her desk. There was nowhere for her to move, up, down, or laterally, except out the front door.

With his raincoat flapping open like a heavy royal cloak, Ray charges down the hall. His mouth is dry, his palms feel clammy, and his temples throb. He has nothing to offer Harry Hill, who he'd love to kill just for the fun of it.

But Jewell Cleary is something else. He wants to touch the skin on the small of her back in the place an inch or two below where her hair did not reach.

He zooms past two crystal pyramid sculptures sitting on the posts canting both sides of the marble staircase. The crystals are of the same ruby color, both sharing the same properties of clarity and good energy. His hand sweeps over carbuncle glaze with ritualistic taps and pats, as he bounds up the steps leading to the conference room. He needs as much good energy as he can get in the November gloom.

He considers Jewell Cleary again. He knows he does not have her figured out. Last night they both had too much to drink. From the hall, he hears Harry Hill's voice louder than anything else. The guy has a big mouth.

The moment he walks into the conference room, he smells fresh coffee, wet leather and hair gel. The first thing he sees is a flash of Jewell's blond hair. She gives him a little wave of recognition accompanied by a smile. Jewell is being overly cute.

That's okay, Ray tells himself. *I can be cute too.* He sees the television is on and tuned in to the noon news. Ray knows the commercial interruptions blare soap products, household cleaners, make-up, food, disposable diapers and panty liners for the incontinent. The noon hour slot is dedicated to young mothers with small children, and old women at home, or shut-ins in nursing homes. Most old women live on fixed incomes without much disposable income. And anyone who does not buy does not exist.

Harry Hill rocks back in his chair, laughing at Dawn Stein. Ray is stunned by Dawn's presence and does not mask his feelings well. Dawn is a line producer who is hired when a job has been given the green light. Ray is deeply embarrassed and dreads telling them the job has been cancelled.

Harry Hill shakes his head, closes his eyes and raises his voice. "What took you so long getting here?" Then he gives him a disgusted look. "You're wasting my time, Ray!"

Jewell is uninterested, checking messages on her phone, tossing her head, flipping her hair, using her long fingers as a comb.

Ray stands at the head of the table. His hands span the surface of shiny black alabaster, leaving ghostly traces from his sweaty palms. Ray loves the table, but Harry Hill is an albatross and he'd like to wring his neck.

"Something wrong?" Dawn asks Ray.

"Why are you here?"

Dawn pushes back her baseball cap, revealing thatches of hair—a brown shag razor cut. "Harry asked me to be here." She pulls the cap forward, almost covering her thin eyebrows. Ray stares at her. The woman never wears make-up, except her brows are always penciled-in.

"How about those Mariners?" Ray is being a smartass and Dawn knows it.

"They're not playing now," Dawn tells him. She's being sarcastic.

Ray wants to get rid of Harry Hill as much as he wants to get rid of the agency. The agency is dying—these days advertising is about algorithms, not good creative. Ray doesn't even know what algorithms are and does not want to know. He can barely understand numbers well enough to balance his checkbook. In the new world of advertising, only a few creatives get to make the cut, but Ray Wachter's agency is not among them.

Ray does not look at Harry as he slides into his seat at the conference table. The smell of wet leather is growing stronger and it is coming from Harry Hill.

In all of this time, Ray still hasn't said a word to Harry, a snub that is noticed by all. Ray reaches over to

Jewell who is sitting to his right, grabs her by the waist, pulls her toward him, and gives her a flat kiss on the cheek.

"I can't breathe," Jewell complains.

"Who needs air when you have me?" Ray teases her. As much as he hates to do it, just to be fair, he leans toward his other side and kisses Dawn Stein too, almost knocking off her baseball cap. "I see your hair," he tells her. "You really ought to go to a different salon to get a better haircut."

Harry Hill puts his feet up on the table and smiles, a move that makes Ray seethe. Harry gives Ray the once over but does not say anything. The room settles into a quiet buzz of padding keys, scratching pens, crunching coffee cups, dashes of electronic TV noise and pings from incoming text messages.

Harry Hill has the bullishness to put everyone on hold like a freeze-frame in a 30-second spot. The sports section of *The Seattle Times* lies open on his lap but he is not reading. He hates to read because he has dyslexia. He thinks that one small fact makes him a great film director. Jewell moves in from behind Harry and plays with his long blond tail, making it into a sort of loose braid. It soothes Hill but it bothers Ray.

The news Ray delivers is not pretty. He tells them the two extra *haircut spots* have been put on hold and are likely to be cancelled altogether.

"It was supposed to be three," says Hill, holding up his three fingers.

"That's why we kept the production cost down," Ray acknowledges. "It was supposed to be a package deal."

"They lied," Harry says.

Everyone lies," Dawn offers.

Ray's voice gets louder. "Who asked you?"

Dawn purses her lips together, almost biting her tongue. "Everyone's entitled to their own reality," she says sweetly.

"That's bullshit," Hill yells. "There's only one reality."

"A director's reality," Dawn demurs.

"It's my circle take." Hill smiles.

Ray sees the splendor of Jewell's hair and a straight shot to the glass doors leading outside to the rain-drenched terrace. He feels instantly depressed. There has to be a way to shake himself free. The rain is coming down harder than it had been in the morning and the day before. Water rushes from heavy aluminum gutters and washes over the surface of the deck. Slick and wet, the deck looks slippery and dangerous, but Ray gets up and opens the door anyway. A rush of cold wet air blowing up from the Puget Sound floods the room.

Ray steps away from the door and slams it shut. "What's wrong with everyone? This place is like a morgue!"

"Do I look like I'm dead?" Hill shoots back. He springs from his seat and places one leg up on the chair. His pant leg draws up, revealing the bunched shin of his cowboy boot that had been covered by his long brown leather coat.

Ray laughs. "When you're dead, you'll look pretty darn good laid out in that coat."

"Oh, don't say that," Dawn implores. "What has gotten into you, Ray? Why are you being so contentious."

Ray helps himself to a cup of coffee and stirs it belligerently. "In fact, if you ask me, this whole goddamn room smells like a sacred cow." He sniffs the air that inevitably leads to Hill's place at the table. "I wonder where it's coming from."

Jewell shakes her head in disapproval and checks her phone.

"Lunch?" Ray asks.

Hill doesn't bother to raise his voice. "Why don't you go out and buy your own lunch?"

"Some other time?" Ray asks.

Harry frowns at him, then laughs. He turns to Jewell and nods *let's go*.

Jewell throws her arms around Ray and hugs him in a tight, playful embrace. "I love you, Ray."

"Love you too, beautiful," Ray says. "Most beautiful," he whispers.

She is indeed the most beautiful. Her long blond hair flows away from her face in free waves that yearn to be touched. Ray thinks Jewell uses her hair the way other people use words or their hands, as a way to communicate ideas and express emotion. He has not figured out the color of her eyes. Last night they glowed in front of the fire.

Her body is luscious but lean, curving in all of the right places. The only extra fat lies in her breasts poking out from her sweater like furry beasts that demand to be stroked. Ray ponders them and grins to himself. He knows the secret of Jewell's breasts.

Ray draws her to his own body. More than anything he is aware of her scent, soft and clean like soap, far from overpowering and definitely not squelched by the falseness of perfume. Last night comes back to him again.

"You shouldn't have let those two other spots get away!" Hill yells.

"You should have told us before today," Dawn says. "We turned down other jobs."

Hill looks at Ray. "You fucked up."

Ray acts angry, but he is faking it. He knows the backstory that Harry Hill does not know. By screwing Harry Hill out of the two extra haircut spots, both he and Sollie Berg stand to make more money.

He watches Jewell breezily find a place to stand behind Harry. Her two hands come up and wrap around the base of his neck. She presses her fingers, bearing down hard into Harry's smooth flesh. She turns to look at Ray as her hair falls forward to the side of her face and stays there, making it look as though the other half of her face is gone. Blown away at close range. From what little he can see of her eyes tells him nothing.

SEVEN

SMPTE TIME CODE 16:20:56:07 After four on Thursday afternoon, Steve Olin leans his head against the window inside a police van. He thinks murder is the most public way a person can die. He wouldn't wish it on anyone, not even Harry Hill. He cannot believe what he has seen with his own eyes. He has repeated the details several times to the police. He can hardly breathe in the stifling heat of the van and feels sweat trickling under his arms, down his chest and off the back of his neck. He thinks he stinks from the terrible sweat that comes from fear, but he doesn't dare unzip his parka.

If only they would let him leave the scene, but they won't. They will not even let him use his phone. He could kick himself for calling the police first instead of calling the crew who desperately need to be told the director isn't going to make it.

He does not attempt to open the van door for air. He knows from past experience that the door cannot be opened from inside. Nor did he have the luxury of being able to roll down the window. The cop in the driver's seat is a woman who seems to be cold and keeps the heat on high. In the rearview mirror, she keeps an eye on Steve, but didn't ask him any questions.

The interrogation is reserved for a detective by the name of Mulcahy, who is wearing a face mask, sitting next to Steve in the backseat. This guy is so tall that his knees buckle into the front seat. Steve tells him everything he can remember. Who he is, his brief record (he was busted for possession of fentanyl in 2008), and his reason for being at Jewell Cleary's house.

People are waiting for Steve who had no way of knowing Harry Hill is dead. "Can I go now?" he pleads. "I've told you everything that I know."

Mulcahy tilts his head to peer directly into Steve's eyes as if he is intent on trying to figure out why something is bothering him. "I'm not finished talking to you, son," he says. "There are other things I have to ask. I have to go slow. I appreciate your patience."

"I'm in an awkward position," Steve tells him. "There is a whole crew waiting to meet up with Harry Hill. We're supposed to be leaving town to go on a shoot. They have no way of knowing…"

The woman cop in front turns around in her seat. "Bad news has a way of traveling fast." Her words are muffled through her face mask but Steve gets the point.

He resents the cops, especially Mulcahy. He didn't even know the woman cop's name. Maybe she had said it, but he did not remember.

Mulcahy looks frankly unsympathetic. "We'll be done soon and then you can go." He stares at Steve as if he intends to make him feel uncomfortable. "I'd like to know about the fentanyl charge, son."

Steve feels himself taking a deep breath but it's due to the lack of air, not because he's scared of the cop. "There's nothing to tell. I was never a user. My mother was and I covered for her."

"We know how your mother died," the woman cop says.

"Your father too," Mulcahy adds.

"That was a long time ago," Steve says. "And I really don't want to talk about them. Do you mind?"

"You don't have to," Mulcahy reassures him. He looks at Steve as if he intends to pat him on the knee. "I'm sorry."

"Me too," Steve says. He knows the cops don't care. They're just doing their job. He feels bad about what happened to his parents. No one will let him forget where he came from. Small towns. Both parents dead. Drug dealer mother. Abusive junkie father. Taking the sleeve of his parka, he rubs humidity away from the window, creating a temporary porthole so he can see what is going on outside.

Jewell's house is more brightly lit than any other tucked-in the neat neighborhood row. Every window shows the sizable form and movement of cops and forensic-looking guys. Steve didn't know, maybe they were EMTs. He snickers to himself. What did they think they're going to do in there, save a life? Steve figures the guys in suits must be detectives.

The crime is still too recent for reporters to show up. Police cars are crammed into the driveway and parked on both sides of the street. The fire engine that had responded to the initial alarm, paving the way for two medic units, is now pulling out and going home. The huge red and chrome truck judders down the slick road without sounding an alarm or flashing its lights. Its big wheels cut through water pooling on the road in an infernal roar of engine.

Steve hears the sound of aircraft hovering overhead, holding a tight pattern. As with all other things in his life, the choppy propulsion of engines and blades reminds him of a great sound bite—the prime avenger of murder. He had seen the violence and could still smell their blood. The scene in front of Jewell Cleary's house resembles a war zone in a great film.

"Do you like the business you're in?" Mulcahy asks softly.

Steve moves in his seat and groans. He simultaneously loves and hates the fascination non-film-people express when they find out what he does for a living.

"Next thing, you'll ask me is if I want to direct."

"Do you?" The cop asks.

"Everyone wants to direct," Steve shot back. He looks at the cop and smiles. "There are a bunch of people waiting for me. Can I at least use my phone and call them?"

Mulcahy smiles and nods. "I'll let you know as soon as we get through to Mrs. Hill."

She has to be told. It's our protocol," the woman cop says. "It wouldn't be right if she heard it from someone else first."

"I feel bad for her," Steve says.

"Think she killed him?" Mulcahy asks.

Steve grimaces. He doesn't know what to say. "I don't see her that way."

"Harry Hill wasn't alone, Mulcahy says. "What do you think about Jewell Cleary?" The tone of Mulcahy's voice sharpens. "Did you have a thing for her?"

"Girls like her don't go for grips, believe me. They're into directors."

Mulcahy drawls as if he's talking to himself. "From what I could see, she had an awful lot of blond hair."

"I don't like blondes," Steve shoots back. I prefer women with dark hair. Black."

Mulcahy nudges Steve in his arm. "So, did you have a thing for her?"

"Look," Steve says. "Jewell's one of those girls who thinks the whole world owes her something just because she's pretty. I worked with her, that's all."

Steve hates the way the cop smells, a combination of wet raincoat and old spice deodorant. "Now can I go?"

Mulcahy shakes his square-shaped head. With his big old hound dog jaw jutting forth in the dark, he resembles

Frankenstein. And Steve feels like he is his bride. No matter what he tells the big cop, it never seems to be enough.

Mulcahy lurches sideways in his cramped seat, trying to pry his long legs into a more comfortable position and lowers his large head like a crane closer to Steve's face. "Okay this guy's married and he's with another woman. Someone kills them both. It doesn't look like robbery. It doesn't look like drugs. What does it look like to you?"

Steve pulls his face away from Mulcahy so fast that he inadvertently bangs the back of his head against the top rim of the metal bucket seat. The vehicle was not designed for comfort. "Hey, I don't know. I mean it could have been some agency guy who didn't like his last spot."

"Very funny," the cop says.

Steve keeps his face at a profile and away from the cop. "I don't know who would blow them away like that. It's sick if you ask me."

"When you saw them lying there like that, what did you think? Who do you think would murder them?"

Steve shakes his head and tries to mutter something but can't at first because he's shocked that the cop would ask him such a thing. "I didn't think. I tried to get the hell out of there as fast as I could."

He walks the cops through the murder scene again, beginning with his arrival at the front door of Jewell Cleary's house. Mulcahy stops him and asks if he touched anything aside from the front door, a few walls and a blond fall wig. Shifting his feet along the cramped floor of the car, Steve realizes the legs of his pants are wet. In the charcoal light, he sees his cuffs stained with blood. Repeating the images of the murder scene renews the odor of blood in his nostrils.

"I'd like nothing more than to go home and take a long hot shower."

Mulcahy is not finished though. "Did Hill have any enemies? Were there ever any death threats? Recent fights?"

Steve moves uncomfortably in his seat and looks Mulcahy straight in the eye. "If you really want to know the truth, there were fights every day with his wife, his producer, his clients and his crew. Harry Hill is, or I should say was, a liar, a cheat and a bully, a shmuck." Looking out the window and nodding toward the house, he says, "Yes sir, a lot of people would have liked to kill Harry Hill."

EIGHT

SMPTE TIME CODE 17:03:44:<u>08</u> After Harry Hill is murdered, on that same Thursday at exactly three minutes after five, the fans of Susan Kauffman are trickling into *Dietro Le Quinte*. Called *Dietro's* by the regulars, the restaurant is owned by Susan Kauffman, a very large woman, who is always visible by the front door. She plants herself on a stool next to the hostess podium so she can see who is coming and going.

As the sky turns from grey to coal black, business in the restaurant is booming. Located close to the Pike Place Market on First Avenue, Dietro's is full of tourists, downtown businesspeople, and regulars from the film industry. Film people tend to cluster at the same place—their preferred flavor of the week—until they find a cooler watering hole.

Susan Kauffman is neither Italian nor glamorous, but none of that manages to dampen her love affair with food or film.

She feels a tingling sensation and her hands shake a little. She is so excited that she launches her huge body into a high-energy shtick. This is her nightly routine and people have come to expect it of her. No one passes by her without getting mothered to death.

Moving into the surge of wet raincoats, she launches her double chin directly into the face of Ray Wachter. He is perched on a stool at the bar wearing a black raincoat. He is the only person at the bar who is drinking something other than beer or wine. His bear-like body hunches over a snifter of Barrell Bourbon, going down fast and smooth. Already he looks like he needs to have another one.

Susan thinks Ray is fabulously successful, and he is also not bad to look at, especially when he smiles at her the way he is smiling now.

She can tell his coat is wet. "Come on, hon," she says pulling on his belt, "Take it off and give it to me."

"For you, Susan, I'd do anything." He gets up to take off his coat. Susan recognizes a Tom Ford coat when she sees one. Nestling close to him, she pulls the coat into her fleshy arms. "God, that's wet. How'd you get so wet? Is it raining out there or what? Here, I'll take it for you and hang it up. You don't want to wrinkle a coat like this."

She motions to a spikey-green-haired waitress and hands her Ray's coat. "Put it in my office, won't you, doll? Put it on a hanger behind the door. No special treatment. Not for this guy. Never! Don't tell anyone, but this guy is my favorite."

Spikey Green Hair gives Ray a captivating smile big enough to show her tongue piercing.

"Hi, Honey," he says to her. He picks up his small, wire-framed glasses off the bar and puts them on. He notices the waitress's nose ring and smiles. He likes girls who are tattooed and pierced. Only most of these girls want nothing to do with an old Ad guy like him. She jostles him as she makes her way through the narrow space between where he is sitting and Susan.

"Make sure you lock the office door, hon," she tells the waitress. "Wouldn't want no one to steal your coat," she whispers to Ray.

Susan notices Ray's eyes look bloodshot. He's giving off some very bad energy. "Oh God," she sighs. "What's the matter with you, you look like you've just killed somebody." She hugs him, hoping it will ward off his demons, but she feels him stiffen. That won't stop Susan. Her whole body comes alive, vibrating, jiggling flesh. Her fingers creep around to the front of his chest as if she is feeling-him-up.

"Will you go out with me?" Ray motions to the bartender for another bourbon.

She slaps him playfully on his ashen cheek. "That's the drink talking. Don't you think I know that?"

"I mean it, will you go out with me?" In a strange way, Ray really does want Susan. He feels scared and searches her face. "I feel like I'm losing everything."

"You just need a break." Susan laughs. "Go on vacation." She hugs him, feeling the steel-rod tension in his back. "And please take me with you. I'll go with you anywhere."

In proportion to the size of his face, Ray's overly large mouth makes him look very sensual as if he's perpetually leering.

Susan rubs his back, noticing his shirt is more than damp but wet. "You smell good," she says. "What did you? Just take a shower or something? What's that cologne you're wearing?"

"That feels good." Ray groans with pleasure. "Don't stop. All I did was order a drink and I get this too. Such a deal."

"Relax, Sweetie," she says, massaging his shoulders. "Pretend I'm that new stylist, you know the one with the long blond hair." Susan places her hand on her own buttocks to show him. "Down to here." She sways her hips.

Ray wants to wretch at the thought of Jewell Cleary, but he can't help but be fixated on Susan's buttocks quivering in a low squat. He likes asses but never in his life has he seen one this big.

Susan's voice gets husky. "You want that blonde so bad. You want her in the worst way.

"Stop it." Ray turns serious. "Wendy will find out and I'll never hear the end of it." Ray reaches for his bourbon and takes a long sip. He looks serious all of a sudden. "We're not doing all that great as it is."

Susan whispers, "I'm sorry to hear that."

"Me too. But what can I do?" He shrugs.

"You know what? She's too skinny anyway. Never liked women that skinny. They don't eat. You can't trust people who don't eat."

They both know the conversation is getting too personal and turn away from one another. Dietro's is filling up. The after-work suit crowd steams into place ordering beer on tap. This bar section of the restaurant is chrome and steel, with splotches of framed dark art on the walls. Light radiates from a barrage of cell phones bouncing off small dark tables and bar stools, and from the flat-black stone floor.

Everyone except Ray and Susan have their faces stuck in their phones. The motors of two espresso machines rumble, drowning the crush of voices and the clink of glasses. There is an onslaught of boys and girls wearing skinny jeans and black, thick-soled work boots. Some girls wear flat shoes with pointy tips that look sharp enough to cut.

Holding her cell phone out like a dagger, Dawn Stein hammers her way through the crowd, looking frantic. "Look who's coming," Susan says. "Dawn Stein forever the line producer."

Ray laughs. "Dawn Stein, the hardest working woman in show business."

Dawn stands in front of Ray and Susan. "Have you seen Steve Olin?" Dawn smiles but only briefly. "Steve Olin?" she asks again.

"Heard you the first time," Susan says. "No, I haven't seen him, Sweetie."

"Great," Dawn says. "I don't know why I bother to hire him. He's always late."

"Because he's got a great butt," Susan reminds her. "A great butt will take you far in life. Trust me, I know." She winks at Ray.

Dawn looks as though she is in pain. Wearing shorts, red-laced shiny red Nike running shoes, and a Seattle Mariners' baseball cap, Dawn could pass for being in her twenties. Susan knows the youthful image is window dressing. Pushing fifty, Dawn is serious, all nuts and bolts, a whirlwind master of organization.

"Where the hell is Steve?" Dawn fumes. "We're supposed to meet here and go to the airport in the same car."

Susan puts her hand on Dawn's arm. "God, you make me nervous, you're strung so tight this business is going to kill you, or else you're going to kill someone."

"It's going to kill all of us." Ray slips his arm around Spikey Green Hair's waist as she sets a new snifter in front of him. Susan nods at the girl to leave, but she waits for him to take his last sip before removing his empty glass. Dawn stabs Ray with her elbow, leaving no room for interpretation. Ray drops his arm away from the girl's back and grins.

Susan presses her cheek to Ray's face. "You're two-timing me already."

Ray kisses her cheek. She heaves her body off the stool away from him and launches into a shtick for his benefit.

Susan roars, "Do you want to see big boobs?" She latches her hands around her own breasts, mighty they are, and lobs them up and down with formidable undulation. "How do you like these babies," she says. "I didn't have to buy them. They're all mine. Check this out." She hitches her hands around the bend of her butt sticking-out like an enormous shelf going wiggle-waggle. "This is mine too. There's not a trace of silicone in this body. Ain't it spectacular?"

People are hooting for Susan, whistling too.

"You ought to be a star, Susan," Dawn burbles from her stool.

"I am a star," Susan says.

Susan spies Koji Matsuno heading toward the bar, which immediately puts the skids on her mood and her move toward superstardom. She knows Koji has a reputation for being a great gaffer, but he gives her the chills. No matter what Susan says, Koji never laughs. When she touches him in the same endearing way that she reaches out to everyone, he recoils in silence.

Koji makes his way to Dawn and nods hello.

Susan zooms in to startle him. "Hi," she yells in his face.

Koji pulls away from Susan and nods to Dawn. "Traffic's pretty bad." He pulls out a vape, instantly taking a hit, puffing hard, watching vapor curl over his head.

Dawn grimaces to herself and checks her watch. "Where's Steve?"

Koji shrugs. "Want me to call him?"

"Don't bother," Dawn says. "I've tried."

Susan squeezes Dawn's shoulder. "Don't worry, hon, he'll show up. Doesn't he always?"

Koji Matsuno gulps water. He's taking up space at her bar, not paying for anything, and it pisses off Susan. "He always takes my water, and never buys anything, and he's got that vape, even though there's no smoking allowed," she complains to Dawn. "He thinks I run this place for free."

Ray gives Dawn a lingering smile that is due to the effects of bourbon, not mutual respect.

"Have you seen Steve Olin?" Dawn asks him.

"No, I haven't, doll face," Ray says, getting up. "I'll need my coat," he tells Susan.

"Take it easy, won't you, hon," Susan takes his hands into her own. "Always remember I love you and I believe in you." She bellies up against his back until he leaves.

Her eyes follow Ray through the crowd toward the front door, where he stops to talk to Spikey Green Hair. Susan likes the waitress but doesn't get the green hair. Ray takes his coat and gives the waitress a ten-buck tip.

The ad guy gets under Susan's skin. She can't stop herself from gossiping about him. "There goes an extremely unhappy person," she says to Dawn. "Look at him. Always driving to land new accounts, he's never satisfied by the ones he scores. He's never happy with anything."

Susan sees the waitress helping Ray with his coat and calls to him, offering him encouragement. "Look at Harry Hill! If he can make the big time, so can you!"

Ray stops dead by the front door. He turns around and stares at Susan. He looks like he has been hit by the explosion of a shell, a blast from a shotgun. Blood is draining from his face, mottling in patches of white and red until he is completely pale. He is shaking, beside himself with anger. A fit of pure rage. There is no mistaking what his eyes are saying. He is telling Susan to *fuck off*. Susan does not know what has gotten into him. She has never seen him this angry, and it scares her. "Oh God, I'm sorry," Susan yells to him. I didn't mean nothing. I've just got a big mouth, that's all." Ray's face begins to soften into a grin. He seems to be recovering. He shrugs and gives her the thumbs-up.

NINE

SMPTE TIME CODE 00:30:03:<u>09</u> At 12:30 a.m. on Thursday, Kenny Kix is loving the way his voice sounds in the editing room. "The dude might not be a good director, but he is exceptionally good at fucking." Kenny is very aware it is him alone, working closely between two attractive ladies. He crosses his arms over his heart in a deliberate embrace of his own body and allows his hands to drop to his crotch, lingering there.

He looks at the girls as if he's asking a normal question. "Did you know that some guys are good at fucking and most are not?"

Ensley Sharp turns away as if she is summoning strength to put up with him. Kenny smiles; he has successfully shut her down. He knows she's nervous and he likes that quality about her. It keeps her on her toes.

"That director," Kenny says, pointing the door. "I happen to know he is very good at fucking."

"I'm not freaked." Ensley shrugs. "If they want to fight in public—that's their problem. I don't know what's going on with him." She nods toward the closed door—the only door in and out of the editing suite.

"The director and that agency guy...the blonde left with him."

"No, I didn't know. Never let their personal shit interfere with cutting." Kenny puts a cigarette in his mouth and lets it dangle from his lips. He looks at the big girl. "So, he went off with the blonde, huh?" Kenny is incredulous. "You mean to tell me that the agency dude took off with the director's bitch? They actually left together?"

Ensley nods, whispering, "She was pretty upset. He was really angry. He was yelling. They were both yelling."

"Never let personal business interfere with the film business!" Kenny barks at her. "That's their business, not yours. I'm the one who gets to freak about stuff, not you."

"Right," Ensley says. She does not seem convinced.

The door opens, letting in a fragmented slant of dingy light. Immediately, Kenny sits straight on his stool and stops talking.

Even the girl turns to look.

"Check it out," Kenny says, affably. "It's just the little chick."

Andy Andrisevic stands in the door frame. "Am I missing something?" She looks surprised. "Where did everyone go?"

"Shut that door and park your butt down. Come here," Kenny tells her. He holds open his hand.

The girl walks over to him calmly and hands him a twin pack of Camels, dollars and some change. Her blond hair is wet, turning into ringlets.

Kenny shoves the money into the pocket of his jeans. His voice is gravelly. "What took you so long?"

With his teeth, he rips open the plastic wrapped around the Camels. "I only asked you to buy one. In case something happens to me and I can't smoke, I don't want to be stuck with two packs. You never know when I might quit."

Andy Andrisevic looks confused. "It was on sale."

Kenny watches the Russian girl while she pulls her own pack of cigarettes out of her purse, some kind of ladies' brand.

"You're just in time," Kenny exhales a long stream of smoke. "I'm just about to make the first cut."

The Russian girl flicks her damp hair behind her ears. "Where did the director go?"

"He went ballistic," the big girl offers.

"Forget it," Kenny snaps. "You're interrupting my train of thought."

The girls look at one another as if to say: *Who is this jerk?* The exchange doesn't escape Kenny, in fact it pisses him off. They just don't get it. They keep acting like it is them against him. When are they going to figure that it is one against one, a catfight? Only one would have the privilege and honor of getting the job.

Dialing the knob forward, Kenny studies the image on the slave monitor. Before he knows it, he is reaching to hit the edit entry key. His hands feel naked without a cigarette, but he is moving too fast to take a drag. Rocking in his seat, he freezes the shot on the fifteenth frame. His eyes pierce the monitor so precisely it is as if he can make a cut with his mind and not have to touch the deck.

"The dude is about to get his hair cut. The soft stubble on his chin looks about five days old. The hair on his face is balanced visually by the wild tangle of blond hair sprawling down his back. This dude is lean, not an inch of fat on his bod. This is a guy who has been corn fed his whole life by the stuff that makes cattle get big. Overall, he makes a statement of unchecked virility. His look is fresh, strong, but not too threatening. The guy could be good or bad, there is no way to tell. Whether he's good or bad, doesn't matter because he's the husband of the dark chick and the blond chick's lover."

Kenny rolls forward on his stool, draws his eyebrows upward, an expression that he knows makes him look quirky and lets his tongue roll sloppily on a retake of the word *lover.*

"Go on. Check it out," Kenny says.

"The actor's real cute," Andy says.

"Cute?" Without looking, Kenny reaches across her lap for his pack of Camels and a yellow cigarette lighter. "Who's cute? Him? Actors aren't anything."

He lights another cigarette and takes a long drag, squinting his eyes at the frame of the blond dude on the video monitor. "Actors rather disgust me. They're just Actors," he growls. "All the world's a stage, but only if I am the one who is creating the stage," he says in a mocking tone. "To an actor, I am God. I can make him look good or make him look like an asshole."

Andy knows he is making fun of her. Ensley Sharp scrunches up her face and sniffs as if she is having an allergic reaction to Kenny's unfiltered cigarettes.

Kenny loves smoking almost as much as he loves editing. "What's cute mean? Am I missing something? Girl, you and I are going to have to speak the same language if we're going to work together."

Doing her best to be jovial, "You know what I mean," Andy tells him. She's gotten this far and intends to stay the course until she gets the job.

"No, I don't understand what you're saying," Kenny says. "Really I don't." He looks at her to let her know he is serious and this is important. "You are not getting it."

"I mean," Andy stammers. "The guy is hot."

"Now hot I understand." Kenny grimaces at the video screen through the haze of his cigarette. "I know what hot means."

He bangs his hand hard on the console, making both girls jump. "Hot, I know," he says, taking a deep drag. "Oh, don't I know hot!"

He takes a long look at the guy in the frame and unloads a billowing plume of smoke into the dark room. "Who's hot? Do you mean me or the dude in the spot?"

"Both." Andy Andrisevic smiles at Kenny and giggles. "I mean both."

"You're both hot." Ensley agrees as if it is an obligatory gesture.

Kenny knows they are both bullshitting him, but he enjoys it anyway. In his estimation, it is Ensley who is better looking with her big hair and red lips, but Andy has got spark. Ensley always looks bored, pained, something, and

Kenny does not like that. She towers over Kenny when she's standing. But right now, she's sitting. He begins to look at her, staring her down, until she looks away. He likes big girls and tries to let Ensley know that. When he's with a big girl, it gives him even greater presence. He could not understand why Ensley was letting the blonde steal all the thunder. Maybe big girls are dumb.

Come to think of it, he had married three dumb big ones, one right after the other. All three of his ex-wives had been assistants. No one else would put up with the hours or the abuse.

He crooks his finger to draw attention to the two video monitors. "Of these two monitors one is called the master, the other the slave." He winks. "I also call the slave monitor *the intern*. Get the picture?"

Of course they knew the difference between the two editing machines. He is being an asshole on purpose. Andy clears her throat and reaches for a cigarette. Kenny pulls the pack out from under her hand and pats the cellophane wrapper with affection. Andy's hand freezes in the position of her attempted reach. Kenny deliberately lets his grasp relax. Slowly he takes a cigarette out of the pack and hands it to her. She draws it to her mouth and nods her head. Kenny moves to light it for her. The first flick of the butane lighter sparks but does not catch fire. He watches the other girl, the big one. She is according him the attention and respect befitting who he is—a Master Editor.

Ultimately the lighter pops a weak flame, illuminating Ensley Sharp's eyes. Big dumb girls have big eyes.

Andy looks over his shoulder to study the monitor. She is so close to Kenny, he can smell her scent: paper, flowers and rubbing alcohol, all rolled into one. She smells like a perfume sample stuck in a magazine. Ensley has the biggest scowl of disapproval he has ever seen, except maybe for his last wife. Seriously, Kenny has to think about it for a while to understand why Ensley is looking so sour. It might be because Andy is blowing smoke too close to Ensley's face. The big ones might be dumb, but the little ones are nasty.

He gives each girl the same type of side-eye glance that is intended to be in sync with the spot they are cutting. Kenny's lighter is failing him. He needs a new one. In a little while, he will send Andy to fetch one at the nearest 7-ELEVEN —the only store open after midnight. Then he will be left alone with the big one. Small metallic clicks from the flatbed are barely audible in the stillness of the room. This is a quiet room. A cutting room. A holy room. The place where movies get made. The first cut is always the best.

TEN

SMPTE TIME CODE 00:20:07:<u>10</u> Although it is Wednesday night, technically it's twenty minutes after midnight on Thursday. Later today Harry Hill will be murdered. Ray Wachter is enthralled with Jewell Cleary. Her teeth are chattering, and her eyes look hazy as if she is tearful and has trouble focusing. She is suffering from a deep chill that has penetrated the marrow of her bones. Ray is feeling the same way, chilled from the rain. He moves closer to her. She backs up a bit and smiles. Ray doesn't know what the smile means. He is giving Jewell every opportunity to ask him to leave.

Their entrance into her house has been awkward. He wants to turn around, bow out, not bothering to try anything foolish. He knows he shouldn't be in this position as much as he knows he has no choice but to be here. He has to find out if she wants him the way he wants her.

They had left the edit session before midnight. After her spat with Harry Hill, he offers to drive her home because it's so late. As they approach the front door to Jewell's house, Ray looks at his watch. It's a cue to give her an out. But she does not do anything to suggest he should leave. Ray takes her hand. She accepts his hand and smiles at him. Her eyes lose their watery glaze and turn dark, wicked.

He places both of his bear-like arms around her skinny waist, drawing her close to his barrel chest, holding her. Before he kisses her, she breaks the embrace. He withdraws, letting his arms fall to his side, giving her some space. She flits away from him like a firefly yearning for freedom from a sealed glass jar. But it doesn't matter. He has already taken ground. He is in her house because he wants to fuck her.

He paces the room while he watches her. Even indoors, he can hear the heavy drone of the rain pounding on the roof. The living room floor is a muddle of papers and electronic video gear lodged close to a USB hard drive. He is careful not to step on bankers' boxes holding dozens of cassettes and microcassettes—old videotapes. Neat piles of DVDs and USB flash drives fill two shoeboxes that are set on the coffee table. The table is also littered with file folders, invoices and receipts.

"Old television commercials," she tells him. "I'm converting everything to digital."

Ray nods and smiles. The room is indeed a graveyard for old television commercials. He picks up an old Betamax cassette from the coffee table and examines it for a title but doesn't find one. "You don't look old enough to have worked with this format."

"I'm working on a project for Harry."

The mention of Harry Hill brings up a touch of rancor for Ray.

"Have a seat. Make yourself comfortable." She gestures, inviting him to sit low to the ground on an overstuffed floor pillow.

Noisily she blows her nose. "I have problems with my sinuses."

Ray thinks she's charming, beguilingly so. "What's the project for?"

"You'll have to ask Harry. Even though it was my idea, I don't think he wants anyone to know—that's why we were fighting."

He sees her crumple the moist tissue and stick it in her pocket. She wrinkles her nose, patting it with the back of her hand. She really is human, after all. He smiles uneasily at her.

"Don't tell me then… but I think you're going to make a film about the history of television commercials. A very short film," he says, laughing.

Jewell nods. "Sort of."

"It's been done."

"Not by Harry Hill."

He walks over to her and touches her arm. She doesn't back away. He can deal with Jewell as a real woman. It is the overblown image, the fantasy, that he has trouble with. Ever since he met Jewell, the very thought of her reduces him to a quivering mess. He feels like a twelve-year-old boy who is experiencing his first hard-on.

"Seriously, make yourself comfortable and relax."

She leaves and goes into the kitchen. A service counter, with a window portal that can open or close, connects the living room and dining nook to the kitchen. Ray sees into the kitchen but does not see Jewell. If he had the gift of foresight, he would see her standing in the same spot in the kitchen where much later today, she will be found dead. In less than fourteen hours, she will be a corpse, with blood-soaked hair, and missing a large chunk of her face.

He feels as though someone is watching him and it puts him on edge. He looks around but no one is there. Her windows are not covered with shades or curtains. The view outside is only of darkness. Beads of water and condensation congeal into cloud-shapes of fog on the glass. Looking into the night is a total blackout, an abyss into the steady cold rain. He wonders if someone can see in.

Jewell is worth watching.

He thinks the layout of her home is odd. The living room and dining room appear to be one large space that is joined to the kitchen. There is hardly any furniture. The dining area is stuffed with clothing racks and boxes of clothes, like a stall in a flea market.

From the kitchen, she calls to him. "Would you turn on the fireplace?"

Ray hears the sound of running water and something else, like the crisp unzip of Velcro. Maybe she's taking off her clothes, he chuckles to himself. He hears the rolling sound of a plastic dispenser and the rip of a paper towel.

He hears her blowing her nose again. Water in the kitchen is running full force. He flicks a wall switch to the left of the gas-powered fireplace, but nothing happens. He pulls open the wrought-iron grill beneath the hearth to see what is going on. Flames suddenly erupt, making the sound of a small explosion, shooting forth close to his face. Startled, he jumps away. Maybe it's an overreaction but he is on edge.

Jewell laughs at him because he has been caught unaware. She carries a bottle of Jack Daniels and two crystal rock glasses. "When you turn on the fireplace, there's a delay before the fire ignites. I should have warned you."

She sits on the floor next to him and smiles. "The fireplace is sort of like my relationships with men. They always take a while to start up, but once they do, they explode into raging fire."

He sees that she has removed her vest, her sweater and God knows what else. She is wearing only a lightweight tank top. He notices she is not wearing a bra. Her nipples look sharp, like they could cut his mouth and make him bleed.

"This will teach Harry Hill to be an asshole with me." Jewell laughs. "Why is he like that with everyone?"

"Do you love him?" Ray asks.

Jewell laughs again. The way she laughs is both musical and affectionate, yet as unsettling as the disquiet of a past dream.

He is starting to have second thoughts about what he is doing. He thinks he should leave her sitting there alone in front of the fire. Beautiful, no, most beautiful, Jewell sitting in front of the fire, alone and free. It is a nice image to hold onto.

Jewell drapes an afghan blanket around her lovely body, leaving her feet bare. Throwing a length of the blanket over one shoulder, she looks like an Amazon warrior. No, Goddess, Ray thinks to himself, Jewell is a Goddess, who has bewitched him, rendering him powerless.

Her hair hangs loose and wild, with damp fronds curling up, cupping under where her breasts lie hidden under the blanket. Whatever resistance he has been holding onto, crumbles when she hands him the bottle. He knows once he loosens up, he will not be able to hold back. He'll talk too much, say foolish things, and tell her exactly the way he feels about her. She stares at him, giving him a hint, and glances at the two empty glasses she holds in her hands. She nods for him to pour the bourbon.

He pours two generous shots, finding himself oddly at a loss for words. Instantly a funny feeling hits him, like who is being seduced here, him or her?

She moves her floor pillow closer to Ray and sits beside him, hugging the afghan blanket close to her body. Light from the fire plays havoc with her hair. Rich in dazzling gold, lemon and auburn highlights, her hair takes on all of the hues of the sun. Ray does not know how there could be so much light from only one source. He helps himself to more bourbon, while he watches her. Jewell is beginning to warm up. The afghan slips away from her shoulder with the pronounced drape of a loose shawl. Her shoulder is bare except for the black strap of her tank top.

"Aren't you going to drink up?" he quietly asks.

She presses the glass to the edge of her lips and smiles. She holds it there for a time before taking a small sip. Ray removes his damp shoes and leaves them on the slate hearth to dry. He takes off his jacket and flings it over the backside of the chair. Then he unknots his tie, loosening it, and lets it slip to the floor.

Her hand dredges through the debris on her coffee table. Even amid the mess, she seems to know where everything is. She brushes a manila folder off of the table and watches Ray's reaction as he quickly scans a pile of alluring photos—swimsuit models.

Watching him flip through the photos, Jewell grins. He settles for a *comp card* of a very pretty blonde in a photo montage of poses and vignettes, showing the range of types the model could play. The blonde is wearing a suit and glasses, another pic on the comp card casts her in riding boots and equestrian regalia. The biggest pic of the model is of her on the beach, glistening with oil. Her long legs are lightly crusted with sand, like a breaded fish filet.

Ray thumbs the pic of the blonde. "Who is she?"

"One of my girlfriends." Jewell laughs. "Is that Melandra?"

Ray flips the comp card onto its backside to see her vitals: 37-23-35. "Melandra," he reads. "Nice name. Exotic."

"Yes," Jewell says, downing the last of her bourbon. "She looks great in pics, but in person..." she holds her glass out to Ray, expecting him to pour. "In person, she looks like white bread that's been toasting too long in the sun. That's why you always have to look at these girls in a casting session, so you know what you're getting."

Ray splashes more bourbon into her glass and smiles. "I know what I'm getting."

Jewell tosses her hair, letting the afghan slip. "When we're casting, Harry always wants the girls' comp cards in his hands so he can make notes."

She waves her arm around the room as if she is performing a cinematic magic trick. "That's why I'm converting all of this stuff to digital. I'm the producer on this project."

Ray wonders where that leaves his wife. After all, it is Wendy Wachter who is Harry Hill's producer, but he doesn't think now is the time to bring it up.

"Look, Harry Hill is very old-fashioned!" There is a hint of contempt in her voice. "Look at the ancient house he lives in!"

She takes a deep breath then smiles as if she is protecting a secret that she does not want to share with him. "I've met Harry's wife, Mia. Even though she is *different*, I like her."

"*Different*." Ray acknowledges the unspoken.

"Harry likes any woman who suits his whims." Jewell grabs the comp cards from Ray's hand and spreads them across the top of the table, like she is dealing a deck of cards. Blondes, brunettes, brown-haired, redheads in every shade of skin and body type. It's so important to see them in person, so you know what you're getting because they all lie. About their age. Their height and weight. Everyone lies."

She looks at Ray for his reaction, but he is listening to Jewell on the octave of a half-note while looking at the comp cards. It is too much trouble to get into a philosophical discussion when all he wants to do is to fuck her.

Jewell points to a pic Ray is examining. "She's nice, but her kneecaps are too big. See how they poke out."

Ray scoffs. "Who cares about kneecaps when a girl looks like that?"

"For some things, a girl has to be perfect."

Jewell tilts her head as if she wants to show the best side of her face. "Look at this one. Nice long legs but look closer. No thighs. No calves. You can't have her walk on in a bathing suit. This girl's been starving herself."

"Anorexia?"

"Yes," Jewell drawls, swilling her bourbon around in her glass. She slips the comp cards back into the folder and runs her hands through her hair in a dreamy sweep.

Ray opens the folder and returns the comp card of Melandra. "Aren't her breasts a little too big?"

"You mean she's sagging," Jewell says. She nods toward the bottle.

Ray sloppily pours her more bourbon. A few drops of the dark amber liquor splatter onto the manila folder. "Don't drink too much." He laughs.

"Oh, I'm not feeling a thing." She smears the bourbon and licks her fingers.

She looks at him and smiles. "Melandra. Big tits. The reason she sags is because she doesn't have implants." Laughing, she looks down into her glass. Her hair is falling forward, covering one side of her face. She turns her head and peers at him from the side of her eye.

"No, don't move your head."

She turns slightly. "Is that what you want?" Her lips part slightly and then contract into a provocative pout.

"Hold it," he says.

Jewell breaks the pose and stares at him. "You sound just like Harry. He's always telling me how I look in different light. Sometimes, I think he's going to pull out a light meter and take a reading."

Ray feels put off by the reference to Harry Hill. "It's your hair. You should see it in this light."

She stares sullenly into her glass before taking a swig. She doesn't say anything as her eyes zone out in the direction of the fire.

Ray picks up the comp card of Melandra. "How do you know she didn't get her breasts done?"

She throws off the afghan and fingers the rising crest above her own breast. "See this. It's high. There's almost a cushiony ridge above the breastbone, like a pillow." She giggles. "Too much plump above the pecs. It's a dead giveaway."

She caresses her own breasts, watching Ray to see his reaction. He looks stunned and sober, speechless.

Jewell isn't slurring but she speaks slowly in an effort to pronounce her words deliberately. "Natural breasts slope down much lower, even when a girl's young. We've gotten so used to seeing breasts all pumped up, everyone's forgotten what the real thing looks like."

Ray kids her. "How come you know so much?"

"We might as well get this over and done with," she snaps.

"I was just joking. Swear." Ray holds his hand up in a pledge.

"Would you like to see my breasts?"

She sets her glass on the table, dispersing small beads of bourbon, then lifts her tank top over her head and arches her breasts forward. "You really can't tell. The best implants are inserted under the muscle."

Ray knows only one thing. He is staring at perfect tits.

"Go on, touch me. Feel me."

She's drunk, Ray thinks. He knows his mouth is open wide because he can feel air coming into his lungs and it is not through his nose.

"Go on." She dares him but does not wait for him. Reaching for his hand, she guides him to her breast.

His squeeze is less than vigorous and tentative because he cannot believe what is happening. This has to be the most unusual *entré* into foreplay he has ever experienced.

"I'm soft." She is wanting him to agree. "Aren't I?"

Ray nods and does not remove his hand from her breast. He shrugs off his glasses so quickly, they could have broken. The glasses might have landed on the table with all her other stuff. He doesn't know, doesn't look, and doesn't care. When he grips her breasts, he sees they are a pair, symmetrical and perfect. She giggles softly, moving her hand over his chest and down to unlatch his belt buckle.

He isn't sure if he is breathing, but he is relieved to detect cold air on his mouth—that is how he knows he is alive and that what is happening is not a dream. His lips cross over her lips in an incoherent jumble of their mouths coming together. The only other thing he feels are her nipples, sharp enough to cut his chest.

ELEVEN

SMPTE TIME CODE: 05:21:16:11 Nearly 5:30 on Thursday morning, Wendy Wachter peers into the face of her black and gold Movado wristwatch. She did not need the peal of an alarm to wake up. She has been awake for most of the night, listening to the harsh Sturm and Drang of incessant rain. She finds it difficult to swallow but forces herself to take deep breaths. The bedroom is too dark for her to see her hands shaking violently, but she feels the tremors. The hand cradling her cell phone throbs. Her heart skips, hitting quick, double-digit beats.

She whispers into her phone, leaving an audio memo, rehearsing what she needs to do.

I'm going to act like everything's normal. No one knows about him or what he's doing with Jewell, trying to take away my job. I can run the company without him! I will find other directors. I've already been looking. We don't need him. Consider Harry Hill dead.

She does not dwell on Ray's absence until she hears the front door opening and the clink of his keys. Alone in her bedroom, she is not alarmed. She knows it is Ray. She hears him creep into the house, quietly padding soft soles along the tiled floor of the entrance hall.

Okay, gotta go, she whispers hoarsely into the phone, ending the memo.

As much as she wants to know why her husband is coming home so late, she quickly decides it is best to pretend to be asleep. She hears him in the bathroom, first peeing, flushing the toilet, then running water in the sink and brushing his teeth. She does not know where he has been and is not inclined to ask.

She stays in bed, pressing her eyes shut, hardly breathing, silently plotting her next move. The moment he settles in and begins to snore, she will get up and dress in the dark. She hears him unbuttoning his shirt, unzipping his pants, freeing one leg, then the other. She can tell he is leaving his underwear on. Sometimes after he removes his underpants, he rolls them into a ball and throws them across the room into the hall.

Very quietly he climbs into bed. Her breath comes in short, shallow bursts. She presses her eyes shut so tight she feels as though she is giving her forehead premature wrinkles. His body is changing shape, shifting around in the bed. Finally, he seems to find a comfortable position and stops moving. She can feel warmth from his body, no part of which touches her. She finds it odd that he did not bother to look in on her to see if she is okay. She listens, waiting for his snoring to begin.

Ray does not know what he feels. He often calls his wife beautiful, even though she is unquestionably not a knockout. The recollection of Jewell Cleary's wild blond hair filling his mouth makes him smile and he does not feel one shred of guilt.

His wife reminds him of a slick version of a little girl. At one time he had been charmed by her propensity to pout. She is also extremely style conscious, fastidious with her appearance and a very successful commercial film producer. These are the things that had attracted him. It was a package deal and Ray had bought in. Four years have gone by. None of the terms have changed. Wendy has remained true to form. And he did not know why that fact alone nags at him.

Wendy thinks getting her stockings will be difficult. That particular drawer has a nasty glitch on its left side and tends to get stuck in the wood groove. She will exercise extreme caution. She will lift the drawer and pull it toward her one inch at a time. Blindly, she will grab two pairs of hose, one to wear and one as a back-up. She never knew when an accident would force her to dip into the spare pair of stockings.

In the kitchen she will eschew her morning ritual of a single shot of espresso, giving her the slight edge of a buzz. Her heart begins hitting excited beats, a wave that ripples up and down the well-defined muscle of her abdomen. She is afraid to look over at Ray. If she makes the slightest move, his hand will thrash around like a paw craving the clutch of her warm flesh. Then she hears what she has been waiting for; his first guttural wheeze and snore signals his entry into a sound sleep.

She pulls her hands from under the covers and holds them up above her eyes. Even though the sun has come up, it is not present in the clot of charcoal sky. The dim grey light of the morning makes her hands look as white as gloves. She turns to look at him. His hair is rumpled and his mouth is open wide enough to catch a fish. Ray looks big and hairy, an old animal, more grey than brown, with frown lines boring deeply into his face. She does not know why she married him other than the fact that the marriage between a commercial film producer and an Ad guy is a good deal. Even Harry Hill had thought so. Marriage to a small Ad guy was better than none. Harry had given them a case of Veuve Clicquot and told them to drink it slow. *Don't let the bubbles go to your head.*

Knowing she has made noise, she half-expects Ray to wrap his arms around her, draw her close and murmur comforting words. *It's okay, babe,* or *I love you.* In the past when he thought she was having a vocally loud bad dream, he would playfully ask, *Dreaming of me?*

She looks toward the window where darkness fails to give birth to the morning. In less than three hours, the most bizarre episode of her life will break loose. Her demeanor will be calm and brisk. For weeks, she has been working on Sollie Berg, making it plain, she can run GASP Productions all by herself.

She needs Ray more than any other time in her life, but he has moved farther away to the brink of his side of the bed. She notes the distance between them and wonders where he has been all night.

Ray has pulled his arms and knees close to his chest in a ball. Tight and embryonic, he is safe and warm in the hollow and does not want to come out. It never occurs to Wendy that his fetal position might be a wholly unconscious attempt to protect himself from her.

TWELVE

SMPTE TIME CODE 00:00:00:<u>12</u> On the Wednesday night before Harry Hill's murder, his wife soaks in the bathtub. Mia is drinking a glass of wine; Vouvray, to be precise, is her favorite, but she will drink any white wine that is dry and has a crisp edge. Harry is in the master bedroom, dressing to go out. Mia suspects it is a date because of the extraordinary care he takes to prepare. He took a shower late in the afternoon, which is rare for Harry. She knows the only time he takes showers in the afternoon is before or after sex. He also spent a lavish amount of time putting product into his hair to add extra silkiness and shine exactly like the television commercial he has been making about a man who is about to have his hair cut by a strikingly beautiful blonde.

Harry shouts at her from the bedroom. "Don't you think I can see that you've been cutting yourself?"

Mia pretends she does not hear him. The entire time she has been in the tub, she feels her blood running cold and keeps running hot water. She cannot make the water hot enough. Her skin has begun to wrinkle in the bath. She thinks of the razor and imagines its sharp blade cutting her skin, but her flesh has been made soft and warm from the water and she fears she will cut herself too deeply, enough to kill herself. Then it will be over. She wants to feel something, anything, but she does not want to die.

What do you do when your husband keeps lying? What can you believe? More importantly, who can you believe? Harry tells Mia she is not only hearing things but seeing things too. It is maddening to be this wrong all of the time.

She must be losing her mind.

From the master bedroom, Harry tells Mia for the umpteenth time that he is willing to pay for a therapist. He thinks something is wrong with her and feigns concern. Harry has gotten a recommendation—his name is Sollie Berg—the same therapist that Harry's producer Wendy Wachter sees once a week.

Harry walks into the bathroom. He looks out of place because he is fully dressed in crisp khaki and cotton, and she is naked in the tub. His expression hovers somewhere between a tight grimace and a mocking smile. Dark eyes probe her face, then rove the parts of her body that are not submerged in water. She shudders while he is looking at her. He is homing in on her flaws, all of the things that are wrong with her body, and she wishes she could sink completely under water.

"You'll love Sollie Berg," Harry tells her. He's a short, little man." Harry uses one hand to emphasize short and his other hand to emphasize little. Mia knows Harry does not like short people and considers them to be inferior and damaged, but he is making an exception for Sollie Berg.

"Sollie loves women and wants to help them be the best they can be."

Harry tells Mia that Sollie Berg is known to be a gifted therapist. He guides women to tap into their inner creative talent in order to recover from childhood trauma.

"You must have been very badly traumatized, very badly," Harry says to Mia, "because you are so terribly fucked up." He gives her a brief, sad smile and walks back into the bedroom.

Mia would gladly welcome death except she cannot bear the thought of leaving her children. She hasn't seen them much today. Viv is with the kids while Mia is taking a bath. Mia is mentally checking out more and more, leaving the kids with Viv for longer spans of time. Soon Viv will go home—she takes Wednesday nights off. Mia hears Harry's phone ringing and concentrates on the sound of the ringtone but does not recognize the caller. She listens to see how quickly Harry will answer, or if he will answer at all.

His ring tones are customized for individuals. Anyone who calls Harry with any degree of frequency gets an individual ringtone—this establishes Harry's pecking order of who is important and who is not. Whenever someone ceases to be important, he deletes the person's customized ringtone. Mia no longer had one assigned to her. Harry told her so.

She notices the new ringtone is a fluttery chirp, like the sound emitted from a rare tropical bird. The ring does not last long. Harry quickly answers his phone. His voice is low and sounds intimate, the same way he used to talk to her when they were first dating.

Earlier he had told Mia that he has a late-night film shoot but by tracking the frequency of Harry's phone calls with the tingling new ringtone, she did the math and checked the tally twice. He is lying. Again. She knows there is no film shoot scheduled tonight. She knows about her latest rival for Harry's attention. This one hurts more than the others. Jewell Cleary is a female version of Harry, tall, a blonde, with perfect hair cascading to her waist like Guinevere. One of his own kind.

She turns off the hot water and listens for her children. She thinks the children are downstairs in the kitchen with Viv. Stay-at-home mothers usually do not have a live-in housekeeper. Most young families can't afford that level of domestic service, but Harry not only comes from money, now he is also making a lot of money.

Six months ago, Mia hired Viv at Harry's behest. Even though he said that he worried about leaving the children alone with Mia, his concern for her seemed to be sincere. He was gone from home, away on film shoots, sometimes for an extended period of time. He wanted Mia to be able to have backup support, so she could get some time for herself. "Feel free to be creative," Harry told her. "It will help you to sort out your emotional problems."

"But forget about working in the film business." The look he gave her was peculiar and cautionary. "No one will hire you without me saying so."

Before Mia met Harry, she had been a production manager with her own aspirations—one day she wanted to direct. She and Harry met on the set while she was shooting stills, documenting what was going on behind the scenes during a high-budget film shoot. Harry was making three television commercials. They were on location at a resort in Cabo San Lucas. Almost immediately she fell in love with him—that was eight years ago.

"Be creative," Harry keeps telling her. But whenever Mia tries something new, painting, pottery, woodworking, Harry makes fun of her. It wasn't fun-loving jiving or jabbing. He said things like, "What are you going to do with that crazy shit?" His comments were so hurtful that after a while she felt like taking the small saw she had used to cut wood, to make a small cut on her wrist. She wanted to experience physical pain to see whether it would soften the blows she constantly received from his harsh words.

From the tub, she sees a blurry image of herself in the steamy mirror. Her skin is flushed from the hot water. She has been in the tub for so long that the bathroom exhaust fan cannot keep up with the steam. Harry is still on the phone. He laughs, not because something is funny, but because someone on the other end is saying something casual and light; it's chatty banter, flirty. Mia knows the person on the other end of the call is a woman who Harry finds irresistible. Mia knows the things that make a woman exciting to him. It's all about him. As long as he is the focal point of the conversation, he will find the woman to be alluring beyond compare.

Mia is hurt by listening to him but cannot make herself stop. Her whole life is falling apart. She never believed she would be so injured by loving a man. She is inured to his abuse, numb. Sometimes Harry is so subtle, she cannot believe that it is really happening. If she talks to him about it, he denies everything and says she imagines things. She wants to stop the madness. She does not know how to break free. She has two small children and no job.

She gets out of the tub. Hardly taking the time to dry herself off with a towel, she puts on an oversized white cotton robe and stands in the entranceway leading from the bathroom into the bedroom.

Harry lies astride on the bed. On the carved oak nightstand beside the bed, she sees the ebony framed black and white photograph she took of Harry long ago when they were first dating. In the photo, his mouth is wide open in a smile that is about to erupt into lighthearted laughter. It is purely coincidental, but he is striking the same facial pose now while he talks on his phone. Whoever he is talking to captivates him the same way Harry used to look at her with desire and say, *I'm enchanted.*

"Who are you talking to?" she asks.

Harry pretends he does not hear her, but she knows he does. He closes his eyes as if he's annoyed, shakes his head and puts up his hand as if to say, not now, go away.

"I'll see you later," he says and ends the call. He looks at Mia with irritation as he slips his phone into a side pocket stitched into the lower leg of his khaki cargo pants.

"What is it about you, Mia, that always seems to be desperate. So desperate. I just don't get what the problem is with you. You weren't like this when I first married you." He waves his hand as if to brush her off. "Jewell is nothing like you. She's blond."

"Why are you doing this to me?" Mia walks carefully toward the bed.

Harry smiles; he's enjoying himself. His wife is a perverse form of entertainment.

"Doing what?" He stares at her, furrowing his brows in confusion. "What am I doing? Tell me."

She is getting closer to him. "Harry, we can work things out. Whatever is wrong. I'm not certain what's happened between us." She kneels before him on the bed and looks up. "Maybe it's something we can fix. Please, Harry, give us a chance. We have two kids to think about."

Harry crosses his legs and looks at her quizzically. "You're doing everything to yourself. You're the most self-destructive person I've ever known."

Mia stands and puts her arm around his back. He returns the gesture and places his arm around her waist. It is the first time he has been intimate with her in weeks, not even a stray touch has passed between them. She kisses his cheek, a light graze across the surface of his skin. The smell of his aftershave is distinctly new, one she does not recognize. He turns his head slightly away from her mouth before pulling away altogether. His rejection is subtle but firm.

She looks into his face so she can see if there is any honesty left in his eyes, but she cannot find what she is looking for. He turns his head completely away from her as if he is turning his back on her for good.

"I wanted to go on the shoot with you," she quietly explains. "I didn't think you would get so mad. What's wrong with that? I just want to watch and observe, to see what it's like to direct."

Harry smiles in a way that is neither kind nor cruel, but jocular. He looks pleasantly surprised, and at the same time as if he is about to laugh. "Why do you want to see me direct?"

"I'm interested, that's all."

"Interested. What does that mean?"

Mia uses her hands for emphasis. "Who knows, maybe someday I'll want to direct." She takes a thoughtful pause. "I want to make movies that matter…that make a difference in the world."

Darkness washes over the golden tone of Harry's long face. He looks very angry as though he might hit her. Instead, he pulls his knee up to the same level as the mattress on the bed as though he is testing his strength and flexibility. He stops his knee mid-air because he can only stretch so far and laughs.

"You're ridiculous. You're just ridiculous."

"I've been thinking about going back to work," she blurts.

Harry stands, leans over her and scoffs. "What about the kids? Do you ever think about anyone except for yourself?"

"I want to go back to what I used to do before we met."

"You've been a failure at everything that you have ever done." Harry looks at her as if he cannot believe what he is hearing. "You can't work in the same business I'm in. Forget it! Don't even think about it." He gives her a big smile that is meant to heckle her. "Besides, you are hugely embarrassing to me."

She can't take any more of his chiding. He's never overtly abusive. He never leaves any marks on her body. He always manages to stay a cut below outright cruelty and remains in a holding pattern of controlled contempt. She walks across the room and looks out the rain-beaded window. A pickup truck is parked on the side street inches from their driveway. She cannot be sure if the pickup truck is black or blue.

Mia suddenly feels cold and clutches her robe close to her chest. "There is no reason why I can't go back to work. We have Viv. And," she adds, before taking a deep breath, "I have always made my own hours. I can easily work with everyone's schedules."

Harry does not say anything. Mia turns around to see his reaction, but he has disappeared from the room. He is gone like a ghost. She worries about whether she will be able to sleep, and does not know what is worse, if she is in bed alone or in bed with him. Whether he is there with her or not is beside the point. Nothing will stop her from dreaming about his death.

THIRTEEN

SMPTE TIME CODE:17:15:27:13 Dawn's eyes flash around the bar but always return to the TV, where the clock on the lower right-hand corner of the screen tells her it is 5:15 p.m. Tuned in to the Evening News, the TV above the bar throws bright white glare and a polish of red light onto the left side of Koji Matsuno's face.

Chewing on her thumbnail, Dawn Stein silently berates herself and keeps a close eye on her friend. She can never tell what Koji is thinking. He rarely vocalizes his opinion. His back is straight and his arms are folded across his chest. He chews on a swizzle stick, clenching it between his teeth like a toothpick.

Dawn admires his ability to play his cards close to his chest. She slaps him on the back, sputtering. "How's my pal?"

Koji ignores her. He is mesmerized by the TV. Dawn casts a glance upward at the news. Only picture, no sound. From a wide shot, a dark-colored house is surrounded by police cars and the night. A reporter with his coat collar turned up to protect himself from the rain comes into frame. Dawn can't make out what the reporter is saying.

Bitten to the quick, the cuticle on her right thumb bleeds into a white cocktail napkin. Her blood runs from the most vibrant red to a faint impression of orange, like small dabs of sponge art.

For the longest time, Dawn has tried to break herself of the habit of biting her fingernails. Nothing has worked. Her nails never grow long enough to cut.

"Koji." She nudges her aloof friend in the arm, but he is bent on ignoring her. *Such discipline he has*, Dawn thinks to herself. Koji is intentionally oblivious to Dawn's frazzled nerves. He is not going to be pressured by her or anyone.

Dawn gets up from her stool and throws the weight of her body into a chaotic line of people coming and going, moving in multiple directions, in front of the bar. She tries to avoid bumping into anyone, turning to the side, saying, "I'm sorry. Excuse me, please," while she keeps pushing to get out of the restaurant. The crowd bottlenecks in the reception area, where Dawn's back clatters against a wall of minimalist shelving holding jars of Dietro's very own branded jams, chutneys, sauces, tapenade, stuffed artichokes and lemon curd. She suddenly craves Susan

Kauffman's signature blackberry pie slathered with crème fraiche.

Susan Kauffman holds court from her stool. "Relax," she says, giving Dawn a worried nod.

Dawn's smile is hardly apologetic as she shoves her way through clumps of people in wet raincoats. Pushing open the front door of the restaurant, she scans the traffic on First Avenue, looking for Steve's pickup truck. He had to be on his way! They're forty-five minutes away from their scheduled departure! In all of her years of experience, Dawn has never been able to hold a commercial plane on the ground for longer than ten minutes, and that was before 9/11 when air travel was more relaxed, and rules could be broken.

"Where the hell is Steve?" She calls out, shivering in the damp night. The cold wet air rushes into her mouth, renewing a faint metallic taste, the residue of blood from biting her nails to the quick. She has a weird feeling that something bad is about to happen. The traffic on First Avenue is heavy, clogged with cars moving at a steady pace, throwing up water from the street. The windshield wipers on every vehicle are in high gear but not rapid enough to clear sheets of rain.

Dawn moves out of Dietro's awning, farther along the sidewalk, where there is no protection from the rain. She hears voices but does not know where they are coming from. Dismembered from their bodies, the voices disappear into the night. No one is around.

Dawn is freezing, getting drenched. Dressed for her destination in a warmer climate, she looks ridiculous in downtown Seattle in the November rain. She wears thin cotton shorts. Her legs sport vivid red blotches like a skin disorder. She hugs herself with her arms, squinting to see through the clot of rain hitting her face. She feels as buxom as a whooping crane, with skinny calves and ankles cold enough to crack off from her body in the next gust of November wind. Her adrenaline has been surging, giving her indefatigable strength and energy. Now she only feels cold and very afraid.

She traipses back into the restaurant, wet and disoriented, shivering from cold and uncertainty. Her push to make a deadline is so consuming that it becomes the only reason to live. Did making a deadline have to mean so much to her?

But no one has ever bailed out Dawn Stein.

Watching faces, seeing no one, she stands still by the door, frozen and mute, suspended in time, like a freeze-frame in a 30-second spot. At this point, no matter what she did, the plane will leave without them.

Koji waves his arm for Dawn to come over. She squeezes through the crowd, bristling against the backs of wet raincoats, brushing against elbows and grazing legs, yet she does not feel a thing.

"Something is wrong," Koji says. "I can feel it. Steve wouldn't do this to us."

"Shit," Dawn says. In all her years of experience never had things gone this wrong.

"You better do something," Koji informs her.

"You're out of line." Dawn seethes.

Koji is not going to get into a conflict with her and turns his head away.

If he has any feelings at all, Dawn couldn't tell, but she tells him she's sorry anyway. Koji nods. He hears her apology, but he will not look at her.

Dawn knows she is adversarial by nature. Consequently, the state of mind oft-described as inner peace will always elude her. Yet, when she looks crises in the eye, always and without exception, she knows exactly who she is, and she is brilliant.

"Come on." She nudges Koji in his arm, pointing to their Halliburton cases sitting on the floor. "Help me with these, won't you?"

Carrying expensive luggage is like having an entourage, Dawn reasons. People part to the side and let them pass. She feels important, like she is somebody. They find a small table in the back corner of the restaurant. It is close enough to the action so she can keep an eye on the front door, yet far enough so they can have privacy.

The thought of making a few brisk phone calls begins to turn Dawn's mood around. She starts to feel in control again. But before she calls anyone, her phone buzzes. The last person she expects to hear from is Steve Olin. She had given up on him long ago. She looks to Koji, mouthing who is on the line and snarls into the phone. "Where the fuck have you been? This better be good!"

"Dawn," Steve tells her on the other end. "Harry's dead."

"Sonovabitch," Dawn cries out. Immediately, she turns off the phone. She's shaking.

Koji asks, "What happened?"

She shakes her head like she does not know. Her voice trembles. "He says Harry Hill is dead!"

"Oh...That's not funny," Koji says.

The phone buzzes again. Dawn's hands shake. She gives the phone to Koji. "I can't."

Koji takes the phone from her. "Steve, It's Koji." His face looks like a blank clapperboard. He doesn't say "ahem, yeah," anything. Dawn turns slightly away from him, backing up several feet away from the table and leans over as if she is trying not to retch. If Steve Olin is joking, she will make sure he never works in the film business again. If he had been a woman, he would never have gotten this far anyway. Women can't act like clowns and get away with it. Knowing she has the power to end his career gives her pleasure, but she is also listening to Koji. "That's not good," he says.

FOURTEEN

SMPTE TIME CODE 17:23:26:14 Steve Olin locks himself in his bathroom after he has been questioned by the police. No matter how many times he scrubs his body clean, he still smells blood. Despite the powerful sound of rushing water, Steve thinks he hears something. He rips open the shower curtain with such force, several plastic rings break off from the bent metal rod. He leans out of the shower stall but does not see anything in the steam. The sounds that have always been familiar have now become strange and sinister. He feels sick to his stomach, as if his guts are being hit by an axe.

Noise attacks him from everywhere: the whining motor of his bathroom exhaust fan, the gush of dusty hot air from his wall heater, and the ping of his calcified bathroom pipes. The floor swells and rolls. His houseboat is an old rental sorely in need of renovation and new appliances.

Until today he always liked living on the water. Even when a storm is surging, the rhythmic ebb and flow of Lake Union rocks him to sleep like a baby. But tonight, there will be no peaceful sleep and he knows he will have to take drugs to knock himself out. He can hear the shotgun blasts that killed Jewell Cleary and Harry Hill and he sees their corpses. The scent of blood is everywhere and overpowers him.

Even though his bathroom door is locked, nothing will stop an intruder who wants to get him. Anyone strong can break down the door. His baseball bat lies on the tiled bathroom floor. He keeps it handy, just in case.

He keeps seeing blood covering the metallic edge of electronic equipment and the beige carpet of the floor. He sees raw exposed brain under Harry Hill's skull and the pulverized face of Jewell Cleary. They are dead, massacred into oblivion. There is no explanation for the horror. Who could have done such a thing?

Fear for his own safety consumes him. He tells himself there is no rational reason why he should feel threatened. The person who murdered them has no reason to come after him. Unless the murderer was still around when he got there and thought Steve might have seen something. *Goddamn it to hell!* He did not see anyone, just like he told the cops.

A tingling pain shoots up one side of his back like sciatica, but it is not borne of bad posture or injury. He is certain that someone is watching him. He is afraid, so very afraid, mulling over the possibility that the murderer has been watching him from a distance, and is still watching him now. His body shivers but he is not cold. The notion of the murderer watching him is too uncanny, creepy, and it makes him nauseous. Again, he sees the inside of Jewell Cleary's house drenched in blood. He begins walking in slow motion through the blood-splattered rooms. "Slo-Mo," he says to himself, using a cinematic term he loves.

His floor rolls in waves, larger than an earthquake. He knows the wake is from a passing boat traveling fast on the water. He has lived in a houseboat for three years and is used to not having land under his feet. The rhythm of the waves soothes him. But tonight, he is unsettled and cannot find comfort. Any unexpected movement makes him nauseous. He throws up his toilet seat and waits to vomit.

Then waits for the moment to pass. "Fade Out," he says.

Steve Olin enjoys violence on the big screen, so far removed from him and reality, looking real pretty, almost beautiful, choreographed and performed to seep in under his skin with the rough carnality of heat. Movies on the edge of death bring out the warrior in him and he likes the feeling. Every time he feels the surge of adrenalin induced by violence, he experiences the essence of what it is to be a man. Violence well done is as significant and as good as coming for the first time. And it is why he aspires to be a filmmaker.

But in the movies, or from behind the scenes—working in the business—violence didn't happen to anyone you knew. And it sure as hell didn't have a smell like the blood that had gushed from Harry Hill's head.

If he keeps washing himself, eventually the fetid odor of blood will go away.

He returns to the shower stall, running the water full blast, as hot as he can take it without scorching himself. His old water heater is not set at a safe temperature. If he is not careful, Steve can scald his skin. He scrubs his body vigorously, throwing out the scent of fresh soap in the rising lather. He is finally getting clean and thinking of the night air, lush with rain and sweet smoke from alder wood burning in fireplaces.

Then the metallic edge of raw blood seeps back into his pores, trying to fill the space where the soap has cleansed him. He will never forget the horrible stench so long as he lives. He turns around in a circle under the shower head. He cannot understand who wanted to kill them. Granted, Harry Hill is an asshole, but the world is filled with people like him. Even to those who hate him the most, he is not worth anything dead. Rinsing away the last vestiges of soap, he fastens his eyes on the bathroom door. It dawns on him that he is afraid to leave his bathroom. He must stay alert to fight for his life.

He turns the water off, steps out of the shower and dries himself. He identifies sounds with greater clarity. He feels the gentle rhythm of his houseboat swaying under his feet. It is a quiet night, light wake on the water. He surmises that a boat or two creeps through Lake Union every hour. Steve's houseboat shares moorage with three other floating homes, docked side by side on the same pier; they all use the same bulkhead.

Steve visualizes the way into his place. There are two approaches to his houseboat: by boat or a long walk down the skinny wooden dock. Either way, day or night, getting there makes noise. Between the familiar motion of the boat's rhythmic rock and the knowledge that he will always hear someone coming, he begins to feel the first sense of calm he has experienced since stumbling upon the murder scene.

If there is one thing he knows about, it is violence. Until this whole thing is resolved, he is not taking any chances. When Steve opens the bathroom door, his own crude action takes him by surprise. His baseball bat swings out first. Pure reflex. His bat chases shadows and strikes the wall, leaving a ding. Small plaster chips fall to the rug under a cloud of humid air. "Fade to Black," he says.

FIFTEEN

SMPTE TIME CODE 00:00:39:15 The night before Harry is killed, Mia puts the children to bed without assistance from Viv. She gives the housekeeper Wednesday and Saturday nights off. Although Viv lives with them, she keeps a tiny studio apartment on Beacon Hill and frequently uses it as a quick getaway when she wants to be alone.

Mia has been in the tub since the end of the late-night news. She spends a lot of time in the bathroom. It is where she hides, trying to make herself feel good. It is also where she cuts herself.

She has forgotten to turn off the TV and can hear a low baritone timbre—the voice of Christiane Amanpour. Mia remembers meeting her once at an event in New York City. Before her life began with Harry, Mia had a career and a life. She was a different person with hopes, dreams and ambitions, not a wreck whose mind has been ravaged by nightmares and madness. Her face feels pinched and contorted from always wincing. Her body feels too soft. She is out of shape, afraid to go to the gym, where someone will see the cuts on her arm.

The surface of her bathwater shows evidence of bubbles and is coated with finely perforated film. Mia's phone begins to ring. It is too late for anyone to be calling her unless there is some sort of emergency. Her eyes drift in the plethora of steam and she finds herself staring at her phone set on a small round glass table on the side of the tub. Whoever is calling her has blocked the number. Harry wasn't home and it might be him. She leans over and picks up the phone.

"Mia, Mia Hill, God, I love the sound of your name."

The person on the other end is not her husband. "Uh. Hello..."

The man emits the soft chuckle of someone who seems to know her. "Mia, I've been thinking about you. I haven't seen you around lately. Mia, I hope I'm not troubling you by calling so late."

"Who is this?" Mia sees herself in the mirror across from the tub. Her forehead wrinkles up in confusion. Her face feels flushed from the heat of the tub, but it does not show.

"So how are you doing, Mia? Did I catch you at a bad time?"

Mia still has no idea who she is speaking with. "Who is this?"

"It's me, Sollie Berg."

"Sollie Berg." It surprises her that he would call so late. "Why are you calling now?"

"I know Harry's not there."

Mia is getting creeped out, yet she did not think she ought to be afraid of him.

"I have been wanting to talk to you. Didn't you call me?"

"Yes, twice." Mia shifts her body abruptly in the tub, creating small waves of water that rise and fall with her breasts. The bathroom is completely white: walls, tile, sink, vanity, tub, only the floor is black, but everything else is blindingly white, as vacant as her heart.

She forgets she is talking on the phone until the man lets go of a long sigh. "Well, how are you doing, Mia?"

She catches sight of her face in the mirror. A smile appears in the place previously marked by a tight line. "Why are you calling so late?"

"I'm downstairs, parked in front of your house. I didn't come to see Harry. I came to see you."

Mia does not respond and Sollie does not say anything, a drift into awkward silence.

"I know he's not home," Sollie finally says. "I was with him earlier."

Mia feels a tinge of embarrassment.

"Can I come up?"

She had never heard of a therapist making house calls, especially not in the middle of the night. "Oh," she says. "I guess."

"You don't have to," Sollie says. "But I think you'll be comfortable with me. I'm very gentle."

"Give me a few minutes to think about it," she says.

She hears him breathing. "I'll come up right now. I'll be waiting at the front door."

"Please don't."

But he has ended the call. She realizes she cannot call him back because his number is blocked.

She stands and gets dizzy from rising so fast. She grabs a plush white bath towel from an ornate silver hook and dries her body. In front of a tall oval beveled mirror, she inspects herself. Her stomach shows the definition of muscle, but her dark skin is dimpling from soaking so long in hot water. An extra layer of flesh jiggles in a place on her hips that used to be all pelvic bone and taut. White, white and still more white, so much white in the bathroom emphasizes the flaws in her dark self.

There was a time when she was proud of her dark body—a companion complementing Harry's whiteness, but now being around him makes her feel ashamed. Age, the metamorphosis of two pregnancies, all of it has taken its toll. She examines a slim stitch of dimpled flesh along the natural curve under her butt as if it needs to be cut off. She wonders if all women are so hard on themselves in the looks department—that place where women agonize over every little aspect of themselves that falls short of being perfect.

She lets the towel fall to the quartz tile floor that is really not black but the color of shimmering coal, where it lands in a heap. The floor is shiny and looks slippery, but it's not. As she bounds into her bedroom, the bed covers are rumpled from where Harry sat, talking on the phone. She remembers him looking animated and having the time of his life while every inch of her was dying inside. And now this therapist comes to her house late at night. It is all too surreal to be believable.

Maybe she is dreaming again and can no longer tell the difference between what is real and what is not.

Mia slips into black leggings and an oversized sweater. Falling off of one shoulder, the sweater accentuates her neck and a nape piercing of two silver studs gleaming like the eyes of a snake. She loves to tell her children she has eyes in the back of her head, and they believe her, laughing the way kids do when they think something is funny but not real.

She checks herself in the mirror, pushing her damp hair away from her face. She takes a squirt of Harry's hair gel and forms stiff black spikes on the top of her head. His hair stuff does not work for her hair. She is not happy with how she looks. Staring at herself in the mirror, she imagines putting herself together to make herself brand new, reassembling a bionic whole. There are boob models, butt models, back models, leg models, foot models, and hand models; some did necks, ears, mouths, eyes and teeth. In a dream, a fabulous woman could be created—like

Frankenstein, monsters, the artificial creatures her husband creates in television commercials. Only the women in his commercials are never real, just byproducts of fantasy— Harry Hill's concept of perfection, one she no longer wants in her life.

She sees herself in every mirror in the upstairs hall and along the wall of the staircase. Her house is full of mirrors and cameras. She is always noticing herself to see if one mirror will cast her in a better light than the last. Having so many mirrors is Harry's idea, and they are all hung correctly in a perfunctory nod to Feng Shui.

She relaxes her body and stands in a tiptoe stance, ready to rise in the air and take off for parts unknown. She makes a promise to stop condemning herself according to the avenging aesthetic eye of her husband and people like him. A different angle of her reflection in the passing mirrors begins to emerge. This perspective tells her what is imperfect, is real. There is truth in imperfection. She slackens her stomach and releases the arch of her back, allowing her breasts to resume their fullness and sag heavily above the outline of her sunken ribcage. She places one foot out in front of the other in a loose rendition of a balletic fifth position.

She clutches the V-neck of her sweater, drawing her breasts together in a hug, and a knot while her fist trails down in between her legs with the flow and fall of a girded loincloth, unraveling. She doesn't have loins. She is not a man, but she wishes she could find out what it feels like to be a man, to have a body that is an instrument of pleasure and power and could care less about this thing called love.

She sees Sollie Berg through the window. He stands under the awning in the front entrance to her home, pressing against the door to shield himself from the wind and the rain. Water dripping from the eaves forms small pools on the steps. She rubs away fog on the glass to get a closer look at him. He stands under the glare of the porch light with only the darkness of the night behind him. Sollie is on the small side. Reedy patches of brown hair barely cover his baldness.

He sees her and gives her a toothy smile. One tooth is crowned in gold. Not knowing what to expect, she opens the door.

"I never enter a lady's home without permission. May I come in?"

Mia would much rather be alone. She is hesitant, but there is no reason not to let him in. She might as well get therapy underway. Maybe some good will come of it.

"I like it when you do that," he says, using both of his hands to brush away water from his hair.

"Do what?" Mia is startled, gasping at the man. "I didn't do anything."

"The way you smile at me. I like it."

She shakes her head with disbelief. "This could not be happening."

"But it is true. Count yourself lucky. You called me twice and now I'm here. I'm at your command." He takes a small stiff bow.

He stamps his feet on the rug to rid himself of water. His suit and shoes look expensive. Despite the heavy rain, he is not wearing an overcoat.

"There's a lot more to you than I can say, isn't there?" He looks at her as if he is trying to cozy up to see inside of her heart.

Mia backs away from him, motioning toward the living room. "Harry told me to get in touch with you. He said you could help me the way no one else could."

"He did, eh? That's very strange." He looks as though he is thinking, trying to figure out something. "But you never know about Harry. No one can ever figure out what he's up to."

"He's unpredictable."

Sollie nods respectfully as if he's writing an epitaph for a dead friend. "I never say anything bad about Harry. I never say anything bad about anybody."

Mia nods her head toward a large sunny yellow armchair with a matching cassock. Sollie sits on the chair striking the same pose the way Harry had done on the bed hours ago before he left to go on his date. Mia doesn't try to understand why Sollie is sitting there with his knee pulling up, bending and stretching, as if he is checking his flexibility. He moves exactly like Harry except Sollie is much smaller. His legs are much shorter than her own legs.

In a strange way, Sollie's pose on the chair is connected to her dreams.

Sollie rises from the chair, surprisingly nimble on his feet. Giving her an effusive smile, he points to the yellow chair. "Sit there, Mia. I want you to be very comfortable. I'm enjoying your company."

He assumes a place promptly in the middle of the handsome cassock at the foot of the chair. "I will sit here." He effortlessly draws his legs into a perfect lotus position.

Sollie is being too familiar with her and she hardly knows him. A part of her is enjoying his attention and she slides into the chair.

"That's it," Sollie says, reassuringly. "Now I can see that you're relaxing."

Mia drifts to a hollow place where she is no longer reeling but still not feeling enough emotion to be her former self. "Do we know each other?"

Sollie chuckles. "You don't remember me, do you?" He rises from the cassock and taps her smooth legs, pausing for a moment, and allows his hand to linger. He nudges her to fully sprawl her long legs to the end of the chair's cushion, where they fall over the edge. He kneels on the floor by the side of the armchair and looks up, studying her face. "I was on the set last month during a shoot. Harry was there too, of course, he was the director. Now do you remember?"

Despite his entreaties to remember, Mia cannot oblige him.

"You must remember," he says, soothingly.

Mia has no recollection and tells him so. "I don't know what you're talking about." Her eyes drift to the window and beyond where a squall of rain is coming down harder and rattles the glass. The rain and wind are picking up and turning into a ferocious storm. The lights will most certainly go out.

Sollie is not dissuaded from continuing conversation that is one-sided. "Harry asked you to leave the set. He was very abrupt with you."

Mia's eyes flutter. Now she remembers the encounter and wishes she did not. Harry had told her to leave the set.

He didn't know she was coming. She knew if she had asked Harry if she could visit him on the set, he would have said no. But she doesn't tell this to Sollie and does not care that there is silence between them. She wonders where she left her cell phone and thinks it must still be upstairs in the bathroom.

"How can I help you to remember?"

Mia does remember now but she has no desire to share the experience with this strange man whose presence feels more invasive than helpful.

Harry's shoot was for Nordstrom—summer sportswear—at a sound stage in Woodinville. Mia remembers the drive to Woodinville as a spontaneous jaunt into the country. Leaving behind the kids with Viv, she savored being alone and getting some time to herself. She drove slowly on the back roads to view the squabbling high color of pumpkin patches looming on flat plots of land as large as farms. Winter squash sat in bins and baskets, some lolling over the ledge, some rowdy, and all of them bumping into one another's thick skin. They were fat, they were golden, round and orange; they were like small suns and kids. And that is where her memory stops. She has no recollection of anything else.

"I followed you out of the studio," Sollie says. "But by the time I got to the parking lot, you were already gone."

Outside, a gust of wind slams an empty garbage can into the street and startles her. Her reflex is subtle as if she is an infant, and not nearly jarring enough to be dramatic. But Sollie does notice and pats her leg. "It's just the wind."

As the memory of Harry's cruelty returns, she hears metal garbage cans rolling on the street, sounding as though they are smashing against the curb. In her mind, she imagines the cans to be dented and banged up like a car in a wreck, any wreck, even a wreck like her. Wind chimes blowing at a neighboring house peal with the frequency of alarm. The overhead light in the living room flickers. The conditions are perfect for a blackout.

Sollie reaches, touching her feet. "You have such beautiful feet. Somehow, I knew that you would. Do you mind if I touch them?"

Mia doesn't move. She is not sure if she is even breathing. She is alarmed but not enough to summon ordinary fear the way a woman would if she had not been so battered, beaten up. She does not stop him as he begins massaging her foot in a controlled, practiced way.

"I think you do remember me," Sollie says. "We saw each other at the shoot."

"No," Mia says. "But I am starting to remember the day of the shoot. It was for Nordstrom. On the set, the models were strutting on the sound stage in their cute shorts, kicking out their legs to show their polka dots and flowers. A few models were making wardrobe changes right on the stage. Most of the guys were looking the other way. No one's going to be caught leering like a dumb adolescent boy."

"Of course," Sollie says. "We wouldn't want that. It would be unprofessional." His fingers penetrate more deeply into the arch of her foot. He has her just where he wants her. What he is doing feels good. She is beginning to desire his touch.

"I remember you standing off to the side. Your dark hair. Liquid eyes, big and brown. I found you to be so beautiful."

Mia leans back and closes her eyes. On the set, she tried to make eye contact with Harry. He did not see her, or if he did, he refused to look at her. He was immersed in conversation with Jewell Cleary over the next shot and whether to mix real fruit with neon bathing suits. Jewell wanted the girls to carry baskets of fruit on their heads, very *Carmen Miranda*. Mia stood alone in the cavernous studio. She imagined the 1940s film star Carmen Miranda, who wore towering mounds of fruit on her head and inspired the kitschy Chiquita Banana commercials. Even then, stark raving out of her mind, Mia had the design talent and sensibility to know the Carmen Miranda look was all wrong.

The crew on the set looked bored, stuck in the *wait phase* of the *hurry-up-and-wait* dynamics of a film shoot. The moment Harry looked up and saw her, his face contorted into anger, turning crimson. As soon as Jewell saw Mia, she flitted away from Harry and disappeared into the sidelines with the gaffer Koji Matsuno. Mia had been unable to collect herself enough to respond to Harry, but she heard his voice boom in the warehouse acoustics of the set. "You look awful," he shouted. And she wished that she could die.

"I do remember. I remember everything. Harry went ballistic. He yelled. He said that I should never show up on a set while he's working. He also insulted the way I look. '*You shouldn't leave the house looking like that!*' That is what he said."

"Do I really look that bad?" She opens her eyes to meet Sollie's intense gaze. "My, my, you really are good. Harry told me you were good. He wasn't kidding. You really got me talking. I have never talked to anyone about what's wrong with me."

"We didn't actually meet that day. You weren't there long enough so I could introduce myself." Sollie moves toward her ankles and presses upward, carefully massaging her calves. "You probably don't get out of the house much. Don't you have two little kids?"

A part of Mia is terrified. He is taking advantage of her and making it look like he is doing her a favor. The atmosphere in the room is tense enough to cut with the fine blade of a knife.

"Why are you doing this?"

"Where are the kids now?" he whispers. "Asleep, I hope?"

"I hope." Mia closes and opens her eyes, repeatedly, trying to get a handle on reality.

She can't imagine having sex with him. Besides a woman is not supposed to have sex with her therapist. It has been a long time since anyone has touched her body with any degree of affection. She craves intimacy but is too afraid to let herself feel anything remotely resembling sex, or, God forbid, love. This body of hers is an instrument of pleasure and power, a gift to offer in the quest of love, but there is no love here. Sollie Berg is sick, a pervert.

Wind bangs against the old wood frame window. Mia sees a twisting snake of shadows dance along the walls. Rain crashes against every door and window in the house. Intermittent creaks sound as if tiles are being ripped away from the roof. The fireplace is cold and bleak. Its earlier fire has gone out. Downdrafts of air trill through the chimney. The flue has been left open, letting in whorls of cold wet air from the violent rain. Small droplets fall onto dying embers that are barely aglow, hissing as they create tiny tendrils of steam.

Sollie is kneeling on the floor, paying homage to her as if she is his Queen. She knows what he is doing is wrong. He is crossing boundaries that should never be violated. While he massages her feet with strong, probing fingers, he speaks to her. "I would give anything to touch the nape of your neck." She knows he wants to finger her nape piercing and revel in the two silver studs that gleam like the eyes of a snake.

A small thump hits the floor, causing Mia to sit up with a start. Not hearing a thing, Sollie continues to caress her feet.

The thump has come from her child. Chloe stands at the foot of the stairs, clutching her blanket. The little girl has toppled her plastic sippy cup. "*Uh-oh,*" she tells her mother, pleading with her eyes. Mia moves quickly to stop the flow of milk from spilling onto the floor.

"Sit down, I'll get it." Mia damns the small pool of quickly spreading milk with a pile of cloth napkins.

Chloe smiles at her Mother. "Are you angry, Mommy?"

"What did you do that for!" As soon as Mia admonishes the child, she knows she is wrong. "I'm so sorry," she tries to smile. "I know it was just an accident."

"Who's that man touching your feet?"

Sollie stands and gives the child a smile, weak but harsh enough to let her know she is unwanted, which strikes Mia as very odd. He is a therapist who hates children.

Chloe wraps her tiny body around Mia's legs and won't look at Sollie. Mia moves her arm around the little girl's back to comfort her, but her hands feel numb. The child's instincts are sharp, more in tune with reality than her mother's ability to detect danger.

Mia finds the right opening to get rid of Sollie and tells him she will get in touch with him in the morning. He agrees, winking as if they are co-conspirators in a stolen but fractured moment of time. Her normal pattern is broken. She is no longer operating in real time and wonders if the morning will come. The wind kicks up a fiercer howl and intrudes her thoughts. She looks into the dining room beyond Sollie's balding head and focuses on a honey color hutch. A large serving platter stands prominently displayed. Pennsylvania Dutch, oxblood red, rich in hex, the platter's two love birds are good luck charms, bringing fortune and harmony to all who dwell within.

SIXTEEN

SMPTE TIME CODE 01:12:22:<u>16</u> It is 1:12 a.m. on Thursday, still early in an all-night edit session. Ensley Sharp strips a match from its pack and sticks it in between her front teeth. Then she starts to laugh. The big girl

swivels in her office chair. Basking in the incandescent
sweep of video light, she throws her head back, allowing
the inertia of turning rapidly in her chair to consume her.
She spins around, cutting through the smoky air, laughing
like a punch-drunk kid. Kenny Kix's eyes stalk her as if he
is getting ready to pounce. He doesn't know why he feels
like he must possess her. It is a strange and wonderful
moment he is experiencing. He feels like lighting the match
between her teeth and pouring gasoline on the fire. He
wants to see her go up in flames.

"No matter how you look at it, all relations between a
man and a woman culminate in rape." Kenny is being dead
serious.

Both young women feel dread and do not want to
hear what he will say next. Ensley pushes her feet off the
floor to propel her chair into spinning faster. Andy looks
into her phone to avoid Kenny's latest tirade. She checks
her messages but does not dare to text anyone. She knows
that will set Kenny off. She also knows, just looking at her
phone could trigger his rage, but she has to do something
to keep herself sane.

"Sex is always a violent act," he says.

"Maybe to you it is." Ensley stomps her feet on the
floor. Jumpy in her seat, she pulls her knees up to her chest
and hugs them like a break dancer. Propelling her chair into
a faster spin, she is making herself dizzy on purpose. She
thinks if she acts out of control, a little bit insane, Kenny
will shut up.

Kenny kicks out his leg against her chair to stop her
spin.

"Why did you do that?" The big girl looks upset. "I was having some fun."

"Do that again and you're out of here." His voice is mellow but his eyes blaze with contempt through the haze of smoke that has built up cumulatively over the time that they have been editing. He doesn't have to look at her to know he is making an impact.

Pulling out a Camel, his hands shake as he flicks his Bic lighter. The flame erupts dangerously close to his hair but goes out before his cigarette is lit or his hair catches fire.

Andy reaches forward to light Kenny's Camel for him. He appreciates her gesture by slightly raising his eyebrow but does not thank her. His eyes shoot her a warning. "You weren't fast enough."

"Please," Andy says. "Where is this going?" She is genuinely upset but does not move from her seat to leave the room. She knows she is a prisoner of her own ambition.

The door to the editing suite thrusts open from outside, throwing a swath of fluorescent light into the dark room. Sollie Berg's large black square-frame glasses overpower his face, making him look intelligent but seedy. Even though he is a small man, he exudes power and money. Of the few strands of hair on his head, not one is out of place.

No one is supposed to be here late at night, but people come and go. Producers, directors, ad guys, and friends of friends show up unannounced.

Sollie's hands are in his pockets, jingling loose change. "Leave the girls alone. I heard what you were saying. Soon you'll be giving them lessons in bestiality."

Kenny spins quickly around in his chair and sneers. "If you want to hear about animals, I can go on all night."

"I'm sure you can." Sollie looks grim. He examines the girls, cautiously eyeing them for some sort of reaction. He doesn't want any lawsuits. He knows the fine line between sexual harassment and admiration, and he knows this line is wider and looser in an editing suite. Behind the scenes or in front of the camera, women will put up with almost anything so they can work in the film business. Whether they work in front of the camera or from behind the scenes does not matter, putting up with abuse—in some form—is a route to entry.

"Pretty," Sollie says to Kenny. "You always get the good ones. Exotic and different."

Ensley is taken aback. "Who are you?" She is making a snide comment more than she is asking him a question. She lights a cigarette, takes a long drag and glares at him through her cloud of smoke. She is sure he is someone important, but his sudden presence makes her feel uncomfortable. Sollie stares her down to let her know that she ought not to be disrespectful. At the same time, he admires her spark. He loves cool black girls.

Sollie rocks on his heels, demonstrating his physical vigor. He's into health, vitality, fitness. Well into his sixties, he competes in triathlons and makes yoga a daily regimen. Andy can feel his eyes travel every inch of her body, seeping into every pore like a viral invasion. She avoids his gaze and renews interest in her phone.

"I don't need introductions," Sollie says. "Do I ever?" he asks Kenny.

"Sollie Berg." Kenny releases his own plume of smoke and shifts his body, squeaking the seat of his chair in a chorus of popping coils and springs. "Mr. Sollie Berg damn near owns the film business in this town, lock, stock and barrel."

Sollie smiles at Kenny, then appraises both women, definitely assessing their finer attributes. Ensley remains unusually quiet. Andy fumbles for her handbag, looking for a cigarette. She is the more assertive of the two and is noticeably indignant. It's one thing to take abuse from Kenny Kix and quite another to be ogled by this strange, creepy man. Andy takes out a cigarette and nods to Ensley to give her a light. They look at each other as if they are sisters in pain. They'd be friends if they weren't trying to get the same job.

Glancing at Andy's neck, Sollie gives her a quirky smile that is meant to be dismissive. "How's the footage?" Sollie asks Kenny.

"There's a lot," Kenny tells him. "Way too much. He overshot everything."

"He always does and that can be a good thing." Sollie pats Kenny on the back. "Think you can get two more spots out of this?"

"Probably three." Kenny releases a plume of smoke into the air above his head. He ponders Sollie's question but doesn't show him any of the footage on purpose or give him any ideas about how he plans to cut. Extra cutting time is involved. He is going to have to negotiate a price and he knows from past experience that Sollie Berg is a tightwad, always looking to cut corners to make an extra buck.

Without turning his head, Kenny gives Sollie the best side of his face Hollywood style. It's his way of being attentive, still playing his cards close to his chest.

Sollie sneezes twice, waving his arms over his head and in front of his face to rid himself of the smoke. "There's too much damn smoke in here," Sollie says. "It's like a bar, or the way bars used to be."

"Don't you know that smoking isn't good for you?" he asks the girls. "It will age your skin. You'll look like prunes by the time you're thirty. Besides, who wants to kiss a girl whose mouth tastes like an ashtray?"

"A guy who smokes, that's who!" Kenny laughs. Smoke pours out of his mouth and nose. He laughs hard, holding onto a blue denim shirt that is slack against his skinny stomach and begins choking on his own smoke. His laughter erupts into a hacking cough that will not stop. He reaches for a can of diet coke on the console but can't stop coughing long enough to take a sip.

Ensley exhales her own blast of smoke in Sollie's direction. "You heard the man. Guys who smoke like smoking girls."

Kenny is still coughing but manages to say, "Smoking hot girls." Then he takes his first sip of diet coke.

Sollie is not amused. He folds his arms and looks at Kenny. "Talk tomorrow?"

Kenny perks up and nods but does not turn to look at Sollie. He won't give him the satisfaction of thinking that he is in a weakened bargaining position. He hears Sollie close the door but does not say goodbye. The editing suite is soundproof. Any sound outside this sacred place cannot be heard, and inside it's as quiet as death. Kenny warns the girls not to say anything. Sollie Berg has been known to linger behind closed doors to listen to see if people talk about him behind his back. Kenny's whisper is harsh, "Don't say anything until I tell you to."

SEVENTEEN

SMPTE TIME CODE 07:01:21:17 Steve Olin goes to GASP Productions every day promptly at seven in the morning. The Thursday that Harry Hill is killed is no exception. He runs from his pickup truck to the front entrance of GASP to avoid getting drenched in the howling rain. The smell of coffee from Café Umbria wafts through wet air, beckoning him to make a pit stop for a double-double Caffè MOCHA Grande, but today he feels too restless to wait in a line of sodden raincoats.

The fine old red brick building housing GASP Productions sits on the corner of First and Yesler in Seattle's historic Pioneer Square, not far from Ray Wachter's Advertising Agency. The street is paved in cobblestone and most buildings are listed in the historic registry. This is the old part of the city that had long ago been destroyed by fire. Steve finds it hard to believe that anything could burn in a city where there is no end to the rain.

Wind picks up and changes direction in Steve's favor, enabling him to yank open a massive oak door and enter the building with cyclonic force. His shoes squeak on a marble floor that is covered with streams and rivulets, chaotic pools of water. A sandwich board warns of slippery floors, cautioning people to watch where they are walking. He stamps on a thick rubber mat, sloughing off excess water. His legs feel strong, like he could run a marathon if only the rain would stop.

As he makes his way into the inner sanctum of GASP, he pauses by the conference room, where a long marble table lies bare. The table has been polished to a high sheen and reflects light from an enormous screen that is actually a video monitor. This monitor is different from the video tap attached to an old fashion 35mm movie camera. The monitor in this room watches everyone who comes in and out of the office. Steve knows where the cameras are located. Hardly hidden from view, the cameras loom from the top corner in every room, unfurling like a series of forbidding eyes.

"Knock knock." He smiles at Yolanda Nez. He feels genuine warmth for her. Big and blond, she's pretty but not enough to be a distraction.

Yolanda smiles and gives him a generous squeeze on his arm. "Take off that coat so I can hang it up to dry."

"It hardly rains in Eastern Washington," he tells her, while he's taking off his coat. "Not like this," he says, smiling at her. "In Wenatchee it's dry and we have four seasons."

"So I hear." She comes up from behind, takes his coat, hanging it on a stark coat tree, a sculpture made from concrete. "How do you always manage to sneak right past me?"

"It's because you're never at your desk, and always flitting around somewhere."

Yolanda takes long lope strides and settles into a cushy chair behind her desk. She assumes her post as receptionist as if she is staffing a battle station. She gives Steve a polite smile, but her eyes dim as she nods toward Wendy Wachter's office. "I'm trying to keep tabs on her."

Steve gets the hint. Yolanda is telling him Wendy is in one of her black moods. Steve gives her what he calls his easy grin. It always works with ladies. He thinks about taking Yolanda out for a drink sometime. She isn't the first office gopher Wendy has kicked around, but he knows why she stays and puts up with the abuse. She's trying to break into the business and is frequently hired as a P.A. on film shoots—another lowly, thankless job.

"Yolanda," Wendy Wachter calls out. "Why don't you leave Steve alone? Tell him to come in here and see me!"

Steve raises his eyebrows, giving Yolanda a dramatic look of false alarm that makes her laugh. He jaunts down a narrow hall, passing Studio-A, where directors' reels are logged and stored on hard drives. The reels are compilations of 30-second spots, showing off a director's genre and unique style. Steve is certain that a time will come when he will have his own reel, but first, he needs a big break—his first job as a director.

He finds her in a large office that is muted in the same color of peachy-beige that she prefers for her wardrobe. An entire wall is a single unobstructed window looking out to the watery blush of the Puget Sound.

"Hello, Wendy Wachter." Even her name evokes a guttural sound. Just saying it takes two hard clicks against his teeth. He stands several feet away from the sharp edge of her desk, but she ignores him and puts her hand up to shush him.

Steve thinks about stretching his body on her plush pink velvet couch, so he can gaze out at the sky that is as grey as the water of the Puget Sound. The rain is taking its toll and without his Caffè MOCHA, HE IS BEGINNING TO FEEL SLEEPY and wouldn't mind taking a long nap. TO STAY AWAKE, he sits in a hard chrome-and-tan leather chair across from her.

Wendy abruptly cocks her small, oval-shaped face and rummages around in her handbag that is as large as a small suitcase with the same intense energy that she puts out to land big commercial deals for her star director. Wendy makes no pretense about the importance of Harry Hill. He is her everything. She could give a damn about Steve—an insignificant Grip.

Steve is not technically an employee of GASP. He's a freelancer who is hired at the director's whim, whenever there is a shoot. The film business in Seattle is much smaller than it is in New York or L.A. Only a few get to work exclusively—in the biz—without having a backup source of income. He shows up at the office every day just to make sure he remains top-of-mind.

Steve watches her as she checks herself in a small compact mirror. She seems displeased, frowns, and continues trying to find something in her handbag. Steve thinks that it's weird because she always looks perfect. People say snide things about Wendy Wachter, but one thing is clear: she is always camera-ready and very focused on getting what she wants.

"Here!" Wendy tosses her bag to Steve, where it thuds onto his lap with the weight of a barbell. "Make yourself useful. Don't just sit there. Find my mascara for me."

Tension travels up Steve's neck as though he is on the verge of getting a muscle spasm. He really does not want to look through a woman's purse. It is a very uncool thing for a guy to do unless he's doing it for his girlfriend. But he will do anything to get in her good graces, so he opens the satchel and looks inside. He finds make-up brushes, a half-eaten roll of certs, two pairs of pantyhose and a set of car keys, but what really catches his eye is a tampon poking out of its thin tissue wrapper.

"Is this mascara?" He holds up the tampon.

"Asshole! Put that back!"

He relies on his grin as a complete way of showing his admiration for her. He wants her to think he is captivated by her beauty and charm. What Steve is doing works every time. He is reaching Wendy. He knows she dismisses him as unimportant, yet at the same time, she has grown used to him and actually likes him. He knows her moods and can see a change coming. She looks at him as though she is seeing him for the first time and is having a revelation, a brilliant insight into how Steve might actually be useful to her.

She startles him with the urgency of her question. "What do you know about this shoot, involving Harry and Jewell?"

"What shoot?" Steve asks. He's lying, but his hands are tied. It is Harry Hill who hires him as a Grip, not Wendy Wachter. On the flip side, it is Wendy who could give him his big break—and make him a director.

"This job in Costa Rica," Wendy says. "Harry hired you, Dawn and others."

"I don't know what you're talking about."

"Weren't you hired?" Wendy asks.

"I'm not supposed to talk about it." And that is true. He has been told not to say anything. He doesn't know why. It's not his business. "I'm just a dumb Grip," he tells Wendy."

"You expect me to believe that," Wendy snaps. She gets up from her desk, walks toward him, and begins to circle. Her heels make dull clicks on the roughhewn-fir planked floor that under Wendy Wachter's extraordinary design flair is unfinished—wood in its natural state.

"Well...I'm ready to listen when you're ready to talk."

A reversal is taking place—it is very cool and not something he had counted on this early in the game. "I'm not supposed to talk about it," he tells her again.

He stands to face her and hands back her satchel. "Here."

"So, I take it that you're not going to tell me anything?"

Steve knows he can only get so far by acting boyish and vulnerable, the guy voted most likely to bring home to Mom. "I don't know any of the details, other than what flight I'm supposed to be on, that and Harry wants me to drive him to the airport."

Wendy slams her handbag down on top of her desk. "Did Jewell tell you that or did Harry? I need to know!"

"Steve is beginning to enjoy himself. "You heard what I said."

"Who told you not to tell me anything?" Wendy yells.

Yolanda whisks into the room, hovering over Wendy; she assumes the position of being her personal bodyguard. She looks at Wendy and covers her mouth with the back of her hand. Steve is impressed by how mature Yolanda is, reining in her boss who seems to be on the verge of losing control. "I'm worried," she tells Wendy. I don't want something ugly to erupt. We've had way too much conflict around her and it's starting to give me a nervous stomach."

"Harry's keeping this whole job under wraps," Steve says quietly. He waits patiently for Wendy's reaction. For the first time in his life, he has something Wendy Wachter wants.

Fear spreads across Wendy's face. She looks tiny and fragile, like a hummingbird poised to shoot straight up into the air. Steve could see the hurt in her eyes.

"It really isn't happening," she says. "Something like this couldn't happen to me."

She turns her back to both Yolanda and Steve, presses her fingers against the steamed-up window to make a minuscule porthole so she can see out, but there is nothing to see except for sheets of rain. The water of the Puget Sound churns dark waves topped with whitecaps. She sees a lone ferry cutting a swath through the angry water and imagines it could easily capsize.

"How dare he cut me out. After all I've done for him," her voice trembles. "Twelve years. It took twelve years to get him where he is today."

Yolanda doesn't say anything. There is nothing to say. She hesitates before turning away from her boss. She respects Wendy and can't bear to see her so hurt, suffering a fall from grace, a brutal tragedy. It always happens to strong women, but never to men, especially to opportunistic bullies like Harry Hill.

"I still don't know what the big deal is," Steve says. "Just because Jewell is his producer on this one job that doesn't mean he is no longer going to be working with you."

"Oh yes it does! Otherwise, he would have told me what was going on!" Wendy turns her back on him to gaze out the window. "God, I feel like killing him and Jewell, especially Jewell. I just know she put him up to this." She sniffs. "I'd like to kill the both of them. I'd like to kill them together."

It amuses Steve to think that someone like Wendy Wachter would speak of committing murder. She looks like she would faint at the sight of a drop of blood.

Steve nods and gives her an extra cute smile. "I'm still going to be working with you."

Yolanda looks at Steve and shakes her head, trying to let him know that he is not helping the situation. She motions with her fingers to keep his mouth zipped shut. "He doesn't really mean that," Yolanda offers.

"Yes, he does," Wendy snaps. She tucks her hair behind both of her ears and lowers her head, donning a posture of humility. She grows quiet and appears to be lost in thought. Yolanda turns to Steve and lowers her eyes in what is obviously a moment of unspoken respect for the humiliation and impending downfall of the indomitable Wendy Wachter.

Then an unexpected development occurs. Wendy realizes how Steve might be useful to her. Her smile grows effusive as she gives Steve a lovely, lingering gaze. Her eyes wander over his body, showing appreciation the same way he has been appreciating her. "We're all creatives. You, me, Harry Hill, we're all in the same game."

She moves toward Steve, springing lightly on her feet. "As long as you've got talent, people will talk you up. It's about the talent. It's always about the talent."

Wendy gets so close to Steve that he could feel her breath on his neck. The strong scent of her perfume is neither offensive nor cloying; it's just Wendy. He knows he can come to like her perfume.

She touches Steve on the arm. "You know, Steve, I've been thinking, I mean the first job would be small. Real small. I mean it might end up being for a car dealership or a PSA for a small non-profit. Anything to get you started"

"I see where this is going." Yolanda is bursting with pride. "You have to get your feet wet," she tells Steve.

Wendy's pearl-drop earrings jingle as she puts her arm around his shoulder and speaks in a low, confidential tone. "We're talking about doing a few spots on spec... you know, just to get your reel going."

"Great idea!" Yolanda claps her hands excitedly.

"Yolanda, don't you have something better to do?" Wendy suggests good-naturedly, but she is really giving her a command, one that Yolanda readily responds to like a trained seal.

"Steve," Wendy says, standing behind her desk. "You know, Steve, I know you've got talent. I know you can do greater things with your life than just pushing a dolly around the set. Your taste is great. And your sense of style has movement. It's fluid. And on top of everything else, you look good."

She sits on top of her desk, crosses her legs and gives him a sincere smile. "All you need is the right opportunity."

"I'm here to give you that opportunity."

She intentionally turns her gaze to the floor to avert Steve's eyes. "All you have to do is follow Harry and Jewell everywhere they go. I want to know who they talk to and everything they do, even if it seems small or inconsequential."

"Take notes." The pitch of her voice eases into a pleasant cadence as soft as a whisper. "I want you to be there for me. And I will be here for you."

Steve cannot believe what he is hearing. He has been working up to this moment for months—charming Wendy, hoping eventually she might give him his first big break. And it is happening, right now, she is giving him a shot as a director. He feels like pinching himself, wondering if this is real, and, maybe, he is only having a dream.

But Wendy speaks to him, assertively, reminding him that this is not a dream. "Sollie Berg will do anything I tell him to do. If I say, 'Let's hire Steve,' he'll say, *Let's hire Steve,* and I'll say, 'Good idea, Sollie.'" She gets up from the desk. The expression on her face registers infinite sweetness, as if she is a little girl. "That's how it works around here. It's always Sollie's idea."

EIGHTEEN

SMPTE TIME CODE 08:53:22:18 Just before nine on Thursday morning, Mia Hill pulls into her driveway and parks. The instant she opens her car door, she hears the throaty noise of an engine. A blue pickup truck speeds out of a parking space close to the front of her house. It's odd for anyone to drive fast in the pouring rain. She did not have a chance to look at the driver or catch the truck's license plate.

Heavy rain obstructs her vision as she runs to her front porch. She tells herself there isn't anything unusual about the blue pickup truck racing away from the front of her home. She does not want to see a connection between the truck and her recurring dream. She looks into the house through the leaded glass window of the old fir front door and sees Viv holding Chloe in her arms.

Her little girl is sucking her thumb, clutching her *bah bah* bear, which she shakes excitedly because she sees her mother. Mia's key easily slides into the antiquated brass lock. At the same time, Viv opens the door for her. Looking bright and calm, Viv is Mia's only refuge in the tumult of her household. Her smile is kind but inquisitive. "How did it go with getting Maxie off to school?"

Mia nods affirmatively. "Fine."

Viv chatters about the steady onslaught of the rain that has not let up for days. "But it is always the wind that is a bother," she says, shifting Chloe from one arm to the other. "It's the wind that causes all of the damage." She looks at Mia as if she is trying to send her a warning.

Mia kicks off her boots, sets them on a mat to dry and hangs her black leather coat on a Shaker wall peg. For a moment she appraises her coat, sleek and modern compared to the stark old wooden pegs hung on the wall in *this old house* that was built over a hundred years ago. One of the older homes in Seattle, it has ghosts, both the living and the dead. Viv blithely mentions the life she had lived long ago on dry land. Mia vaguely hears her talking incessantly about the spate of bad weather, likely to last another week, not unusual for November in Seattle, but completely unlike the small farming community in Idaho where Viv grew up.

"Stop that," Mia is telling Chloe to pull her thumb from her mouth.

Mia takes Chloe from Viv's arms and nestles her face into her daughter's blond curls before giving her a kiss. Her daughter feels as warm as summer sun. She forces herself to concentrate on what is here and now, and grounded. Deciphering the meaning of her bad dreams can wait. So can Viv, and so can Sollie Berg, whom she has not yet called.

Her dreams had never come up when Sollie Berg unexpectedly showed up last night.

She wishes Viv would stay by her side, but the woman hurriedly leaves the hallway, where the scent of Harry's hair wafts down the fir-planked steps, permeating the house with the aroma of patchouli and coconut. Harry takes good care of his hair and uses the most expensive hair products. As of late, Jewell Cleary has been providing him with a steady supply of new samples: mousse, hair sheen, laminates, gels, and texturizing spray.

"Please stay. I want you to stay." Mia calls to Viv, but the woman is already gone, roaming somewhere in the house in search of new chores to do.

Mia feels a quick rush of dread. She knows Harry is closing in on her and she does not want to be around him. She will only get hurt.

Doing her best to avoid Harry, she turns to Chloe, looking at the child with baleful eyes, shaking her head; it is a way to deflect from her fear. Viv also makes a habit of avoiding Harry. If the woman knows what is going on, she has also made it a habit not to ask questions. Mia does not feel obligated to tell her anything. For Mia, her feelings are as inexplicable as her dreams. Confronting her feelings makes them more terrifying. It is like breathing energy into them and giving them a life of their own.

Suddenly Harry is there, standing in the hall about six feet away from Mia. He gives his child a wide grin, baring his teeth, bobbling his head like a silly cartoon character to make Chloe giggle. When he turns to Mia, his eyes narrow, turn cold, dead. Mia shudders; she can't believe she had ever been intimate with him. She backs up to get away from him.

Utterly unprompted, Chloe bursts forth in glee with a small clap. "The funny man. I saw a funny man."

"Is that right, honey?" Harry says in the sweetest, child-like voice he can muster. "You are my little girl. My good little girl. I'm so proud of you."

Chloe pulls her thumb out of her mouth, without being prodded to do so. "I saw a funny man. The funny man hugs Mommy goodbye."

Harry throws his weight against the banister causing the wood to creak. "What is she talking about?"

Mia sees the pointy toe of his cowboy boot poking through the slats in the railing as if he is getting ready to kick a horse. Rarely has he been physically violent. Instead, he assaults her with his words, always cutting her to the quick.

"You know, Harry, I really wish you wouldn't lean on the banister like that. I tell Maxie the same thing all the time. It can't take the weight. One day it's going to collapse."

Harry shakes the banister. "Seems fine to me. It is a little loose." He looks at Mia. "Maybe you can find someone to fix it? In your spare time?" He waves his arm around. "You have all this that I gave to you. You even have a housekeeper, a live-in babysitter. Can't you manage to find the time to call someone to fix it?" He gives her a snide chuckle, but he does ease up on the banister, setting his foot to rest on the bottom step.

"I saw a funny man," Chloe says. "Mommy saw him too."

"What is she trying to say?" Harry asks Mia. "I don't understand what she is talking about. Do you understand what she's talking about, Mia? Don't you understand your own daughter?"

He happily shakes his head at Chloe throwing around the weight of his hair. His goofy expressions make the little girl laugh, at first. Then she pulls back, playing shy.

The little girl turns away from Harry. Mia hugs Chloe closer, pressing her cheek to her daughter's face. "Sollie Berg came here last night. I didn't know he made house calls at night."

"What?" Harry clutches his hands to his chest, but the shock does not last long. He starts laughing; then it turns uproarious, huge hoots causing his entire chest to heave. The laughter comes from the core of his being and he cannot stop, not even when it makes Chloe squirm in her mother's arms.

Mia holds Chloe tighter, first releasing her then shifting the child, propping her against her other hip and speaks haltingly. "I don't see what's so funny."

"I never thought Sollie would show up here, not in a million years. What did he want? Don't tell me. I don't want to know. It's too bizarre to think about. You and him?"

"He's a therapist."

"Uh, what?" Harry looks incredulous. No kidding. Seriously? You're kidding me, Mia. Please, tell me you're kidding."

Mia insists. "You told me he's a therapist, so I called him. I told him to come by." Chloe arches her small body away from Mia. She presses her small fingers on Mia's cheeks. Normally, Mia would kiss her fingers or playfully pretend to bite them.

Harry puts his hands in his pockets and steps closer to examine Mia's face. She recoils from his proximity and backs up.

"I did what?" Harry asks. "I did no such thing. You're crazy. Sollie Berg, a therapist! He owns the goddamn studio

I work at and everything connected to it! He owns half this town. You mean to tell me you don't know who Sollie Berg is? What makes you think he's a therapist?"

Then he leans closer to Mia, leering at her. "He's also a sex addict. Kinky," he whispers, "or so I hear." He throws his hand over his face to cover another belt of laughter. "You and Sollie Berg! Oh my God, who would believe it?"

Stumbling over her words, Mia is obviously shaken. "You don't remember recommending him to me?" She cries out, "Even last night before you went out, we talked about him." Chloe turns in Mia's arms, wriggling to be free. "I go. I get down, Mommy." Mia sets Chloe on the floor, where she scampers away, dragging her stuffed bear along the floor.

Harry draws closer to Mia. His clumsy gait is amplified by his cowboy boots that add two inches to his already impressive height. Nearly on top of her, his stare is confrontational. If he had a knife, he could easily cut her. She can feel his breath and picks up his scent, minty now and unlike the fetid odor from earlier in the morning.

Mia, you're really sick. You're out of touch with reality. I'm going to have to have a talk with Viv. I'm seriously worried about leaving you alone with the kids."

Mia flees to the living room. She hears the clomp of his cowboy boots driving hard into the wood floor, traveling in the direction of the kitchen. She is so scared, she cannot think. She cannot be sure if she is losing her mind. Her throat is parched and she knows no amount of water will quench her thirst. There have been times in her life when she has been afraid, but this is different, so terribly different; terrified, she is unable to move freely. She does not know who to ask or who to call. She is paralyzed by the notion that maybe she is losing her mind.

She turns off the TV that has probably been left on by Maxie since early this morning. Toys litter the floor: Matchbook cars, a dart gun, Chloe's plastic picture books, and loads of Legos—itty-bitty geometric shapes, self-contained units with pegs and holes in red, blue, yellow and green. A kid can build anything with Legos. Maxie loves to build robots that kill bad guys with laser weapons. Mia gets down on her hands and knees, scooping small chits of plastic into her lap as if that would somehow restore her sanity. The small pieces are sharp enough to cut someone's foot.

Harry's voice booms from the kitchen. "She's mentally ill and I don't know what to do," he is telling Viv. The old woman speaks so softly, Mia cannot hear what she is saying. Scared, she cannot swallow. Her mouth stays open so she can take in air. She wonders if they are conspiring against her, and while a part of her knows it is preposterous to think this way, she cannot stop the terror inside from robbing her capacity to think. She can no longer hear their voices rendering the decisions being made about her—that could be so patently final. For a long time, all she hears is silence and the rain.

Harry's phone emits the fluttery chirp ringtone. The ring does not last long and it relieves Mia to know he will be preoccupied with something other than saying terrible things about her to Viv. She considers for a moment that the phone call might even put him in a good frame of mind. It makes him so happy when he's about to leave for a shoot. Happy, yes, if he's happy that would be good for her, good for everyone. She stops gathering Legos, so she can concentrate on listening. His voice on the phone is light, flirtatious banter. She looks down at her long, outstretched fingers and sees the heart-shaped diamond in her wedding ring that looks dull and does not reflect light. She listens for Harry's footsteps, praying that the knot in the back of her throat will loosen and subside, maybe go away altogether.

Viv walks into the living room with Chloe tottering beside her. She looks at her mother, jumps into the air, and bounces on her tiny legs that stretch like rubber bands. Bounding toward her mother, she playfully rolls along the floor until she reaches Mia, where she settles in her lap.

"I'd like to talk to you in private," Viv tells her. Mia fears that Viv is planning to leave. *Say nothing,* Mia tells herself, giving Viv a sympathetic nod. Viv wrings her hands in her apron as if she is terribly upset. Mia examines Viv's hands, finding them to be smooth, unblemished, and unlined, unusual for a woman well into her sixties. Viv's face wrinkles with worry while she looks toward the hall, where Harry plods in his boots, talking on the phone. He scuffs the toe of his boot into the railing and kicks the wood, causing the banister to wobble. The two women look at each other but do not speak as they listen to him gathering his things in the hall, unzipping linings, buttoning down the clasps on his luggage, and the dense drag of his coat being lifted away from a Shaker peg. "Maybe after he's gone?" Viv queries Mia. "That way we can have a better conversation."

NINETEEN

SMPTE TIME CODE 10:40:17:19 Mid-morning on Thursday, Wendy Wachter sits in her light gold Mercedes sports coupe, staring vacantly into the concrete walls of an underground parking garage. The interior walls are saturated with water, bleeding dark stains. Pools of water cover most of the ground. The drainage system cannot keep up with the rain. Everywhere she turns, her entire world has taken on a mottled grey texture that is as swollen with the viscosity of water. The waterlogged pocks in concrete conjure the image of a bullet-riddled corpse that is swollen with blood.

And she does not know why she sees blood.

She checks her watch. Sollie Berg's yoga class is over. By now he has showered and dressed. Any minute, he will walk through the double-glass doors. Wendy is parked next to his Emerald Green Mercedes-Maybach G650 Landaulet. Even in dim light, the long lines of his SUV flash a metallic sheen that leaves an indelible impression of extreme wealth and luxury.

She squirms in her seat with minimal discomfort; her petite limbs are feline in movement or at rest. She pushes her black Prada coat into a soft heap in the back seat and checks the rearview mirror to make sure she did not mess the tight knot in her hair. She wants to be perfect for Sollie Berg and one way to entice him is to leave her neck uncovered.

The moment she sees him enter the garage, she jumps out of her car, yelling, "Sollie, it's me! I've been looking for you! I miss you, Sollie."

Initially, he doesn't seem thrilled about seeing her, but his mood quickly shifts away from being stern and irritated. Curiosity drives him. He is interested in knowing why Wendy Wachter would be lying-in-wait for him in the garage under his health club.

He presses his key fob to open his back door, but his eyes never leave the double-glass exit doors. Even as he tosses his green rolled-up yoga mat into the back seat of his car, he is still keeping an eye on Wendy and the doors. He likes knowing he has an exit strategy. He pulls out his phone. While he texts, he talks to Wendy. "What brings you here, Wendy? And why so many phone calls?"

"Can we talk?" She feels both rage and gut-wrenching fear because if things don't go her way, she will be out of a job. Despite her inner turmoil, she feigns a long inviting smile that accentuates her overbite and worries about getting lipstick on her teeth. "I'd like to talk to you about Harry Hill."

"What about Harry?" Then Sollie answers his own question. "I know all about Harry. You don't have to tell me anything about Harry Hill." He checks his phone to see if there is a response to his text.

Wendy gives Sollie a playful tap on his arm. "I'm concerned about what's going on with him and Jewell Cleary."

"Why should that concern you?" Sollie's eyes twitch with a touch of nastiness behind his black-framed glasses. "It's not our business. It's between him and his wife, a private matter. Let's stay out of it. Okay, doll?" Sollie draws her closer to him, a gallant gesture to keep her safely out of the way of a slow-cruising car that turns into the space across from where they stand. His kiss on her cheek lingers longer than a routine peck and he nuzzles her neck. "You always smell so good."

She sees his eyes scanning her button-size-breasts. His expression lies somewhere in between the mirthful gaze of a pixie and a pervert. A part of Wendy recoils in disgust. She feels one slender tendril spring free from her top knot into a curly-q onto her neck. The loose hair bothers her. She feels like getting scissors to cut it off. His fingers travel to her neck, entwining her stray strand of hair. He whispers into her ear. "I bet you taste good too."

His words always go right up to the edge of decency. "What's going through your mind, little girl? I've known you long enough to know when something's brewing." Sollie's touch makes her shiver but she does not stop him.

"What's the matter with my pretty baby?" Sollie croons.

Wendy is unable to restrain her tone. "Harry's gone mad. He's going AWOL. He's going off on a shoot of his own with Jewell Cleary!"

"So let him go." Sollie shrugs.

Sollie is relieved. "Harry has every right to be mad. We cancelled his production."

"He doesn't know that yet. I haven't told him." Wendy clutches her pearls to her chest, holding onto them as if she is using them like a rosary to pray to an unseen and shallow God. "I can't tell him he's been cut out of the deal.

I don't want to lose him. Where will that leave me? How can I be a producer with no director?"

Sollie touches her, tracing her brow to the nape of her neck. The sweep and span of his fingers possess the incoherent feeling of a bad dream.

He nods reassuringly. "Ray will tell him. Agency guys are always good at delivering bad news."

If we keep screwing Harry out of jobs that we bid on, that he expects to get paid—his full day rate, plus a percentage, then he'll walk."

"Not Harry," Sollie insists.

"He's going to make Jewell his producer." Reaching below the arch of her back, she manages to check the back of her pinstripe skirt to make sure her zipper is intact.

Sollie laughs. "Harry's not a fool. He'll be mad for a while, but he'll be back. Trust me on that." Sollie moves to get into his car. Look, I gotta go. I'm meeting someone and I don't want to be late."

Sollie gets into his car, and pulls out slowly, careful not to ding his car. He stops before he reaches the lane to exit the garage and rolls down the window. "This thing with Harry's no big deal," Sollie says. "It happens all the time. It's just business. Show business."

Wendy crosses her arms and nods. Her smile is wan but it is the best she can do because she is overcome by dread. Staring at the concrete walls, she wonders how much pressure is needed to jam on the gas pedal to pummel her car into the shape of an accordion. She's always been shrewd but she's not keen about screwing Harry out of getting paid for his work as a director. GASP Productions has already been paid for the work by the client. Harry has been cut out of the deal, so Sollie and Ray can skim more money off the top. It's not that Harry cares about the money, he has plenty of his own. Wendy did not want to deal with Harry's bruised ego and his rage.

The view from inside of her car is bleak, mirroring her turbulent thoughts. She feels shadows surrounding her, falling flat, one-dimensional dark energy, an omen portending trouble and misery. Something bad is going to happen. She doesn't enjoy competition with the only thing she sees, which is a concrete wall, saturated with rain. Pocked with uneven holes, the concrete suffers from premature wear and tear. With one foot on the gas and the other on the brake, she plays stop and go, on and off, in a demented form of *red light, green light*—these are the buzz words describing the financial backing of a commercial film job.

As a producer, she never knows for sure whether a job will go until she has a purchase order in her hot little hand and the check has cleared the bank. Pumping her feet, alternating the gas, the brake, like pedals on an organ, she did not know which foot would get lucky. She continues to court death, gagging on gas fumes and her own exhausted outrage. *Green light*, she mouths.

Or is it red light? She defines living and dying according to the color of a traffic light. Living or dying goes both ways. All along it has been a game, the same game along the lines of an *all new and improved* Proctor & Gamble product. Only in real life, the stakes are always higher. She considers how much force is necessary to send her car careening so fast that her head would crash through the windshield. Total wipeout. She does not know whether she would choose to live or die. Red light or green light. The game is up.

TWENTY

SMPTE TIME CODE 09:10:22:<u>20</u> Ten minutes after nine on Thursday morning, Jewell Cleary sits in her Karmann Ghia sports coupe that is parked in front of Harry Hill's home. Her windshield wipers are turned off. Every so often, when she gets cold, she starts the engine, turning the heat on high. She rolls down the window several inches. The welt of cold rain splatters against her cheeks. From the street, she sees Harry standing in the hallway, talking to the old woman who takes care of his kids. She sees no signs of Harry's wife.

Jewell has been waiting for Harry for fifteen minutes.

Inside the house, Mia is in the living room. She feels a stab in her chest, similar to all the other times she told herself to trust her husband when her gut groaned, warning her to rely on her own instincts—adultery. Serial adultery. Jewell Cleary is not the first. There have been so many others. She does not know why she feels so dependent on him.

From the living room Mia calls to Harry, "There was an earthquake this morning, did you feel it?"

The tone of Harry's voice is blasé. "No, Mia, I didn't feel it."

She runs to the hall, not knowing what she can possibly say to him to stop the madness. The dream is coming true and she has to come to terms with it. Without stopping to catch her breath, she blurts, "Harry, please stop."

Viv ambles herself out of the hallway. She does not want to be in the midst of a brawl between the two of them. Amber light flickers from the antique bronze wall sconces, casting shadows across Harry's face. The borders of the walls are stenciled in a Fleur-de-lis pattern, resembling lilies or wild irises, but in the damp, grey morning, they eye Mia like daggers.

Mia walks toward him as if she's meeting him halfway. "Please don't go," she implores him. "Harry, please. If you leave here, you're going to die. Please. This morning I had this dream. I know it sounds weird but it's true. I keep having this same dream. Please believe me. Please don't go."

"More psycho shit, Mia. What the hell are you babbling about? Why do you always talk nonsense to me?"

Harry looks away from the window, craning his neck to see the street, where Jewell sits in her car waiting for him. The sight of her blond head lowered into her phone makes him smile. He expects any second, she will call him again.

Mia tries to compose herself. She thinks if she is calm, then maybe he will listen to her. "Harry, let's forget all that has happened. Think back to when we first met? Remember how I would predict things and they'd come true? You used to kid me. Remember? Remember how you'd flip coins, heads or tails, and no matter what I always guessed right? I scored one hundred percent, remember?"

"Why is it I can't ever understand what you're saying." He turns away from her, but before he leaves, he jerks the banister and shakes it. His look is cruel; he is on the verge of laughing at her. Her first inclination is to block the front door so he cannot leave but she knows that will lead to a shoving match, or worse, great violence. Mia has always considered overt displays of anger to be deep-rooted self-hatred, which is what led her to cut herself. She'd rather hurt herself than commit an angry act against Harry Hill, even if he richly deserves it. She sits on the hall steps, forming a tight, closed ball. The door opens, letting in cold air made fresh from the rain.

Jewell sees the front door heave open against the crush of wind and just as quickly the door slams shut behind him sealing off the wind. Harry clambers down the steps in his long leather coat and cowboy boots. Weighed down by two brown leather Ghurka bags, one bag is thrown over his shoulder; he carries the second bag with his free hand. A black flap bag lying across his other shoulder holds his laptop. Jewell knows Harry well enough to see he is not happy about being a pack animal.

From inside the house, Mia sees Jewell jump out of her car to help Harry. The two of them are swapping bags, both shielding their perfect blond hair from the rain, jostling into cars, and before long, they are driving away. Jewell's Karmann Ghia follows Harry's BMW in a procession heading to parts unknown.

Mia's hands cling to the edge of a step. It is too late; she has lost him. The position she finds herself in is humiliating. Viv walks into the hallway and looks at Mia. While her face is flush with sorrow, she can no longer bite her tongue.

"Good riddance," she spits out. "Now you can be free of him."

"Then you know?" Mia asks her.

"It would be hard not to see what is going on." Viv sits on a lower step, two steps down from Mia, thrusting her knees to the side to make herself comfortable. "Unless you live through it, you can't expect anyone to understand what you're going through."

She looks up at Mia. "I've been there. I know how it feels."

"There was an earthquake this morning."

"Yes," Viv says. "It was very mild, hardly noticeable at all unless you were lying awake in bed, as I was." Viv stops talking for a moment and looks at Mia. "Actually, I was thinking about you and what's been happening around here between you and Harry. I don't want to say anything. It's none of my business, but it might seem obvious to you that your marriage is over, but it's not."

Mia feels uncomfortable under Viv's gaze. She presses her fingers along the wood close to where it abuts the wall. Finding a thin trace of dust, she rubs it between her fingers and lowers her head into her knees.

"It might seem as though he wants to get rid of you, but he just wants to control you. It can go on this way for years until he completely destroys you. That is what is so cruel. He's trying to make you think that you're crazy, and you're not. You do know that, don't you?"

Other than blinking her eyes, Mia remains still. Air is cut off from her lungs. It is too shocking to think that Harry is intentionally trying to drive her crazy. As much as she never wanted to believe it, she does know it is true. In this moment of finally admitting the truth to herself, she wants to disappear from the earth and die.

"I hear him talking about Sollie Berg," Viv says. "He's doing everything in his power to make you believe that you've lost your mind."

Mia feels a quick succession of chills traveling up her spine and settle in the two cold studs pierced in the nape of her neck. Her stomach seizes up in tight contractions, unseen concentric rings constricting her inside like thick metal bands.

"Why? But why?" Mia calls out. "I'm the mother of his children."

"I don't think he knows why," Viv says. "Men like him enjoy destroying people, especially women! They thrive on it!"

Mia is taken aback by the old woman's strong language. It's not as though she has not heard these words before or even spoken them herself; it is so unlike Viv who always presents herself as being calm, mild mannered.

"What about the children?"

Viv's voice grows louder. "Wait until you see what he does to them! He doesn't care about the children! To him, they're just props!"

Mia's voice is hoarse and rises in alarm. "Where's Chloe?"

"She's taking a nap."

"I have to take her to school soon."

Viv nods, returning to her usual state of composure, looking pensive. "Children feel everything."

Mia closes her eyes. She does not want to see the hall, her surroundings, this old house, or Viv. She thinks of Chloe and the look on her face in the playground every time she attempts to go down the slide alone.

Mia waits at the bottom of the slide, crouching in position, waiting to catch the child and cradle her in her arms. Except it never happened. Chloe would not go down the slide. She'd climb the steps all the way to the top and stand there, blocking the slide from the other kids. A long line would form on the steps behind Chloe. The kids would grow impatient and yell *go, go*, but Chloe remained unfazed.

She stood at the top of the slide, twenty feet in the air, spellbound, amazed at how small everything else could be when she had grown so tall. Eventually, Mia would climb the steps, brushing past the flanks of other kids and fetch her daughter from a less than certain fate. Then one day, Chloe came down alone. Even now, Mia could hear the excited patter of Chloe's laughter. *I did it, Mommy,* she said. *"I did it all by myself."*

Mia cannot believe it took her so long to see what Harry has been doing to her. Now the only image she can see is the expression on her daughter's face the first time she shot down the slide. She hears Viv pushing herself up from the floor, so she does not have to reach for the rickety banister. A dense hush passes between them that is louder than rain. She hears Viv gathering toys from the floor.

Opening her eyes, she sees Viv carefully looking at her. "You will have to brace yourself for what is yet to come. If you think he's been ugly up to now, you haven't

seen anything yet. Trust me on that. I've been there. He will
do anything to cut you out of the picture."

TWENTY-ONE

SMPTE TIME CODE 17:58:47:<u>21</u> Steve Olin is not sure
how much time has elapsed from when he found Harry and
Jewell. Showering has not washed away the scent of their
blood. He wants to be alone, away from Dawn and Koji,
Wendy Wachter, the cops, anyone who wants to know
what he saw.

His houseboat offers him sanctuary, his only port in
the storm. Normally rain tapping on the roof is comforting.
But on this night, the rain is an intruder interjecting
violence within the context of his thoughts, the same way
bullets rip gaping holes into flesh, eviscerating guts. He
stares toward the ceiling at a skylight; it is dark outside, and
darker in his living room. A bottle of Corona sits on his
chest. His tongue is thick and numb, not only from beer
but from fear. The rhythmic rock of the houseboat, fueled
by the wake of a passing boat, is not lulling him to sleep.

He is going to do what he has always done after a
difficult and long shoot—drink and sleep for a day, maybe
two. The frequency with which he beats the path from his
couch to the refrigerator depends on how bad he feels.
Right now, he can't imagine staggering toward another
bottle of Corona. He balances a vial of Ambien on his
chest. He's not a big fan of Ambien but he does need to

sleep. The longer he sleeps the more time and distance will be put between him and the murder. He takes two 10 mg tabs, washing them down with a slug of warm Corona and drops the vial onto the floor.

A six-pack stays close to his side, but he's done drinking. Ambien and beer don't mix. He doesn't want to end up like Heath Ledger, *who took seven tabs and never woke up.*

Steve's feet hang over the arm of the couch. If luck is with him and he suspects that it is, by the time he is done with this binge, the stubble on his chin will thicken into the first stage of a Nordic beard. He knows most women like beards. Women and working are the two most important things in his life. Yet there is a priority. If a woman interferes with his work, she's done. Breaking up with a woman is good for a two-day binge. So is the end of a shoot. But murder didn't have a precedent. Maybe three days will make him forget what he saw.

He blows across the rim of the beer bottle, making a slight whistle. Beer will soon wet his floor like piss. He waits for the Ambien to kick in. His phone is on the floor, set on silent. Every so often a call or a text comes in, lighting up his phone, but he doesn't bother to look. He isn't up to talking to anyone.

The image of blood flares up in his consciousness, vivid in the quiet moments between his first dream and deep sleep.

In the last year, he has been away on shoots in Anchorage, Lake Tahoe, Reno, San Diego, Fort Worth, Texas and Lafayette, Louisiana. The jobs and locations merge together, making one indistinguishable from the other, except for the job in Louisiana.

From Baton Rouge, he had taken a commuter shuttle into Lafayette. Driving thirty miles south to the heart of the Bayou, he landed in a small backwater town called Patoutville. More humid than hot, relief always came late in the afternoon with a surprisingly brief but fresh burst of rain. The rain was different in Louisiana and came in the form of a thunder shower with a distinct beginning, middle and end. There was a peak moment when rain came down as hard and as fast as it could fall. Then it would gradually peter out and stop.

Rain is different in Seattle. Large cold drops fall from the sky for days, flooding an unsuspecting earth, overflowing drains, sewers and waterways, saturating soil, turning into mudslides. He listens to the drone of rain, two hundred and fifty beats per minute—the relentless precision of a metronome. It is hard to find a measure of silence within the beats. Thin shards of stillness come and go, cutting into his heart. Given what he saw, he feels as though he has a right to expect something bad will happen any second.

He hears the scratch of metal on his roof. The skylight overhead reminds him there is so little sun from October through June. For nine months, the soles of his boots sink into the earth. Rain is why Steve prefers to live on the water. No matter how high the water rises, his houseboat is made to float. He hears footsteps outside on the dock and hopes it is an illusion cast from the wind.

He drifts back to the shoot in Louisiana—for a new Jambalaya food product made by Kraft. Out on the backyard Bayou, the setting was classic live oak choked with black moss and swamp. The Kraft spots were *slice-of-life*, resembling the Cajun bands at FAIS-DODO—the Saturday night country dances held in southern Louisiana.

Harry Hill had cast twenty-five Cajun extras with no acting experience. Once the camera started to roll, Hill directed them to sit at a thirty-foot-long table and to eat expressively—this kind of spot is called a *bite and smile*.

In Steve's stupor of half sleep, between limbo and a dream, he smiles. There had been a woman at the Jambalaya shoot. He couldn't remember her name. Black hair, dark skin, full lips, eyes like ink, she resembles Mia Hill. Both are dark angels.

He hears metal clanging in the wind. Despite his rattled nerves, he reasons it away. Last summer, he had replaced his rotting-wooden downspouts and gutters with the kind made from corrugated tin. It's cheaper but no less durable. Eventually, the metal will wear out and rust. As an afterthought, he had added the skylight. He's not a skilled carpenter. Now his handiwork haunts him, making fun of his impatience and the way he swore every time he had drilled a crooked bit into the metal frame with his Machida, the wireless drill that grips use to skillfully put up walls on a set.

He's been dozing but does not know how long. Another sip of beer would feel good going down, but he is too tired to reach for the bottle and lift it to his mouth. There is light wake on the water and the wind can no longer be heard. Every so often, he experiences a weird sensation in his chest, skips sharper than a startle reflex.

In the Jambalaya shoot, the Michot Brothers played fast, hard-driving Jambalaya music while a whole lot of Cajun hot sauce was slathered on ribs, steaks, shrimp, crayfish and oysters. The only problem with the goddamn shoot is that it would not stop raining.

The Cajun extras spoke their own patois, a combination of French slang with words borrowed from Spanish, English, German, Native American and African. The woman with black hair tried to teach him but he had forgotten her and the words. The Cajuns were superstitious, and one man had spooked Steve, accusing him of bringing rain to the Bayou like a curse. The man had been the black-haired woman's friend. His eyes were darker than hers.

On the day before the Jambalaya shoot, the rain had been coming down as cold and as steady as the rain in Seattle. Harry Hill got wind of the Cajun man's superstition. He got so spooked, he ordered Steve off the set and sent him packing home to Seattle. Dawn Stein hired a Cajun shaman who had the power to cast spells. She paid him a hundred bucks. It stopped raining just long enough to shoot the spot.

A Cajun shaman could make a lot of money in Seattle.

Metal whines, grating overhead. He does not remember hearing this sound before. Something on the roof has shaken loose in the wind. He stands on the couch, clumsily tapping the skylight with the tip of his baseball bat. Drunk and drugged, he stumbles on the cushion of the couch. The glass pane moves a notch in its frame but seems to be secure.

The rain has not let up. Shadows drift across his walls, darker than his room, darker than the night. He does not know where the shadows are from. The light on the dock turns on, activated by motion. Living on the water exacerbates every sound, distorting reality. He thinks the footsteps he had heard earlier and had dismissed were real because now he knows for sure someone is coming.

More than one person is on the dock; two distinctly different types of walks, one, a crunching gait, another light-footed and rubber-soled. Shifting himself on the couch, a wedge of wood comes up between his legs.

Steve gets up from the couch, swinging his baseball bat. Now someone is knocking on his door, calling his name. He doesn't care who it is, even if it's the cops, he is not going to talk to anyone. He picks up a bottle of Corona, presses it to his lips and drinks it all in one thirsty chug. He grins at the front door and belches. "Go away!" He drops the bottle to the floor and lets it roll.

He clearly hears Dawn Stein and Koji Matsuno calling his name. Dawn Stein yells at him through the front door. "We want to know what happened, Steve! Would you open up and talk to us?"

TWENTY-TWO

SMPTE TIME CODE 13:48:03:22 Before two on Thursday afternoon, Harry's car splashes up torrents of water that are rushing downhill from Jewell Cleary's

driveway. He parks his BMW close behind Jewell's round
bubble of a Karmann Ghia, slightly touching her rear
bumper. Harry and Jewel pop open a large black umbrella,
which is immediately attacked by wind, turning inside out,
bending spokes. Harry clutches the umbrella to his side as if
he is wielding a shield. Holding onto one another, they run
from the rain, stumbling toward her house. After a quick
lunch, they had enough time to take care of personal
business before heading to the airport.

The steel grey light in the sky makes it difficult to see.
Rain washes over them, dampening their faces. A gust of
wind flings a small wooden planter against the side of the
house. Jewell lets go of Harry and runs toward the planter,
but Harry grabs her by her hair. "Come on, Jewell," Harry
yells over the din of wind. "I don't want to get wet! Let's
get inside! Hurry! What's taking you so long?"

Harry almost bumps into a large green recycling bin
blocking the path to the front steps. "You should really
move this thing!"

He is shocked to see her pull out a key from inside of
her mailbox. She turns the key in the lock and pushes open
the door. She drops the key back into the mailbox, making
a metal ping.

"You really shouldn't leave your key in the mailbox.
Anyone can get in."

Jewell gives Harry a coy smile as if he is being unduly
alarmist, and playfully pushes him into the house. Harry
steps inside the hall and tries to shut the door but the wind
works against him. He leans against the door, forcing it
shut. She hears the steady thumping of rain on the roof and
an occasional swish from cars passing, throwing off water

on the road. He takes the bent black umbrella and drops it into a stand.

Harry notices details; even when he's not on the set, his mind functions strategically as though he's staging a shot for the camera. Jewell has already packed her bags. Her Ghurka luggage is set on the floor in the living room by the fireplace. Harry smiles to himself. The luggage was a good buy and probably the only gift he will ever give to Jewell.

He pulls out his phone and texts Steve Olin: "Where the fuck are you, cowboy?"

Jewell doesn't bother to turn on the light. She smiles and takes him by the hand. Guiding him into the living room, she flips a wall switch by the fireplace, igniting a dim blue flame that erupts into full amber fire. She leans her body against Harry and pulls his weight toward her. He opens his mouth in a kiss that is meant to linger, but she stops him, presses her fingers to his lips, tracing the line of his mouth. "Don't talk," she says. "Don't ever talk unless I tell you to."

He loves it when she does this to him. He leans forward to kiss her again, but she does not accept the offer. Prodding him to a cassock stool in front of the fire, she slowly squats to the ground in a rocking rhythm. He is sitting too. She looks into his eyes, a serene but provocative stare, nary a flicker or a blink. He returns her look with a bemused expression on his face as if to ask, *what's next?*

"Do you still want me to do it?" She thinks her gaze is a way of peering into his soul.

Harry doesn't see it quite that way. He runs his hand along the line in between her breasts. He knows he is going to get laid and it's going to be one of the greatest fucks of all time—that's what he always says to himself until the next one comes along.

"Your hair," she says, running her fingers lightly, twisting a few select pieces of his slightly damp hair into loose curls. "Are you sure?"

Harry nods. "If that will make you happy. Why not?"

"What about Mia? Won't she mind?"

"I'm not thinking about her. Why should you?"

Jewell runs her hands along the inside of his thighs and lowers her head toward his crotch. She gives him a sweet kiss, inhales deeply as if she is intoxicated by his scent and traces her finger along his zipper.

"Good design thinking," he says, as if he is trying to hold himself back. "I thought I was supposed to do that to you."

"Don't get me started," she says, rising to kiss him.

"Don't stop," he says.

"Give me a sec."

"You're magnificent." She is the most enchanting woman who has ever walked on earth; the only woman who can sap his strength and tame him. *His Delilah.*

She breaks contact with him and walks toward her dining room. Her feet pad through a thin trail of wispy bonsai leaves, making a papery rustle.

She unwraps her shears from a flat grey box and holds them up for him to see. "They cost me nearly three thousand dollars."

They do look expensive and very sharp. He wonders if there is enough time to fuck and get his hair cut. He cannot decide which one he wants more right now. He always wants to fuck, but he can wait until they get to Costa Rica. He knows she will never get her scissors through airport security in their carry-on bags.

Her shears catch light from the fire, bouncing images of glowing tongues in orange and yellow around the grey walls. The blades look more than sharp, as if one precise cut would whack off a finger.

Jewell's lips are thick with nude gloss. "Hello." The smile she gives him is wide and generous, but with her, that is always a compromise. She only appears to be giving of herself. She wants to take everything she can get. For a moment, she sets the shears to the side. Pulling the sweater over her head, she drops it to the floor. Now she is only wearing a thin T-shirt, no bra and a lacy thong. Black. Everything Jewell wears is black.

She holds the shears by the side of her face, which gives her a seriously witchy look. He thinks about wrestling the shears from her and whacking off her hair before she cuts his.

"I can put a bowl over your head." Her smile is *off*, slightly crooked.

Holding the shears along the side of her leg, she walks around him, appraising him from every angle. To him, her walk feels like a stunning pivot. He can feel her breath and detects her earthy fragrance. Even her hair throws out its own brand of heat. He does not know how long she will linger before she glides around him. He never trusts anyone standing behind his back, but, in this case, he feels like he is wearing a blindfold and loves the suspense of not knowing what she will do next.

She stops moving and takes a deep breath. He sees the shears at rest on top of the fake-stone hearth, where the blades catch light from the fire. She parts his hair into three sections, banding his hair into long sheaths, three ponytails.

She stands behind him, so he cannot see what she is doing but he can smell her earthiness and detects her movement. She slowly raises the shears and cuts from only one section. The first few strands fall to the floor like the golden locks that a woman would carry in her locket as a keepsake to hold close to her heart forever.

Jewell is not interested in having him forever. She has already shown herself to be purely selfish, lacking in conscience. She will take any man or any woman she wants. She touches him under his chin to tilt his head up toward her face so she can look into his eyes. In her other hand, she holds the shears toward the light of the fire. "Aren't you afraid that cutting your hair will sap your strength?"

Harry feels himself easing into a smile. It's an intentional response designed to be both sarcastic and sexual. Even in his submission to her, he is still the one in charge. He is looking at eye level with her pussy and reaches forward to stroke her, but she stops him with a firm hand and keeps pressing it there. "I'll be the one to decide," she says. "I'm always the one who decides."

He enjoys this charade. He would never let a woman have this much power over him if the game was about something practical and more powerful than sex. In all other aspects of his life, he is always the one in control.

The movement of her hands is intended to be playful, not careful. The blades of the sheers come together in a slender sharp point. She cuts off each ponytail. One, two, three, each tail falls to the floor in a hush. "I've decided to cut your hair dry," she tells him. "This way I can see every small detail."

She uses her hands to brush all of his hair forward, creating a long pompadour, but it is only temporary. He can hear her cut and sees pieces of his hair, fine and fragile, falling on the floor. "I'm giving it slight texture on the ends."

He breathes heavily, not sure if it is due to the excitement of having her so close, bearing a lethal weapon, taking control over him, or if it is anticipation of what he will look like once the cutting is done.

"Don't move," she sternly tells him.

"If I was moving, I wasn't aware of it," he says, but he's lying. He is only willing to be subject to her whims for brief glimmers of time. It's a game. She thinks it's her game, but it's really his call. He's in charge.

From around his back, she walks toward the fire and turns to look at him. "It's coming along. I'm keeping the angle in mind and giving it length on top and on the sides. The back is shorter and very slick."

He is growing hot in front of the fire. The fireplace kicks out too much heat. He wants to move but has been given strict orders not to do so. "May I take off my shirt? It's so hot in here."

Jewell tilts her head, smiles and stands slightly away from where he sits. "Leave your shirt on until I tell you it's okay to remove it."

He folds his arms across his chest, and stares ahead, where he sees the clutter of empty Starbucks cups heaped on overstuffed floor cushions and the frame of a director's chair missing its canvas seat. He remains still as if he is completely giving himself over to her.

"I want you to cut my hair. Just like the spot," he says.

Jewell smiles as she walks toward Harry; her gaze never wavers. "You have great bone structure." She reaches toward his face and runs her fingers from his ear, along his jaw, to his chin and places her fingers in his mouth, beckoning him to close his lips. She wants him to suck her fingers and he does. Her free hand lifts the shears and snips his hair in front of his face, close to his eyes. "I'm taking it right up to the edge," she tells him. "Isn't that where you want to be?"

TWENTY-THREE

SMPTE TIME CODE 02:17:10:23 At 2:17 a.m. on Thursday, cutting spots about haircuts has got Kenny thinking about getting one. Yet he knows once he's done cutting this spot, he's not going to do a thing to his hair. He likes his hair just the way it is. He crushes an empty pack of Camels and tosses it onto the Electronic Cutting Board (ECB), the school-room-size yellow table underneath the two video monitors and the control deck.

He doesn't like cutting in video, but few directors these days shoot in film. He crushes another can of Diet Coke and tosses it onto the table close to three other cans. He smokes the same number of cigarettes whether he's cutting film or video. His ashtray is not overflowing. The ladies keep track of the butts. The big one empties the ashtray every time he makes a new editorial decision. The blond one is gone, off to 7-ELEVEN to buy him a new Bic.

Kenny has reason to glare at the big one. Ensley Sharp's eyes are blinking too often for his satisfaction. She's losing the fight to make it through the night. Until Andy returns from 7-ELEVEN, he is down to one pack, and that is a scary place to be. Kenny has plenty to track: cigarettes, the spots he is cutting, the ladies, and the Master.

Oh, he could go on and on about the Master.

The Master always wore sunglasses, the shiny, *can't see my eyes*, mirrored kind. No one could see the Master's eyes. Kenny mimics covering his eyes. If Ensley notices his odd gesture, she doesn't react. Thinking about the Master excites Kenny. Day and night, the Master wore mirrored sunglasses and he wore jeans everywhere, even to fancy Hollywood parties.

The day Kenny met the Master, he wore dog tags around his neck like a broken-down war veteran. The Master had not served in combat though. The U.S. military doesn't get a guy like that. The Master had too much talent. Real talent stands out, like the suspension of time in an editing room.

Kenny laughs to himself. He feels a touch bitter and doesn't know why. He holds his hands up and moves in on Ensley's face. She does not know what he is doing and leans back.

"Real talent shines for the whole world to see," he says. "Ever meet a guy who's got it? I mean real presence?"

Ensley's nose flares as if she is getting itchy and about to sneeze. Kenny feels like he needs to slap someone hard.

He'll wait until the blond girl is back. He doesn't think
Ensley can stand a good shaking. He feels his lips twitch
and his nose is getting itchy too. He wonders if he is having
a physical withdrawal response left over from the days of
craving toot. Back in the eighties and nineties, he could not
cut without snorting cocaine. He snorted so much coke
that he ruined his sinuses and lost the ability to feel
pleasure, and that, too, is a scary place to be.

Kenny could really lose it once he got to thinking
about the Master. He spins on his stool. "The Master could
stop you cold with a look," he tells Ensley. "Make you drop
your panties too." He keeps talking, swiveling and smoking.
"The Master could make you drop your panties before you
even knew they hit the floor."

Kenny didn't stop to look for her reaction. He vividly
remembers the Master, so powerful and strange; it is as if
the Master is there in the editing room with him. The
mirrored sunglasses did the trick—that's what got him
hooked. It's like the Master didn't want anyone to see his
eyes. Kenny took a long drag from his last cigarette. He had
to think about the Master for a while. There was more to
the mirrored sunglasses—Kenny never did get to see the
Master's eyes.

Kenny is pivoting on the stool. He didn't mean to
home-in on the big girl, but he feels as though she belongs
to him. The effect of the Master's mirrored sunglasses is
strange. When Kenny looked at the Master, he was forced
to look at himself.

Kenny grabs his nose and pulls on it as if he's clearing
his nostrils. "When the Master wore those glasses, you got
to see yourself reflected in his eyes," he tells Ensley. "And

you know how it is.... You've seen yourself in somebody's mirrored sunglasses. Your features look distorted." He stretches the skin on his cheeks as if they are made from putty. "It's like looking into a mirror in a fun house."

Kenny stops talking and is filled with loathing. Ensley does not laugh at any of his funny faces. He zooms his face close to hers. "Maybe the Master wore those glasses, so he could show us how stupid we all look."

The big girl didn't pull away as if it was too much trouble to avoid him. Although she did close her eyes and exhale a long warm breath to the tune of a faint sigh.

Kenny is close enough to smell the coffee she is drinking to stay awake. "Wake up," he nudges her.

She opens her eyes and yawns. "I am so sorry, but I really don't know what you are talking about." She takes another sip of coffee. Her eyes wander to the monitor where the young blond dude's smile is huge but frozen.

Kenny knows the look he is giving her will give her a good kick in the seat of the pants. He is giving her the regular old short shrift of indignation. The girl feels his gaze without looking at him. Kenny doesn't know why but he finds himself hating the big girl. The Master would have fired her by now, even if she was his favorite. The Master didn't play favorites. Kenny doesn't play favorites.

"The Master fired his own daughter from the set of *The Getaway*," Kenny blurts in a supercharged voice. He knows he is getting heated but that doesn't mean he can stop it. "The Master fired his own fucking daughter! I mean the *sonovabitch* was awesome. He fired his own fucking daughter and you have nothing to say!"

The big girl has a face like a mannequin. Kenny can't tell what she's thinking, and he doesn't like that.

"You don't know who I'm talking about, do you?"

At first, the girl doesn't say anything, then she licks her lips as though she's gathering courage. "Nope, Sir, I don't think I do know," she says, turning away from him.

"Don't think just because you're pretty to look at and because I like you, you've got a leg up on me." Kenny points to himself. "Me and the Master are the same. We think the same. We do the same. We are the same."

She closes her eyes, cringing. She is too afraid to say anything, but it's not a primordial fear. Ensley Sharp is getting worn down like the dull blade on a knife.

Kenny is enraged beyond what he can bear. His fist comes down and hits the top of the bright yellow table. "I'm talking about the fucking Master and you're not hearing me!"

The girl's words squeak. "You're talking about the monitor. Right? The master video monitor?"

Kenny jumps off of his stool, picks it up and starts thumping it against the floor. The girl puts her hands on top of her head, bracing herself for a blow. It's good Ensley is shielding herself because Kenny does not know for sure what he is going to do. He takes the damn stool and slams it upside down onto the floor. Banging the stool repeatedly, the blows are buffered by the stool's cushion seat. He stands there, staring at the silver spin of the stool's metal ball wheels.

Kenny screams in a hoarse voice, "I'm talking about the greatest filmmaker who ever lived!"

Being overcome with profound grief is enough to make him shut up. The stool's wheels stop spinning and catch the silver glint of light from the monitors. The big girl still has her hands on top of her head to protect herself. Kenny doesn't have any energy, no fight is left in him, and he has lost the will to live. Thinking about the Master is serious. Very serious.

Blubbering like a fool makes Kenny's nose run. After years of going without toot, his whole body is fighting through another long night. Tears come into his eyes. He's going to break down and totally lose it. He doesn't want this to happen, but it is. His voice is cutting up, skipping words, and he is finding it hard to breathe. Whispering, he is whispering in the cadence of pure devotion. "I loved him. I would have done anything for him. He is the greatest filmmaker who ever lived. I would have died for him."

The door to the editing suite blasts open. Andy Andrisevic whisks a stream of white light into the dark cavern of a room. "What's going on?" Carrying a white plastic 7-ELEVEN bag, she immediately takes charge of the situation. "Where are we?"

Ensley feels grateful for Andy's reentry into the fracas but at the same time, she wants to cut her throat. The only thing standing between her and getting the job is Andy Andrisevic. While she hates the girl, she is relieved to have a companion in misery. They are frenemies in a perfect storm.

"Animals, bestiality?" Andy quips.

"Girl, is that what's really on your mind? If that's the case, just say so."

Ensley looks serious. "I'd rather not. Really."

"The Master knew how to use animals," Kenny says. "More animals were killed on one of the Master's shoots than you could shake a stick at."

"Please," Ensley says, "I think I know where this is going."

Kenny points his finger at her. In her own way, she was telling him she had a special place in her heart for animals. It was a mistake.

"Remember *Pat Garret*? Think those birds were props? They bled real blood, man. Think them horses going down didn't hurt? Horses died on the Master's shoots, man. It was cruel but necessary. The Master took the trouble to do violence right."

Kenny makes the sound of an implosion of air being sucked into his windpipe. He puffs up his chest and flaps his hands in the air. "Spilling blood meant something to the Master. The dude was not a pussy. Nor was he ever pussy whipped."

Ensley winces and reaches for a cigarette. Smoking might be the only way to calm her inner turmoil.

Kenny catches Ensley's visceral response and nudges Andy like a pal. He knows it is just him and him alone, working two girls, one against the other. Andy gives *good smile*. He likes the way she laughs in response to his jokes. They are starting to connect. In twenty-two years, Kenny Kix has had his share of assistants. Some good, some bad; the good ones have gone on to cut on their own. He is trying to figure Andy. Is she good or bad? He only knows she is not as fine looking as the big one. Her frizzy blond hair looks like a bad dye job.

"The women in the Master's films always had great breasts. Susan George, Madge Sinclair, Marete Van Kamp: their breasts were awesome, very white and throbbing with female power. The Master knew what to do with *Woman*."

"Right," the big girl says. She pulls a knife out of her purse and flicks it open. It's not a switchblade, but close. She repeatedly stabs the plastic encasing the Bics to free a lighter.

Kenny wonders if he has pushed her too far but no one has ever stabbed him in the editing room, and his assistants have never slit their wrists. He whispers to her. "Life isn't all about fucking. It's really about cutting. That's all I know. I like to cut. Looks like you do too."

With the knife still in her hands, Ensley closes her eyes. "I think I'm going crazy. I'm really starting to lose it!" She makes a noise in her throat as if she is gagging.

They wait for Ensley to regain composure.

"Who is the Master?" she asks.

Andy looks at Ensley as though she is insane. "How could you take this job if you don't know about the Master?"

Ensley intends to *head butt* her.

Andy shakes her head, feigning shock. "She doesn't know who Sam Peckinpaugh is!!"

"Sam Peckinpaugh?" Ensley's voice quavers. "He's dead and creepy!"

Kenny looks right at Ensley, giving her a smile that is deliberately sinister. "Lady, you have made an erroneous jump cut!" Then he laughs.

Andy punches him on the shoulder like he is her pal. For Andy to touch him is not cool. He is the one who gets to do the touching. "You are so seriously twisted," he says, throttling her by the shoulder, giving her a good shake." He hears Ensley gasp, but he is focused on Andy's eyes rolling, fluttering whites. It is a very emotional response. She understands his message in the core of her Russian heart. The way she jiggles in her seat, even after a good shaking, Kenny could swear she is trying to show off her breasts...which aren't bad...as if he could give a shit. *Hot damn*! Kenny has been through these play-offs about a thousand times. Like the Master, he had his priorities and *Woman* isn't it. He didn't always allow the winner to warm his bed.

Cutting is the real hot seat.

TWENTY-FOUR

SMPTE TIME CODE 12:33:01:24 Mia Hill goes grocery shopping at 12:33 p.m. on Thursday. She bursts into the Metropolitan Market on Queen Anne Hill, stamping her tall black leather boots on a rubber mat to shake them free of water, dead leaves and the hard-bitten chill of her husband's abuse. Her face is on fire, yet the sting of his incessant cruelty brings tears to her eyes. The two incongruent forces of anger and grief operate as twin engines propelling her from the safe nest where she has stayed cowering for days, weeks, months—she cannot pinpoint the precise span of time tracking her descent into despair and a desperation so pronounced that she cuts herself to feel something, anything, even if it is only a fleeting stab of pain.

She does not understand how she allowed it to happen. The first warning signs were subtle. He didn't treat her badly every day. In the beginning, his cruelty seemed uncharacteristic. She made excuses for him, blaming his behavior on the pressures of work. She repeated a saying she had extracted from a book of wise but anonymous quotations. *This too shall soon pass* became a daily mantra. But his nastiness grew frequent and more overt until she stopped making excuses for him.

Then it was too late.

She was broken.

People swarm around her. Even though she doesn't make eye contact with anyone, she can feel them, nestling close to the polished sheen of her black leather coat. Wheeling her cart through the produce section, she scans the bounty of vegetables, apples and pears, and the wonderful gourds of the season. The sight of golden delicata, butternut and acorn squash falls heavy in her heart. She stares into bins full of sugar snap peas and string beans, as though they have the power to give her new life.

Normally, she would lower her head, scrunch her chin to her neck, and try to hide her swollen and splotchy face from the world.

But things have changed.

The realization of knowing what her husband has been doing to her, intentionally and diabolically, takes her breath away. For the first time in many months, her malaise lifts, floating away like fog dissipating in the distance, across the Puget Sound.

he is waking up from her own very bad dream.

Pinching the heads of raw cauliflower into a plastic produce bag, she turns sharply to the side, creaking her cart forward along the ledge of a bin holding jumbo potatoes, some bakers, some red, and yams. She shakes, not from fear but from the rage that used to be hidden and repressed but is now unbidden and about to explode. She fumbles with the grocery cart, banging it against her own leg, which further enrages her.

She is not willing to hurt herself ever again!

The cutting is done.

Two large white potatoes fall to the ground. One hits the tip of Mia's toe, then rolls away. She does not know what causes the potatoes to fall but stops to pick up the one that hit her foot and returns it to the bin. From the corner of her eye, she feels someone watching her. Normally, she would pay no mind, but today is different. Today she is starting a new life. Anything can happen.

An Asian man picks up the other errant potato and places it back into the bin. His black leather gloves are the same texture and sheen as her coat. A fresh surge of blood swells in her cheeks. The man's skin is pale and luminous as though it has been washed in the soft water of Seattle's insidious rain. She recognizes him from somewhere but can't be sure. His stance is cold, unsmiling, but not unfeeling; there is warmth in his eyes. She detects he is being polite. He wears all black, a turtleneck under a leather jacket on top of black pants. He gives her a small nod of recognition, then walks away into the hustle of fast-moving shopping carts and throngs of lunch hour shoppers.

She turns around to look for him, but he is gone—disappeared through the store's automatic doors, swallowed up by the gale-force wind and the rain that is slanting sideways from the sky. Her previously faint recollection of him grows sharp. She remembers him. Koji Matsuno is a gaffer. Harry hires him for every shoot. He was on the shoot the day Harry banished her from the set. She remembers Jewell leaving Harry, going to the sidelines, talking to Koji. The thought of Koji being an eyewitness to the public humiliation she had endured at the hands of her husband enrages her the way it should have on the day that it happened. She was dead then.

She is no longer dead now.

The store is packed. Every check stand has a line five deep, six feet apart, seeping into the back aisles. The electronic hum of registers vibrates. She catches the video monitor overhead. A video loop demonstrates how to toss asparagus over macaroni to make an all new and improved instant supper, *Supreme Chicken de-lite*. Visual intrusion into her psyche is everywhere. She tries to remember why she came here.

Her hands lock onto the handle of her grocery cart but do not tremble. She is growing very sure of herself. A new confidence is rising. She is not reverting to the woman she had been before sharing her life with Harry Hill. What is evolving is someone new. She surges forward with the cart and begins to move. Warm venom seeps into her hands like an urge. She jostles someone in the thigh and another person in the back. She hears a pissed-off groan but does not stop to apologize.

It is their own damn fault for getting too close.

Glossy images of insanely beautiful people scream at her as she careens by the magazine counter. Small palpitations prickle her skin. Too much information. So little time. Mia could not tell hype from bald-faced lies and the truth, as if any truth could be had at all. Perfect images of perfect people of the new world order leak a flood of propaganda as oppressive as the Seattle rain. Images of shining bare skin mount, one after another, congealing together and percolating like a subterranean demon emerging from the depths of her consciousness. Every image is designed to seduce, the same way her husband uses sex to sell products in television commercials.

Something physical overtakes her body. It manifests itself in the core of her gut and cuts her to the quick. She is feeling sick, something intestinal; it is nausea, similar to morning sickness as if she is preparing to give birth. The first wave rolls through but when it comes to pass, a terrible anger foments in the core of her being that is neither kind nor good.

"Why can't women be angry?" she yells.

If anyone hears, no one pays attention.

A genie of freedom cuts loose in the fragile place she calls a soul. She feels anger, rote anger, brutal anger, the primitive anger locked down deep in the maidenhead of all genes traceable back to a woman named Eve. She unleashes this gust of pure fury, fuming and foot-stomping, aiming toward no one in particular but away from the polite fortress of her stomach, and most certainly away from the self-concocted nest she has made by cutting her wrists. She is surprised at the intensity of what she feels. For the first time in months, she is filled with passion and outrage.

She slams into the dairy product aisle, where the dairy case holds more varieties and flavors than there are milk-producing animals. She picks up a gallon jug of non-fat and throws it into her cart, bellowing, "Milk does the body good!"

People stay away at a safe distance, giving her space. She feels crazy but powerful. Whisking her cart down the next aisle as fast as a car out of control on the freeway, she finds herself surrounded by two insurmountable walls of cereal. She begins to hear the litany of her husband's reel shout from the shelves—the full power of his sexy *bite and smile* spots inducing America to buy, buy, buy. Always be on the lookout for something new, something fresh, something better. Don't ever be satisfied with what you have. Never rest on your laurels.

You're only as good as your last spot.

Full of high fructose corn syrup and artery-clogging saturated fat, with palm oil modified to give it sugary flavor, cereal is poison, poison to people, poison to children. Delirious with rage, she plunges her cart headlong into a crisp lined floor display of Cracklin Oat Bran. Two boxes tumble to the floor. The mishap makes her even more furious. Manning her cart like a machine gun, she lets the pile of cereal boxes have it. She rams them over and over, yelling, "Crackling Oat Bran, the crunchy baked cereal, more please." The cereal boxes topple from their display, maimed, pummeled into a twisted heap of mashed and dented cardboard.

Speeding forward, "Honeycomb. Nutritious corn cereal with a crunch kids love," she belts out in a big voice, aiming her cart into the center of the well-stocked shelves.

Hurling the boxes into her cart like a lunatic who has won the grand prize of an unlimited shopping spree, she yells, "If they want me to buy, I'll buy!"

"Total cornflakes," she squeals. "More nutritious and better tasting than the leading cornflakes!" Rows of cereal boxes fall flat on the shelves like dominos. "Kellogg's Cornflakes, America's only cornflake," she yells, kicking the boxes down to the shiny floor.

She raises her arms high above her head to reach the tallest shelf. Swooping down boxes, she tosses some into her cart and most onto the floor, "Cinnamon Toast Crunch, less sugar than most cereals. Cocoa Pebbles, nutritious rice cereal your kids will love!"

Every ad slogan Harry Hill had manipulated through the perfect lens of his video camera echoes in the chambers of her broken heart.

"It's all a big lie and it's called Advertising!"

A small bead of perspiration forms above her upper lip. The store is too damn hot. But heat did not account for the other afflictions that beset her. Her entire face begins contracting in the unmistakable motion of a spasmodic twitch. Like a stroke victim, she flares her nostrils, is unable to breathe, and her eyes are unable to focus.

Using her feet and arms, head and back, she kicks and bashes hordes of cereal boxes. "All new! New! All new and improved! Introducing! New system! Free! Save! Try! More! Fewer! Better! Best! Fast! Quick! Low! Light! Low fat! No fat! Reduced fat! Special! Loaded! Nutritious! Delicious! Delicious and good for you!"

An alarming wave of nausea attacks Mia. As she waits for it to pass, she gains some semblance of sanity. She tells herself: *anger is but a brief madness.*

"How many fucking brands of cereal do we need? Is this America or is it the fucking end of civilization?!"

Sinking to the ground, she kneels before a thunderous pile of Quaker Oats and cradles the broken canister to her lap as if it is a newborn child. Picking up dry oats by the fistful, she asks in a calm voice, "Why did they have to change the lid and get rid of the little string? I mean why did they have to go plastic?"

She hears the murmur of incredulous voices. She didn't have to look up to see the crowd. At the forefront, store personnel stand with their hands on their hips, observing her. No one moves to arrest her, not even the store's security guard. After so many years of shopping there, they recognize her face, and some know her name. She gets up from the floor, shaking off dried oats. Most of the crowd is losing interest and trickling away. Damage settles everywhere. The floor is covered with broken cereal boxes and a glut of crumbs, flakes, crispy wheat things and oat bran. The store manager asks her what happened. Without the slightest hint of embarrassment, Mia's voice pipes up like a mighty organ in a dead church. "I think I had a heart attack," she tells him. She's not lying; it's as close to the truth as she can get.

TWENTY-FIVE

SMPTE TIME CODE 13:17:26:<u>25</u> From the old brick
building housing GASP Productions, Steve Olin takes a
short walk to the J&M Cafe in Pioneer Square. Steve rarely
drinks during his lunch hour, but today is different. He's
celebrating his amazing score with Wendy Wachter—she's
going to give him a shot to direct his first spot. His big
break is one patch of blue among the many dark clouds that
have descended. Time slows for Steve, allowing him to
revel in the moment. He has time to kill before he picks up
Harry Hill and Jewell Cleary.

From inside the tavern, through its wide store front
window, he sees cold grey water spreading across
cobblestone. He's glad to be in the J&M Café, taking refuge
from the rain, washing down his burger and hand-cut fries
with beer. He gazes at the antique bevel mirror behind the
bar where he cannot see his own reflection and hangs his
parka on a brass hook. Claiming to be Seattle's oldest bar,
the woodwork in the J&M Cafe is a relic dating back to the
late 1800s. The bar was one of the first built shortly after
the Great Seattle Fire had torched most of Pioneer Square.
He still finds it hard to believe that this gloomy, wet city
could catch fire.

The comfort of taking his last bite of a thick burger
slathered with bacon and cheddar, gives him a sense of
well-being. Winning over Wendy Wachter is a stroke of

good luck and an amazing accomplishment that makes him ache with pride. And he's not going to let anyone take away what he's earned fair and square.

His thumb grazes over the Corona label once or twice. The beer is solid gold, the same color as his waitress's hair. Steve keeps glancing in her direction, hoping to catch her eye, but she does not notice him. He retreats and reads the label on his beer bottle. He prefers Corona over any other beer. His father used to drink Bud and crunch each can when he was done.

The waitress stands in front of the service end of the bar, waiting for an order. Steve can see her from a different perspective in the mirror. Long black lashes, thick black eyeliner, her blond hair is ratted into a loose top knot. Wearing a lacy baby doll camisole over black leggings, she works hard to create the look of messy chic. Her attitude says *I don't care if anyone looks at me.* But Steve knows that is a lie.

Out on the street during a shoot, he sees girls like her all the time, craving attention, wanting to be noticed. They walk on the street and act nonchalant, but as soon as they get close to the camera and crew, they assume a special way of walking, offering themselves like sacrificial lambs being led to slaughter: hips, legs, tits and hair, pretty packages on the verge of being discovered.

Steve always hears their voices. *Are they making a movie? Who's in it? Is anybody famous?*

When they learn it's only a television commercial, they lose interest and disappear.

Non-film people think film production is only about making movies and don't know a fortune can be spent on a single 30-second spot. Making a commercial is a very cool thing to see. More crew members are on the set than it takes to populate a small town. P.A. grunts are running with their walkie-talkies, asking people to be quiet until the take is done. Cops are hired to manage crowds of onlookers and to guard the talent, the crew, expensive equipment, and the huge Winnebago holding wardrobe and dressing rooms. There is always a dreamy mixture of excitement and anticipation in the air—the feeling that at any moment, a star or two could turn the shoot into an Instagram moment.

Steve smiles at his waitress for longer than he intends. If he had seen her on the street during a shoot, he would have made it a big point to ignore her. Pretending gawking onlookers don't exist is the foremost rule of crew etiquette.

The waitress takes his smile to mean he wants another beer and returns his smile to show she gets his message. His eyes cross the expanse of the long wooden bar, pausing to rest on the back of the waitress's legs (they are no big deal) and up to the television, tuned in to CNN without sound.

A couple of guys are sitting at the bar. Wearing dirty jeans and sweatshirts, they have the rough animated look of men who work with their hands. Not talking much, they stare at the TV. This bar could be anywhere. Steve knows bars. He's been to a few.

His eyes fasten on the TV screen. He can't help it; his eyes keep drifting there. The fast flicker of images holds his interest and continues to catch his eye even when he tries to cut away.

The picture is distorted and bounces ghosts. The jumpy images irritate him. He wants to turn up the sound.

More than anything, he wants to adjust the picture. For the first time since he got here, he is aware of the stench of stale beer. Every time someone opens the door, fresh air competes with the stink of the bar.

He tries to get the waitress's attention and flags her. "Can you fix the TV? Look, the picture's out of focus."

The waitress walks around the counter behind the bar, taking her time before she looks up at the screen. "I can't reach it," she says, off-handedly. "I'll tell the bartender when he comes back." This time she smiles.

Steve smiles back. Sure, you will, he thinks. At least she's warming up. Keeping an eye on her, he decides he will give her a chance. She's a little on the heavy side, not fat, but thick and compact—stocky. Whatever she is, *her look* does not translate well to film. The camera prefers long lean angles and is unforgiving of small round curves.

Good direction, Steve figures to himself. A good director takes the small episodes of life and transforms them into believable bits on the screen. And when you've only got thirty seconds, the images have to be tight. This is the true essence of good directing. And before he knows it, he is looking around the room, using his hands to frame shots.

His eyes return to the TV. The waitress still hasn't gotten it cleared up. He looks around the room but doesn't see her. He feels disappointed. The fact that she hasn't done anything to fix the TV makes him angry. He reaches in his back pocket for his cell phone and realizes he left it in his truck. There is no other place where his phone could be.

The spot on the TV shows a young dude walking down the street wearing jeans, no shirt, in pursuit of a cold beer. The babes are watching him pass by. This boy walks for a long time and he looks good.

Harry Hill has done the spot for Miller Lite. Good images like that work with any product. Great director. Harry Hill thinks he's great, but it does not mean he has the right to put down Steve Olin. Whatever Hill is, he isn't great at anything except being an asshole. The great director bit is hype.

When Hill is on the set, he has an annoying habit of looking through the camera and shaking his head, muttering, *I don't know, let me think about it.* Then he walks to the sidelines and lowers his face into his hands as if he's in deep artistic angst. He walks in a circle like a jungle cat scoping his prey. Everyone on the set feels the intensity of his deliberation. His hands cover his face, then his eyes, occasionally rubbing his temples. He is letting everyone know that the director is making a creative decision. No one can make a move, even breathe too loud until Harry Hill comes out of his trance and gives the green light. His decision is always received as astonishing, pure genius.

The waitress walks into Steve's field of vision and blocks his path to the TV. Steve feels a quick flood of anger. She never did anything about the ghosts. She said she would. To make matters worse, she is standing in his way. He takes a deep swig of beer and clenches his teeth, but he will not show his anger. She stands right in front of him. Looking at her close-up he sees she is actually pretty. He is tempted to ask her if her natural hair color is black. When he checks to see how he is cutting it with the girl, she leaves. From a long shot, panning camera, she is walking across the room, away from the mirror behind the bar and away from him.

TWENTY-SIX

SMPTE TIME CODE 19:03:56:<u>26</u> At 7:03 on Thursday evening, Wendy Wachter is surrounded. A small coterie traps her in the front lobby of GASP. News that Harry Hill has been murdered is blowing up cell phones, spreading like a plague. Wendy backs up to get away from Dawn Stein, Koji Matsuno and Yolanda Nez, but they are so close she can feel their breath, which conjures the image of the headless horseman and Ichabod Crane from Washington Irving's *The Legend of Sleepy Hollow*. She can't shake the image of Harry Hill with his head blown off. She imagines him showing up at his next shoot, carrying his head under his arm.

Dawn's eyes are dark, moist and are barely perceptible in the office suite where Wendy has purposefully not turned on the lights.

"Harry wasn't wearing a shirt." Dawn shivers and protectively clutches her arms to her chest. "No pants. He didn't have his pants on."

"Spare me the details," Wendy tells Dawn Stein.

"I really don't know anything." Dawn protests. "They only person who saw anything is Steve Olin."

Wendy just smiles. Throwing off water from their wet rain garb, all four of them corral into her office, talking at the same time. *He's dead. Murdered. So is Jewell Cleary. Both dead. Their heads blown off with a shotgun. Only rednecks have shotguns. Who would do such a thing?*

The conditions are not favorable for Wendy to take charge of the situation, but she tries.

"Steve?" Wendy asks. "Where's Steve? He should be here."

There is dramatic intensity in Koji's eyes as though he's fearful he could be the next to die. Wendy feels like choking him with his ridiculous wild rose black belt, but that would take too long. She'd rather slit his throat with her silver letter opener that glints on her desk in the otherwise dark office.

Yolanda frets about Steve's safety. "I hope he's okay."

Dawn shakes her head "We talked to him briefly but he wouldn't let us into his houseboat. He's really shook up." Dawn Stein sloughs off her very wet North Face rain parka and much to Wendy's dismay throws it on her soigné ROSÉ-colored velvet couch where it is bound to leave water marks.

Yolanda looks at Wendy with alarm, seeking her guidance. "Should I stay here, watch the phones, or go for coffee?"

"See if anyone wants coffee." Wendy turns away from Yolanda and looks up to the security monitor in her office. She is not interested in any other image aside from herself. Her profile is to the camera. She thinks of herself as quite striking from the side, perfect, except for the one loose strand of hair that has been giving her trouble all day. She brushes it upward and it falls back down.

"Make mine non-fat decaf, almond, please," Dawn says.

"Nothing for me, thanks." Koji Matsuno leans against the far wall of Wendy's office next to the couch. Wendy watches Koji whiles she uses her hand to smooth the lovely apricot and taupe stripe wallpaper, a *Nina Campbell*. Wendy congratulates herself on the choice. She observes Koji as being more quiet than usual and preternaturally pale, a sure sign he is about to disappear into the fine lines of the wall and leave behind a human shadow.

She walks over to the front desk to unplug the cable connecting the television monitor to the camera. Holding her Mikimoto pearls to keep them from getting caught in the tangle of wires, she pulls the plug. The monitor makes an electronic pop and turns black.

"Make it sweet, but non-fat," Dawn emphasizes. "Tell them almond milk, not flavoring, decaf."

Wendy does not know how to play this. She is winging it all the way. "I'm sorry Harry's dead," she says to everyone in the room. Avoiding making eye contact with anyone, she fixes her gaze on her custom lacewood *Mezzaluna* Desk. "Really this whole thing is very shocking. Tragic." She centers herself by tracing her fingers along the Eames coffee table in front of the crushed velvet couch. "I know I look like I'm doing okay, but I'm really not. I feel like a nervous wreck.

"Don't forget. Double tall, sweet, non-fat, almond," Dawn calls to Yolanda.

Wendy quickly walks toward Dawn as though she intends to hit her. "Why are you here?"

Dawn's arms cross over her great barrel of a chest. "I have a right to know what happened to Harry Hill. We all do."

"I told them to be here." Sollie Berg walks into Wendy's office. Under his green woolen beret, his face is grim, ashen and wet from rain. He sniffs to stop his nose from running. His eyes narrow to dark slits. With his disproportionately long arms, he reaches for the wall switch and turns on the lights. An amber hue glows in the room but it does not light up Sollie's eyes until he puts on his glasses.

He stares at Wendy, stating his words carefully. "Your husband is in the loop about what's going on."

He removes his beret and gives it a slight shake. "I'm just learning about what happened. I can tell you this, I'm not happy."

Wendy gives Sollie a weak smile. "Where's Yolanda? Did you see Yolanda out front?" She knows Yolanda would have given her warning about the approach of Sollie Berg.

Koji Matsuno nods. "I think Yolanda left to get coffee."

Sollie flings limber energy as if he is about to do a somersault, a flip and sustain a pose in mid-air. "I'm getting hot," he says, removing his moss green Irish Sweater. He gazes out the window where the black water of the Puget Sound is swallowed up by the wind and rain. His back faces Wendy and it is intentional. He wants her to understand the gravity of the situation. "This is going to be a mess when it goes public."

He turns to face Wendy. "You know how much I dislike having attention drawn to myself."

"I can't help but notice that Harry's murder is a terrific opportunity to publicize GASP," Wendy blurts to everyone. "I mean aren't your ears burning?"

Koji looks upset. "That's sick."

Dawn's eyes scan Koji. "Funny but not funny."

Sollie's eyes blaze with alarm. "That's exactly what I'm afraid of!" His tone is accusatory, as if Wendy is guilty of murder. "What are you going to do about this little problem we're having?!"

A slight smile creeps across Wendy's face. "I'll prepare a statement and send it to you for approval—that will be the foundation for everything, what we say to clients, vendors, talent and the press."

Wendy turns to face a tall copper and bronze lamp. As she turns on the lamp, she notices her hands are trembling. "We didn't do anything wrong."

Light falls from the square parchment shade in a muted tone of gold. Wendy loves this lamp; it enhances the color of her skin. Good lighting will give her the edge to handle Sollie Berg. "What happened to Harry has nothing to do with GASP Productions."

"And Jewell," Sollie mentions. "How are you going to handle that?" Sollie doesn't tell Wendy that Jewell Cleary was going to replace her as a producer. No one knew except, maybe, her husband, Ray Wachter.

"What about Jewell?" Wendy feigns innocence. "I didn't realize she's dead too! You didn't tell me that," she yells at Dawn.

"Yes, I did," Dawn yells. "You never listen!"

Koji nods to himself. His face is drained of blood. He takes two foil packets of Nicorette gum from his shirt pocket, uses the edge of one to break the seal on the other and pops a small square into his mouth.

Sollie finds a place to sit on a Stickley stool. Hammered together with copper wainscoting and tough brown leather, it quickly becomes apparent that he's uncomfortable sitting there and hops off. Dawn beckons him to sit beside her on the couch but he chooses instead to stand, facing Wendy.   "You've got to firm things up with what will be said."

"What happened is just personal, not business."

Sollie shakes his head. "You can make it a little softer than that."

"Harry has a family. Little kids who won't know their father." Dawn drops her head into her hands. "What about his wife? Her husband's dead. She has two young children."

"She's probably the one who killed him," Wendy snaps.

Dawn looks at Koji. "God, how awful."

Wendy drops the box of tissue onto the Eames table in front of Dawn, walks away from them and looks at Sollie. "I really am sorry. I can't believe Harry's dead. I mean I worked with the guy for twelve years. I did everything for him. In some ways, it was like a marriage. Maybe..." She feels herself getting emotional. "Maybe our relationship was more solid than a marriage. A lot of marriages don't last as long as we did."

"Bravo," Sollie says, clapping his hands.

"I'll get a statement to you by morning," Wendy reassures him.

"I'll need it in an hour so I can run it by my attorney."

Wendy nods, brushing off the top of her New Delhi side table as though she's ridding herself of street soot, dust. She studies the Nymphale vase on top of the table. A small section of the Lalique crystal bears a brown ring, slightly stained from flowers of the past.

"I'm really glad to see you," she tells Sollie. "All of you," she mumbles while continuing to stare at the vase, annoyed that she cannot get decent flowers this time of year. The gold and brown mums of November are boring.

Sollie smiles at Wendy's effort to rise to the occasion of managing a crisis of huge proportions. "I'm really glad that you're here. Without you, I don't know what I'd do."

Wendy basks in the warmth of Sollie's attentive gaze and smiles. She circles her index finger inside the silver rimmed neck of her cobalt blue vase. Sollie Berg is a creepy, little man, but he is the one who pays for everything.

"You are the glue that holds everything together," Sollie says, pointing to her, then looking at everyone else, knowing they have no choice but to affirm his proclamation.

Dawn nudges Koji good-humoredly. "Let's face it, Wendy is the best, head and shoulders above Jewell Cleary."

The mention of Jewell Cleary makes Sollie flinch. "She as a very pretty girl." He folds his beret precisely in half as though it's an envelope. "And talented," he adds. "Such a shame."

"Harry Hill is my director!"

"Was your director." Sollie gazes at Wendy as if he's making a complicated assessment. "There's no use agitating everyone, Wendy." He turns to leave the room.

Then he looks back at Wendy. "It's important that whatever we say in public is consistent." He scans everyone. "All of you. Even if you're not an employee, you all worked with him and Jewell."

Wendy is irate beyond words. "I'm the one who's shit out of luck! I'm the one with a dead director." She sits at her desk in front of her Mac and begins typing. "I'll have it for you in an hour."

Sollie Berg leaves the room with the energetic gait of a man that takes pride in his sexual prowess. He waves his arm behind his lithe body to bid everyone farewell.

Wendy is glad to see him leave. He sucks away everyone's life force. Sollie Berg's world is pure, antiseptic without gore or guts. No blood. There is no blood shed. There is only sick sex and money.

Yolanda rushes into the room, throwing off pellets of water. Carrying a cardboard tray holding coffee, she pants from under the hood of her raincoat. "I saw Sollie Berg in the lobby."

Wendy frowns at Yolanda and turns her back to everyone. The screen on the overhead monitor is black, dead. She forgets that she had disconnected the cable. She doesn't need to see the monitor to know her face has gone white. She remembers falling down the steps in front of Jewell Cleary's house, desperately trying to get away from the blood. She says out loud, "None of this is happening. I'm really having a bad dream."

Koji is in the same place, hardly moving, barely breathing, a Hiroshima dark shadow—a victim going about his daily life when a bomb suddenly drops from the sky, incinerating his body, leaving behind a haunting outline on the wall. Wendy can't shake the reality that Harry Hill is dead. She imagines him showing up at his next shoot, carrying his head under his arm. Then she realizes his head is gone. There is nothing left for him to carry. He'll have to rent a head as a prop.

TWENTY-SEVEN

SMPTE TIME CODE 17:43:49:27 Mia Hill arrives home close to six on Thursday in time for dinner. As she pulls into an open space in front of her house, she realizes she has driven all the way home without turning her windshield wipers on. The car's windows are fogged-up, covered with winding runnels of rain and cascading sheets of water. The windshield presents an impenetrable glaze to the outside world. She turns off the ignition and puts her head on the steering wheel to summon strength, bracing herself for what is next to come. She bolts out of the car to avoid getting drenched. She doesn't see the police car parked in front of the house until she steps into the street, where cold wind rips through her coat.

She immediately thinks of the children. But the children, or at least their arms and legs, are flashing in the front window, indicating robust good health. As far as she can tell, a visit from the police does not have anything to do with them. Every light in her house is turned up all the way, like a private sun on a block of dark homes. Other homes are only illuminated by small portals of light, a random table lamp or backlit from a kitchen. The comparison of her home blazing among others is a dead giveaway that something is very wrong. She feels terror that lodges in her stomach and throat. Because of the recurring dream, she knows something terrible has happened and she feels compelled to run.

But there is nowhere to go.

Her wet hands shake as she turns her key into the front door. Fumbling with cold metal, she nicks her knuckles and misses the keyhole. She drops her keyring onto the thick door mat bearing Pennsylvania Dutch-style partridges, blue ribbons and letters spelling out *welcome*. As she bends over to pick up the keys, her hand sinks into wetness. Her welcome mat is completely saturated with water. She inadvertently bangs her head into the copper facing surrounding the doorknob. The blow is what she needs to regain her sense of self-preservation. It is fitting for the police to be here on the day she has decided to end her marriage.

As she again tries to insert her key, Viv intercepts her and opens the door. Her face is as grey and as lackluster as her hair; her perpetual smile is noticeably absent.

Mia," the woman whispers, motioning toward the living room. "I'm so glad you've come home. The police are here."

"What's wrong?" Mia asks.

Viv shakes her head as if she does not know. Mia thinks Viv knows more than she is letting on. Sometimes, Mia thinks Viv knows too much. As she moves into the hall, Mia is not ready for the exuberant assault of her children. Max tackles her head on. Chloe hitches herself a ride on Mia's legs. Jumping up and down while their mother mutely tries to walk forward, both children cry, "Mommy, Mommy. Mommy's home!"

Mia bends down on one knee, cradling them both close in an open hug. She can tell that her children are agitated. Mia presses her face into Chloe's hair. The familiar sweet scent emboldens her to press on.

"Mom, is Dad a bad guy?" Maxie asks. "Do the police want to take him to jail?"

Mia's eyes seek Viv in a beat yearning for understanding, but Viv's face registers coldness and confusion. She looks away from Mia. "Chloe, Max, come with me now, please," she says, trying to scurry them away.

Chloe squirms a small defiant, "No," complaining, "I want my Mommy."

"No," Max protests. "We want to stay with our Mom."

Viv is imploring the children, "You'll have your Mom soon enough." She takes each child by the arm, leading them upstairs. "Don't give your Mom so much bother. Come along. She'll be with you soon."

Mia sees their feet resisting the climb upstairs, skipping steps, then reversing, two steps forward, one step backward, a bunny hop and a recalcitrant run in place. At the same time, a man appears in the opening to the living room. "Mrs. Hill?"

Mia strains her head toward the ceiling. The man is dressed in plainclothes and well over six feet, closer to six-eight. He bears the correctness of an ordinary bureaucrat. She finds him bland, non-descript in appearance, notwithstanding his amazing height.

She laughs out of nervousness. "Aren't you a little tall to be a cop?"

If he appreciates her humor, he doesn't show it. "Can we go somewhere and speak privately?"

"Has something happened?"

The man shakes his head as though doesn't want to say too much. "Mrs. Hill, my name is Detective Mulcahy, Seattle Police." He hands Mia his card.

She hears the detective say her name again, as though he wants to confirm that she is indeed *Mrs. Harry Hill.*

Mia knows she is about to hear bad news. "Here," she says, rushing into the living room. She pulls two French doors shut. "This way we'll have some privacy." She whisks around the room as if she is mustering comfort for unexpected company. She makes small talk as if that will somehow normalize the abnormal.

"Have you noticed the rain? Well, how could you help not notice the rain?" She laughs. "We've had so much rain, everything's rotting and there's flooding everywhere." She turns around and sees a woman police officer by the fireplace, eyeing her with rapt attention.

Mia feels compelled to cry, the spontaneous eruption of the emotion that has been shut for so long. With infinite wisdom, she chooses not to reveal her inner hysteria.

Mulcahy makes introductions. "Mrs. Hill, this is Officer Joanna Keating." The woman cop politely nods. Mulcahy looks around for the closest seat. Mia directs him to a sturdy wingback chair while she tries to keep her arms from shaking by gripping them across her chest. "Can I offer anyone anything to drink?"

Mulcahy shakes his head, awkwardly spanning his long legs across the floor. Officer Keating calmly beckons for Mia to sit. Showing terrible fear of the inevitable, Mia backs away from them, awkwardly finding her own place in a window box seat perched under rain-streaked glass. As she sinks into the thick cushion, she tucks her hands into knotty fists, digging her nails into her palms.

Mulcahy's stare is unwavering and fixed. She is a hard mark on the wall. "I'm sorry to be the one to tell you this, but something terrible has happened. I'm afraid your husband is dead." Now that Mulcahy has delivered his message, he takes a deep breath. "I'm sorry."

He nods to Officer Keating, indicating it's her turn to talk.

"He's been murdered."

Mia does not react. There is no quiet sob or shriek of hysteria. She sits still in a placid state as if she is completely alone in the room. All along, the dream has prepared her for this moment. She stares into a window where visibility remains nil in the flood-lit mask of water. She sees her own reflection in the glass. There is no anguish evident on her face at all. She is waiting, waiting to hear more. She knows more is to come. She knows that although the cop has completed a most painful task, one of the most difficult parts of his job, for him it is really a matter of routine. She knows she is being scrutinized, the subject of abject curiosity. The cops need to see how the bereaved wife responds. They need to find out if the bereaved is a suspect.

The tone of Officer Keating's voice is apologetic. "I'm sorry. There is never an easy way for us to do this."

Mia's eyes settle upon the fireplace where orange embers smolder in a bed of coals. Yellow light leaps over two fresh logs that hiss because the wood is wet. Her calm might be unnerving to the police. They might think she is one of those people whose strain of denial runs so deep that she pretends she does not hear the message of death.

She feels like she should say something, "Oh... I-I....," but she can't manage to say anything.

"It's okay," Officer Keating says. "We understand."

"Uh," Mia begins to talk, clutching the collar of her leather coat. "How did it happen?"

Mulcahy clears his throat as though he expects the onset of an annoying cough. "Mrs. Hill whenever there's a homicide, we can't release all the details."

"Mrs. Hill," begins Officer Keating, "It is difficult to tell you this, but at the time of your husband's death, he wasn't alone."

Mulcahy interrupts Officer Keating and continues. "There was a woman with your husband. Her name is Jewell Cleary."

"Was she...," Mia starts to say. "Did she murder Harry?"

Officer Keating's words are deliberately intended to be understated. "There is no evidence to suggest that. Jewell Cleary was also murdered. Both of them were discovered in Ms. Cleary's house this afternoon. Before we release your husband's body, we will require confirmation from the coroner's report."

"Did you know her?" Mulcahy asks.

A rush of blood rises to her face and constricts her throat. She grips the top of her leather coat to cover her neck.

"Did you know Jewell Cleary? We understand she worked with your husband."

Mia shakes her head.

"So, you didn't know her?" Mulcahy asks.

"There have been so many through the years." Mia's voice trails away. Quiet resides among all three, a gift capturing relief in the midst of great discomfort. For what seems to be a considerable amount of time, no one speaks. The logs in the fire are drying, crackling with heat, emitting small pops. The drumming echo of rain running from the gutters and downspouts outside the window takes precedence, mounting attack like a heavily armed intruder, steadily advancing in the stillness of the moment.

"Harry liked fresh energy as he put it, fresh talent, fresh faces, new things. Look at this house. It's so old, one of the oldest homes in Seattle. Funny, isn't it?"

Both cops fail to catch the irony and stare at her. Mia fluffs her black hair with her fingers, pushing it away from her face. "I'm sorry," she says. "More than myself, I'm thinking of the children. How do you tell your children their father is dead?" She stands, walks toward the fireplace, keeping her back to the cops. Thinking out loud, she says, "Unless you need anything else from me, I'll walk you to the door."

"I have numbers for you to get in touch with." Officer Keating offers her a standard packet of forms that are thin, smell of carbon and are wrapped in plastic. "These agencies are for family crisis counseling and victim assistance."

Mulcahy stands, dodging the full erection of his height. Even from under his raincoat, his shoulders appear to be too round; his back slopes as he walks out of the room. His slow lumber is a method to scope out and avoid doorways, awnings, furniture, all things that could stand in his way before he sees them. He is a man who has never grown comfortable with his height.

Mia follows them out of the living room and into the hall. Mulcahy looks over the woman cop's shoulder, scanning her paperwork. Joanna Keating exudes the solid aura of a woman who would be happier working on a farm in Nebraska rather than riding around in a Seattle police car. Her eyes are large, light brown and speak of a compassion that her position will not otherwise allow.

Mia feels that they are on the verge of a physical touch, some small act of concern, but both of them stay at a safe distance. She is certain they had to know how horrible this whole thing must be for her. No words or expressions are exchanged. They stand still long enough for the passing of time to become awkward.

Mia's hands reach for the door. She desperately wants to get them out of her house. She needs to grieve violently, loudly and alone. All three of them can hear the same things in the silence, sounds of the house, wood snapping and hissing on the fire, childish patter from upstairs, Viv's calm voice and the immeasurable force of the rain.

She flings open the front door, bathing the hall with the sweet fragrance of wet air. Officer Keating presses another item into her hands. Mia looks at the reference card

with the cop's name above a long sequence of numbers.
"The case number," the cop says. "In case you have
anything you want to tell us."

Mia wonders, what is the point? Are they letting her
know that Harry's murder has turned into an official
spectacle, pegging her as the chief suspect? The woman cop
pats Mia on the sleeve of her coat and tromps out of the
house into the night. Mulcahy doesn't budge. He looks at
Mia. She thinks she can hear the questions he has not
asked. He wants to know if she and Harry had fought.
Were they having difficulties? He wants to know if she
knew her husband was having an affair with Jewell Cleary.
Mia avoids Mulcahy's eyes, fearing he will see all the
symptoms of her chilling guilt.

She looks at the card again. Seattle Police Department
is printed in raised blue letters. Harry Hill had not died
quietly at home in his bed. He died violently for all the
world to see. Mulcahy appraises her leather coat. She thinks
he wonders why she has not taken off her coat in her own
home. She cinches it tight around her waist. It's none of his
damn business. Mulcahy seems satisfied about something
and walks out. As she watches him descend the front steps,
she wants to do anything to make her appear innocent at
heart. She runs onto the front porch. Her feet slosh water
damming on both sides of the steps.

"Are we in danger?" she cries after him. "My
children!" Mulcahy never answers her. The patrol car is
already pulling out, driving away. In the cold night hear she
hears the sound of gulls circling overhead but cannot see
them in the black sky. At that moment, Mia knows the
police will be back.

She runs into the house, closes the door, and latches the chain lock, which seems to be a necessary precaution. Pressing the weight of her body against the door, she shakes. Tears come, an inability to breathe and horrible thoughts. She sees the image from her dream. Harry's corpse, minus hunks of flesh, his hair cut and his head gone, a naked and foul thing, made obscene with blood.

"Stop," she whispers to herself. "Don't think of him as dead, think of him as gone."

The sheen of her leather jacket catches the reflection of fire. By the fireplace, she sees his face in the flames, laughing at her, mocking her. She grabs an iron poker and beats seared, blackened portions of the logs into wood chips and chunks of glowing embers. The embers dissolve, burning the outline of his heckling face. She isn't afraid of him anymore.

Unbuttoning her leather coat, she allows the fire to warm her. She places a new log on the hearth as the fire shoots sparks and small flames in chords of blue. It's really over, she thinks. He's dead. Without turning around, she knows someone is watching her. She looks up and sees Viv. Viv walks toward her. With her arms opening to embrace her, she says, "I'm sorry he's dead, but it's much better this way. For you as well as for the children."

TWENTY-EIGHT

SMPTE TIME CODE 14:31:03:<u>28</u> At two-thirty-one on Thursday afternoon, dusk falls as the grey day slips into a charcoal sky. Seattle is far north and the days of November are short; any light is worthy of worship and adulation. And on this particular afternoon, darkness blankets the warm honey-hued flesh of Harry Hill and Jewell Cleary. They are in her living room, sitting close to the fire. Harry admires his own reflection in the silver-handled mirror Jewell has brought to him. His newly shorn locks wave and cluster together in a band around his head like a golden crown of laurel leaves.

Harry's hand dangles along the length of her hair and meets the indentation in the curve of her back. "Come here, Jewell." He pulls her forward to brush his lips along the curve of her breasts. With his other hand, he pulls up his cell and begins texting. *Where the fuck are you, cowboy?* It's the third time he's texted Steve Olin, and he is quite mystified why he is not hearing back. Again, he texts Steve. *Wherever you are, give me extra 30 mts to get ready. Thx.*

Jewell takes the phone from his hands and places it on the arm of the director's chair that has no seat.

Harry smiles at her. "Do you realize it has not stopped raining for three days?"

"Why does it even matter?" She laughs.

He takes comfort in the nearness of her warmth and her scent sets him on fire. He takes her shears, holds them up to the light of the fire, inspecting the blades to see how sharp they are. As he opens the blades, the slim V-shape is the precise line of sight to Jewell's flashing eyes. She sticks out her tongue at him, flicking it lightly. He uses shears to cut open her black thong panties.

It's always the prelude to sex that matters most—how intensely and how quickly heat builds-up to the climatic explosion of a furnace. Harry imagines seeing the two of them how they look this very minute, grainy in texture, muted in their nakedness, like an old silent movie, never once delivering sound bites, only raw image flickering from the couch to the floor, banging against the wall, back onto the floor, up and down, up and down, in a slow fluid jut of limbs, intertwining skin, rotating slippery asses, heaving forward on all fours in a celebration of flesh quivering in a crazed melee of interchangeable wild blond hair, drinking up bodily fluids through mouths bowing and bruising in a salient tribute to a long grand fuck.

The aftermath is always the same. Harry considers that it took longer for Jewell to cut his hair than it took for him to fuck her. He forgets his hair is short and wonders if it is too mussed to be seen in public but smiles to himself because whatever is wrong with his hair, Jewell will fix. She takes the shears, playfully waving them in front of his eyes as if she aims to cut him. He shows no fear. Two rapid blinks, that's all. He knows she is not dangerous that way— physical violence is not her nature.

They hear a bang outside but don't move, thinking that it must be another gust of wind, flinging a garbage can against the front steps. Nothing is safe in the wind. Jewell gives Harry a grim smile that could be playful or secretive. He does not know for sure what she has in mind. As far as he's concerned, he's done and has no further reason to charm her.

She talks, a chatterbox, about her house and her life with her first husband, an insurance lawyer who is feckless and boring, always playing by the rules, assuming there are rules to abide by when there are none.

"We're not quite divorced," she says. "Almost but not quite."

"But you've got the house." Harry smiles approvingly. He grips his hands under the edge of the stone hearth and props up the weight of his body as if he is about to do dips.

"Although he's a lawyer, he's not a very successful one," she says.

"Did you leave him or did he leave you?"

"What do you think?" She gives him a snarky smile.

"I think I ruined your panties."

She leans over, cups her hands around his mouth to kiss him and mounts him. "Don't mention it."

There is little light except for the fire. Grey gloom settles everywhere. Their bodies and their hair bounce shadows against the walls and above from the ceiling. Harry rises up from beneath her, takes her hand and guides her to the cold stone hearth where he sits.

"It's hard for a man to lose a blond wife," he says.

Pulling her astride, he thinks he can make one more ride. The steady thump of rain on the roof recedes to the background as a car engine revs then comes to a stop. Jewell rises and falls on his lap. He holds onto her by her breasts, twisting and pulling her nipples. Footsteps, a ping of metal, and the door opening and shutting is masked by the pitch of Jewel's cries.

If Harry Hill had been given more time, he would have again said, *You really shouldn't leave your key in the mailbox. Anyone can get in.* He only knows his hair is short and wonders how long it will take him to get used to it. Jewell, with her scissors in her hand, is getting the ride of her life.

Harry lets go of Jewel's breasts and reaches for his phone. He sees his last text to Steve, but there is still no response from him.

TWENTY-NINE

SMPTE TIME CODE 13:35:4:03:29 Steve Olin is at Jewell Cleary's house around three-thirty on Thursday afternoon. Every door to the house has been thrown open. Harsh light blinds him. Standing under the hot lights is nowhere near a dimension called heaven. The intensity of the heat makes his face burn. Sweat and rain soak the collar of his parka. He is also shivering from exposure to the damp air. How is he cold when the lights are so hot? No one needs to tell Steve how to capture a poorly lit room on film. Steve trains himself to notice details in case he can use something for a shot. But he is not on a film set, shooting on location or in a studio. This is a crime scene.

And it is not the first time he has been here today.

Early afternoon. Less than an hour ago.

Steve remembers seeing Jewell. Her lush mouth moves against Harry's ear; she's whispering. Her lips part as though she intends to kiss him. Red flushes up on Harry's face and he smiles. She tosses her hair. A strand gets caught in Jewell's eye. Harry touches the fallen strand, moving it away from her eye, making her blink.

Neither one had on clothes. Sweaty and spent from sex, Harry threatens Steve, and Jewell is brandishing a skinny pair of scissors in her hands.

He wasn't scared because they were pissed. He'd be pissed too if someone walked in on him. It's what Harry said that sent him for a spin. *You need to leave. You won't be working for me again. Thank you for your time.* Steve tried to explain that he had misplaced his phone and thought it was in his truck, but it wasn't. In the film business, a missed text is a matter of life and death—another cardinal rule.

Steve knew he had been a bit careless, playing fast and loose, because of his extraordinarily good luck with Wendy Wachter. He mentioned that to them. *Wendy is giving me a shot at directing.*

Harry and Jewell laughed at him. Steve had hedged his bet on Wendy Wachter, not knowing she would soon be out of a job. *Keep dreaming,* Hill had told him.

Harry Hill is not a nice guy. Steve finds the whole scene with Jewell and Harry to be confusing and he isn't thinking clearly. Steve was supposed to pick them up to take them to the airport. The first time he showed up at the house, Harry and Jewell were most definitely alive.

He doesn't remember what happened between the time he left the house and then came back again only to find them dead. When time is lost in the stillness of a frozen frame in a 30-second spot, it is easy to forget. He remembers wading through water to get to the street. He got into his truck and drove. If a man is a real man, he has to move physically. He has to be free and unhampered, so he works with his hands. He must accept the inherent violence of his nature and use it to his best advantage.

Working in the film business means moving from battle to battle. Getting to wrap at the end of a shoot is winning a war. The director is a general plotting camera angles with the majesty of a major offensive. Crew people are like soldiers. They have the same hurry-up-and-wait work routine and rank and file as troops in the military. Steve is a corporal hell bent on becoming a general.

Harry Hill is the only barrier to his ambition.

Steve's cell phone wasn't on the console where he thought he might have left it. He pulls over to the side of the road, lets the truck idle, and examines the floor. He checks his glove compartment, the truck's side pockets and the back seat, all of the places where he knows he would never toss his phone. His eyes catch the drift of water splashing up from the road. Water pools on both sides of the road. Angry rain lashes the windshield of his truck. He remembers his last stop at the J&M Café when he had taken off his wet parka. His recollection is dim, but his hand deliberately probes the inside layer of a rarely used pocket to fetch a phone that had been there all along. He had put it in a deep pocket to keep it safe from the rain.

He checks his last text messages from Harry Hill. *Where the fuck are you, cowboy? Wherever you are, give me extra 30 mts to get ready. Thx.* He doesn't check the time of the messages. He mistakenly thinks the great director wants him back in the fold and isn't going to fire him, and still wants Steve to take him to the airport.

To the best of his recollection, this is why he returns to Jewell's house the second time.

After Harry Hill's barrage of texts, the last text, simply a question mark, is from Wendy Wachter.

He found Wendy at Jewell's house around the time of the murder.

Now cops are everywhere, doing forensic things with tape, chemicals and cameras—taking measurements and pictures of everything, including the bodies of Harry and Jewell. Steve is told to stay out of the way and is led outside to the front porch. Blackness hems him in from both sides of the exterior of Jewell's house. Stray beams of faint light trickling from inside of the house are caught in swells of mist. He is surrounded by water. He feels for his cell phone in the pocket of his parka but has been told not to call or text anyone.

The giant detective with the long jaw tells him, "I'll let you know when you can go."

Steve isn't especially afraid of violence. He links violence to his concept of maleness, and it defines why he aspires to be a filmmaker. Aside from his deep abiding love of the craft, he is out there, doing the wild thing, liberating himself from all of the traditional jobs that keep men indoors, in offices and in boardrooms, shuffling paper with flaccid arms and soft hands.

Harry Hill was the only barrier to his ambition, but no longer.

While he's stuck waiting for the big cop, he sees a fresh dam of rain cut loose from the sky and assault the

legion of rescue vehicles parked on both sides of the street.
Rain hammers the roof of his pickup truck like a hail of
bullets. Flashing red lights cause traffic to slow on the road
but not to stop. No one is curious enough to leave the dry
comfort of a car. Water is as maddening as the encroaching
night, wrapping around his body like a black tarp of tears.
There is too much water, too little light. He could easily
drown in this water.

THIRTY

SMPTE TIME CODE 15:03:15:<u>30</u> Wendy Wachter sends
a text that only contains a question mark at three minutes
after three. She sits in her car waiting for Steve Olin to
arrive. The rain is so fierce that she does not know for sure
if she has found Jewell's address. She has never been to
Jewell's house before today, yet her GPS tells her she is at
the right place. Curtains of rain completely cut off her field
of vision. She cannot see a thing through the windshield or
through the car's windows.

Scant light can barely cast shadows in the grey
darkness. She cannot clearly see her hands but can feel
them trembling. She is going to confront Harry Hill. No
one dumps Wendy Wachter without paying a price. A
surprising rush of warmth sweeps up her throat to her
cheeks.

GPS can be wrong. Not knowing if she is in the right
place floods her with anxiety. She gets out of the car,

slipping in shoes that are a whole size too large for her feet. Moaning and cursing to herself for not having an umbrella, she pulls her coat up around her throat as if she means to preserve it for a later showing in the sun. Even the best cashmere doesn't take well to water. And an umbrella is no match for this wind.

She knows she looks like a wreck, but for the first time in her life, she does not care. Battling ferocious gusts on the southeasterly side of Madison Street, she tries to keep her head down to protect her head and face. Even though her vision is compromised, the rich copper color of Harry's BMW stands out in the enormous grey, like an old penny stamped on the side of an elephant. Harry's fender touches the rear bumper of Jewell Cleary's Karmann Ghia. The linkage of the two cars is a powerful symbol of Harry's lust for power and Jewell's ambition. She knows power and ambition are usually the same thing. Sex and money cement the deal.

Scrambling up the steps to Jewell's house, she feels her feet coming loose in her shoes. She reaches for a handrail to steady herself up the steps. Arriving on the porch, she sees that the front door is open. She walks right into Jewell's house as if it is her own home and yells, "Harry?"

And again, "Harry?"

Slipping awkwardly in her oversized shoes, she walks down the hall, yelling his name. "Harry! Harry! Jewell?"

She hears buzzing, the white noise of channels stuck in between stations. A cross current of fresh, cold air gusts through the hall. The house is unbearably cold, causing her to shiver. From the corner of her eye, a wad of blond hair

overflowing from a box startles her. Long and tangled, the
hair is not attached to a head or a face. She can tell it is a
wig, and it gives her the creeps, but it also gives her a
strange thrill. She would love to scalp Jewell Cleary.

"Harry," she cries out. "Where are you?"

The small, box-shaped room is crammed with
theatrical clothes, props and thrift store stuff and smells
spicy like mothballs. It dawns on her that she has not been
invited here and is trespassing. But it is the same as Jewell
Cleary trespassing on her turf at GASP Productions,
interfering with her relationship with her star director, and
vying to take her job.

"Harry," she screeches.

She wraps her arms around her chest to steady her
legs. On the floor, her feet brush up against soft fabric, a
woman's black thong sliced in two. She wrinkles her nose
in disgust, embracing what this might mean.

"Harry," she calls. No wonder he isn't answering her.
"Harry," she whispers.

She is certain Harry is otherwise engaged and looks
for a way out. Walking backward down a thin section of
hall, she begins to have second thoughts about fleeing in
retreat. Even in the absence of warmth or light, she is able
to think clearly and is pervaded with renewed cockiness. If
she found him with his pants down, so much the better. No
one wants to be in a weak bargaining position.

At the end of the hall, the back far corner of the
house puts out the sound of white noise. She feels a
powerful and biting rush of cold air and pulls her coat
tighter to her chest. She does not make it inside of the last
room. She stops dead at the door frame and screams a

single piercing blast. Blood is splattered on the walls, the floor and the furniture. Blood is everywhere, covering everything. Every opening of her body pricks up and receives blood.

Her mouth contorts, choking back aborted pants and terrible, long moans. Running breathlessly, running blindly, twisting her skinny ankles in her oversized shoes, she is sobbing and shrieking without shedding tears and gasping for air. Tripping on her own feet, seizing up in fierce panic, she throws her entire body, headfirst through the open front door. The entire burst of airtime that it takes her to get out of the house is less than a 10-second lift from the average 30-second spot.

"Wendy!" Someone calls her name. "Wendy!"

Scrambling down the front steps, she skids on the next to last step, twisting her ankle. She tries to catch herself from falling, clawing the wooden ledge of a flower planter, but it does not stop her. Her palms scrape splintered wood, leaving nasty welts, lacerating her fingers. She lands on the ground, sprawling the right side of her body. Disoriented and shoeless, she manages to sit up and feels rain cooling the heat of her face. Her stockings are torn. One big toe protrudes through a hole in sheer black mesh, looking large and foolish.

A man comes out from behind a hedge bordering an adjacent yard. She cannot see the face of this man as he moves toward her.

She recoils, crying, "No."

He heaves aside a large green recycling bin. "No," she cries again, shimmying her body into the planter. The man wears a parka with his hood up. Uncoiling her body, she springs to one side, crawling on the ground. The man stops her and reaches to help her stand. "Wendy, don't worry, everything's going to be okay. You just slipped, that's all."

Steve Olin stoops to her height, grips her by the shoulders, whispering, "What happened to your shoes, lovely lady?"

Then she starts sobbing. "Do you know what's in there? What's happened?"

Wendy hobbles in her stocking feet onto a concrete landing, closer to the street. Her soiled shoes are in her hands that are chafed and raw. Dirt is trapped in her fingernails.

"Wendy, Are you alright?"

Dazed, she turns around and looks at him. "Go away. I'm okay."

"Oh my God." She isn't okay. Someone is probably dead. She doesn't know what to do. She uses her wounded hand to slick back her hair that has come completely undone from its tight knot. She lifts her hand to her mouth, pressing her lips. What has happened? Had Jewell killed Harry? Had he killed her? Were they both dead? She starts crying at the sight of their cars in the driveway. The two cars parked so close together have taken on the cold surety of their union in death. All along it has been a tragedy waiting to happen.

Steve kneels down on the ground beside her and touches her arm. She is mortified that anyone should see her in such a state. "Leave me alone," she tells him, pulling away.

Steve removes his hand but stays close. He looks genuinely concerned. "Did you break anything? Can you walk?"

"No!" She told Steve to be here, but it seems wrong somehow that he is here. She must get to her own car and call the police. But what would she say to them? "The police will think I did this," she cries.

"Did what?"

"In there," she yells, pointing toward the house.

"Wendy! Stop it! Just stop it. I don't know what's come over you!"

Wendy would not look at him. She keeps walking, not knowing what to do. She knows she is in shock. She knows she has shut down her ability to make any kind of decision—even one to save her own life. She is stunned at the notion of having to call the police. She couldn't possibly incriminate herself in this mess. She has to get out of here! She is walking away from him, shaking her head as if to say *I didn't see a thing.*

She did not see Harry Hill or the details, just blood. "I just saw blood."

Steve feels confused and laughs. "Wendy? Are you okay? Wendy? What's the matter? What has happened to you?"

She lifts her face to the grey sky and receives the full brunt of rain. Steve is talking to her, but she does not hear what he was saying.

She looks toward the street with selective vision. What she sees frightens her. Cars are not moving but are parked with round wheels made shiny with chrome rims. Windshield wipers are stuck to glass like flicking sticks.

Other things peer out at her: the half sawed-off limbs on a bare oak tree, dead rose bushes, mud sliding off the back of an old wheelbarrow that has been turned over on its belly, and a rotting jack o' lantern smiling the last of its evil grin as it collapses into the sodden earth.

The tires on Harry's BMW and Jewell's Karmann Ghia show signs of wear and tear, a significant loss of tread. The silver grill on Harry's car is tarnished. She sees part of things, fragments, disjointed images that have no hope of being spliced together to create a visual story that will stand the test of time. She sees the stray and distant beam of headlights that are too far away to be of her world, a world that is a 10-second lift from a 30-second spot.

And she remembers the black thong sliced in two like a cut in an old-fashioned negative of film. The world she sees is blurry, out of focus, a stylized view seen through the lens of a shaky camera, nothing more than a string of broken images.

She is being left for dead with the rest.

Her whole body is shaking so hard that she can't focus. Steve didn't look like himself. His hair is wet, plastered back, accentuating two narrow eyes, and his nose is running.

"Harry's dead. I think. I don't know."

At first, Steve's eyes widen, growing large and alert, but then narrow again to a steady fix as if he does not believe her. "How?" he asks, wiping his nose with his sleeve.

Wendy yells at him. "I said I don't know. Something's happened. There's blood all over the place." She starts sobbing. "There's so much blood. No one could possibly live after losing so much blood."

Steve hoists himself from the ground. "We better call the police or an ambulance. Where's your car parked?"

"No," Wendy wails over his voice. "No! I don't know how to play this! I'm concerned how this looks! Don't you see? The cops will think I did it because I did want to kill him!"

"That's absurd." Steve looks around toward the street, where no one is around. He gives her a long look like he is trying to figure her. "Come on Wendy, you don't have anything to worry about. You couldn't do anything to Harry Hill. You're not big enough," he scoffs lightly.

She can't catch her breath long enough to say anything. She uses her hands, pointing back to the house. "I-I. can't." She continues walking away. "I'm not going to talk to the police! I'm not!"

She sees the beast within her own self for the first time. Only a beast would run from violence without trying to find out if anyone is still alive. She is more fearful of being implicated in a scandal than she is afraid of death.

Steve doesn't pursue her and laughs. "Harry put you up to this, didn't he? He's always messing with me. This whole thing's just a joke."

Wendy licks her lips that have gone dry. Her lower teeth scrape away the last residue of lipstick. All of her make-up is gone. She is sure to have black smudges under her eyes. Her hair and clothes are drenched beyond recognition. Even her perfume has washed away. It takes all of her strength to summon the essence of a vulnerable girl.

She does her best to appear fragile, delicate and almost pretty.

She pulls on Steve's arm, imploring him "I didn't see anything. Whatever happened, happened before I got there. I'm terrified of police. It will kill me to talk to them." She clutches the arm of his parka, whispering, "You go in there and see for yourself. You call the police. I'll just go home."

She waves her arm toward the house. "Forget them! We have a deal. Next week we start developing your reel. Sound like a plan?"

Even through the exhaustive din of the wind and the rain, Steve's voice is positive and upbeat. "Okay, sounds good."

He backs away nodding, letting her know that he gets what she is saying. He does not look normal. Soaked with water, his coat is black and shiny. His lips are pinched to a thin blue vein. Only the tip of his nose is red. All along there has been a strange look in his eyes, now it has gotten worse. Wendy keeps mistaking his behavior for concern or confusion, but now she isn't so sure. All she knows is that she is drowning in water. As she stumbles away from him and toward her car, she knows she is in shock and her clothes are ruined. The coat, the shoes, her hose and her dress, everything has to go. Losing her clothes is the only way to assure herself that this whole scene has been nothing more than a horrible dream.

THIRTY-ONE

SMPTE TIME CODE: 03:03:24:<u>31</u> At three minutes after three in the morning on Thursday, Kenny Kix is happy with what he is seeing. A babe throws back her blond hair in gales of delight. Lots of smile, big happy teeth, sunny disposition and so much blond hair. The pic is the POV from the perspective of the young dude who has just walked up to her front door.

Kenny is liking the concept. It isn't violent but it is staying with him. The spot is looking cool enough to put on his reel.

Cutting this spot is a snap. Kenny Kix could cut blind, he tells himself, or better yet, in his sleep, but make no mistake, Kenny Kix wouldn't be caught dead blinking or batting his eyes in an editing room.

"Get me a smoke," he commands. He didn't care which one of them got it for him.

Watching the monitor carefully, Kenny jogs the image forward three frames, then backing up a bit in reverse, before locking off on the fourteenth frame. He pushes the key and enters the edit into his master deck. As soon as his hand comes off the deck, a burning cigarette comes between his fingers like a wand. Kenny doesn't bother to say thanks. The blond Russian girl knows her place.

He works the slave deck, tracking both monitors. He is moving, he is hot, and he is onto the next bit of fluff to fill out the scene. Kenny watches the images spinning forward, distorting picture, spilling quarreling squeaks of tape.

"Sounds like mice chewing a slipper," Andy tells him. She is grinning like she loves him. It is almost too much for him to take. He didn't love her so much.

The next shot he wants is coming up. The blond babe is putting her arms around the neck of the young dude. It is the only way to spell out sex cinematographically and in less than thirty seconds. The same snippet flashes over and over. The blonde hugs the young dude, again and again.

The little girl tells him there are eleven takes of the same shot. The tone of her voice is very cool, unflappable. Kenny is starting to appreciate her.

"I used to do this on a flatbed," he mumbles, keeping his hands on the deck.

"I know," the girl says. "And that would have meant a helluva lot more work for me to do. I know. You told me."

Kenny is about to chew her out, but she flips him professional edge like a sword.

"Scene 106, circle take nine," she is telling him.

"Very cool, very competent, shoulder to shoulder next to Kenny, the Russian girl's eyes dart back and forth between the two video monitors. She is scribbling notes on the edit log.

Kenny feels unusually generous. "It's the Editor who really makes the film," he tells her. "All you need is coverage and sometimes you don't even get that. Everything else is just photography."

"I'll bet," the girl says. She gives him a look of both complicity and respect.

Kenny's eyes shift over to her slave monitor. He is waiting for his two-shot to come up. He is searching for the young dude and the blond babe hugging from a reverse POV—how they look from the street's perspective. The blonde's arm is slung over the dude's shoulder and falls down his back, where her hand comes to linger on the young dude's butt.

Kenny turns away from the monitor and snarls at Andy. "If a director doesn't have a good DP and a good editor, he's fucked, got it?"

"Right," Andy says.

"Directors are shit!" Kenny glances to the door to make sure the director whose spot he is cutting isn't around to hear him.

Confident, completely certain his words are private and held captive by a select audience, Kenny goes on. His tone, however, is not discreet. "The Master is a real director and he is not a shit. The Master never made a fucking television commercial! And he wouldn't have, even if his fucking life depended on it. The Master is the greatest fucking filmmaker who ever lived!"

Kenny is waiting on Andy's slave monitor to give him the image he wants. "Who am I talking about?" he yells. "Who the fuck am I talking about? Who is the fucking Master?"

He swivels all the way around on his stool with gale force and gives Ensley Sharp a nasty look. She sits in the far corner of the room out of the stream of video light. It makes his eyes sore looking at her, not being able to see her face. She wouldn't oblige him by looking up. This big girl was staying out of his way on purpose. She is playing with his head, man.

He takes a deep drag from his cigarette. He doesn't trust the big girl. She still hasn't finished her homework assignment. For all Kenny knows, she might be in shock. She keeps her head down. Her pen moves across a pad of paper. Kenny can tell she is a lefty. Ensley is doing what he told her to do—writing Sam Peckinpaugh's name one hundred times in bold block black letters.

"Have I got a story for you," he says, warily. "It's about rape."

The Russian girl's eyes get big, but Ensley Sharp does not move.

Kenny looks right at Ensley. "Did you hear what I said? I said rape."

Andy bobs her face forward into the stream of video light and smiles. "*Straw Dogs.*"

Kenny is so taken with her he damn near falls all over himself. "Did you hear what she said? Did you hear? Did you hear it?" he cries to Ensley. "That is so cool. *Straw Dogs*, man. She said *Straw Dogs*. I love it. *Straw Dogs* is the preeminent masterpiece on rape."

Kenny can hardly control himself. "You have fucking made my day, Lady!"

He feels like going over and kissing her. "*Straw Dogs* is like my fucking favorite film of all time."

Andy shouts, "I know all of the Master's films!"

He is beside himself with pleasure. He likes nothing more than to talk about the Master's work. It is better than sex, better than cutting, better than death. "Name them," he shouts.

Andy knows she is hot. "*Pat Garret* and *Billy the Kid*, *The Ballad of Cable Hogue*, *Bring Me the Head of Alfredo Garcia*, *The Wild Bunch*, *The Getaway*, *The Killer Elite*, *Bloody Sam*." She stops and looks at Kenny who appears to be drooling. "And what's the name of that film nobody saw?"

"*Junior Bonner*," he says so softly that his voice turns hoarse. "*Junior Bonner* was great, not his finest, but great." Kenny feels like sobbing. "It was great. What the fuck do critics know?"

Taking a deep breath, he sighs. No one has ever mentioned most of the Master's work all at once. Had he had the time to anticipate the scenario he would have figured he would be going ballistic with joy. This was not the case at all. The cigarette he is smoking has burned down to his fingers. He flicks it away into the ashtray and puts his knuckles into his mouth. Made hot by the cigarette along with the cumulative effect of all the others, his middle fingers taste bitter. Hearing the litany of Sam Peckinpaugh's films makes him quiet and he cannot figure why. He bows his head in a moment of silence.

"Weren't you going to talk about rape?"

Kenny is a little blown away. He couldn't figure the dynamics here. He didn't want the little one to win but she had nosed out in front of the big girl by far, like Secretariat running the race in the Belmont Stakes.

He didn't want to be telling a story. He wants to relax and think about the Master. On the edge of rawness, his words keep coming back to haunt him. He is trying to win the minds and hearts of young girls, but his voice will not cooperate. Instead, he hears the rasp of an old man.

Kenny knows the score. The film business is a young business. He is getting too old to cut. In front of the camera, behind the camera, to the entrails of the cutting room floor, no one is spared from the indignity of growing old.

He is feeling like he is a character right out of one of Sam Peckinpaugh's films. Living from one job to the next, there is nothing in between except the despair of waiting. Having his rough cut in hand is like having a ticket to get back in line and hang around until things happen all over again.

Ensley Sharp is not smiling. She knows she has lost her edge over Andy Andrisevic, who is now going for the jugular. She will slit Ensley's throat and be done with it. "What about the story you were going to tell? Your story about rape? Tell me about it."

Ensley Sharp does him an ignoble turn. She rolls her eyes. It is very unbecoming.

Kenny goes off the rails, a train wreck on a wet track. "What's the matter with you? Sunset Boulevard is jammed with dead bodies, man. It is paved with the stinking carcasses of those who thought they would be rich, famous and powerful! They are the wannabees, man. The has-beens. And this business fucking ate them alive! You may think you have all the time in the world, but you don't. Just yesterday. the Master was sitting there! Right where you are! He was paying me to edit his film! You tell me where the fuck he is at now! Go on! Tell me where the fuck is he?!"

"He's dead," Ensley says with fixed, unblinking eyes. "He's an old-time director and he's dead."

She has cleaved his heart in two. Kenny places his hands over his heart to stop the bleeding. "You're fucking nuts, lady. The Master's not dead. Sam Peckinpaugh has more lives than a fucking cat."

He couldn't bring himself to pass a gander at the big chick, this incredibly stupid big chick. He thinks he is putting on an awfully good show, rolling his eyes, making verbal pops with his mouth. Everything he does is evidence of total wipeout. He is a basket case on purpose. No one can ever sue you for sexual harassment if you're insane.

"Don't you know an assistant is as important to me as a wife," he yells.

"I know you've had plenty," the big girl mumbles. She gets up from her stool and waves her hand around the small smoky room. "This is your life. Not mine."

"Lady," Kenny calls after Ensley as she is walking away, "make some more coffee."

"Make it yourself," the big girl tells him. "I'm done."

Kenny goes on as if he has not heard Ensley. "If that's the fucking level of your commitment, then you are like seriously fucked and you should not, I repeat, you should not, be working for me!"

He rotates in his chair to lend a bit of frenzy to what he is saying. "I'm going to do you a favor and pretend I didn't hear what the fuck you were saying and attribute your delusional statement to a complete mental aberration."

"You go ahead and do that." Ensley Sharp opens the door leading out of the editing suite. She stands in the door frame and faces Kenny. Leaning against the door, she tilts her face into the white light and looks pensive. She pulls her leg up, kneeing the air briefly in a stretch before her foot comes back down, crossing over her other leg and settling on the floor. The back of her heel taps against the door frame. Her hands reach into her pockets. She seems to be feeling around for something and pulls out a small tube, opens the cap and smooths a thick line of clear gloss over her lips.

Backlit by a slant of crisp halogen fill light, the thick shaggy sides of her black hair take on a bluish tone. Looking at only Kenny, avoiding Andy, her brown eyes glow the color of a red-bellied snake. If she didn't look so tired, she would have reminded him of a bad girl he had seen in an old black and white movie from the 1940s.

She juts her chin toward the monitors before retracting back into the straight line of her own slender neck. Her eyes now begin to shine softly as she waves her hand in the air. "You talk like a fool. All this is nothing but fool's gold and after a while it loses its shine."

Kenny knew he had pushed her too far. To make matters worse, she was the one he had wanted.

"I'll find another job," she says on her way out.

Kenny hears her but doesn't watch her walk away. The door of the editing suite slams shut, sealing the room, quiet and airless, a tomb.

Andy doesn't say anything and closes her eyes from either lack of sleep or stress. Kenny does not know why Andy makes him crazy with anger. Her eyes look like slits and spook him. He runs his fingers through his stringy hair, fluffing it up. Andy is completely unaffected by his proximity to the edge and not doing a thing to help him feel better. In the monitor, he sees his own image. His hair shines with more grey than black and covers most of his face like a mask. In the flat plane of glass, his eyes disappear into the deep sockets of his skull and look more tired than otherworldly. The longer he stares into the light of the monitor, the more the image of who he is grows sharper in his own mind. This screen is two-dimensional and it lies. It shows the pic of a mean-looking dude who cuts film, but it does not show his enormous fear.

THIRTY-TWO

SMPTE TIME CODE 13:41:19: <u>32</u> Sollie Berg wants all women, including Mia Hill, who walks into his office unannounced at 1:41 p.m. Sollie Berg's ideal woman does not look like Mia Hill. She has honey-blond hair with a tint of gold. Her lips part in a slight pout and are painted the color of champagne grapes. She taunts him with her bold mouth that is open, eager and promises of pleasure and of pain. Her innocent eyes implore him to be cruel. All of her power lies in her mouth and her eyes. Winsome eyes, brutal mouth, together she uses them as a single weapon. He wants her desperately. Only she can make his craving go away. He wants to crush her mouth with his own. He wants to please her, subdue her and possibly even strangle her. If he did not take her, his erection would throb in pain for an indefinite amount of time. His ideal woman tosses her hair and laughs at him. She looks exactly like his ex-wives, all four of them, and Jewell Cleary.

He clutches his small, knobby hand around a Swarovski crystal paperweight and crushes the image of his daydream.

Mia is dark, dark hair, dark complexion, dark eyes. Completely clad in black leather literally up to her neck, she is not wearing any makeup and her hair is askew as if it has been blown by the wind and flattened by the rain. Her boots are interesting, finely crafted black leather rises slightly above her knees. He is stunned that she easily got past his receptionist, but he is willing to relinquish his concern if only she would pull off her boots and show him her feet.

Necks and feet are his two favorite body parts, both of which Mia Hill has unwittingly concealed from his sight. He does remember the indentation of her high arches and the shape of her even toes. "We can pick up right where we left off last night...if you like?"

Mia would have preferred to wait until another day to ask him for a favor, but she fears if she gave it too much thought, she would talk herself out of it. She sits in a handsome chair that is plush, in the color and shape of a pumpkin. She does not say anything to him on purpose. There is no way to fool her. She is going to get what she wants from him.

The only light in the room is blue and emanates from a large aquarium filled with several large conch shells, crushed coral, bright-colored rocks, and green gossamer threaded plants that look like sea grass. Mia estimates the tank to be at least seventy-five gallons, maybe more and thinks it is strange that there are no fish. From the tight flat pocket of her leather coat, she pulls out a Camel and lights it with a miniature pink Bic.

Sollie immediately takes umbrage, wrinkling his nose with contempt. "I didn't think of you as a smoker."

"I'm not," she says, letting go of a stream. "But today's special."

"You do know, smoking's not good for you."

"Damn it," Mia snaps. "You really ought to be careful about how you talk to me."

Sollie has always been able to recognize when trouble is afoot; it's his greatest strength. Calm and business-like, he sits on the banquette behind his desk, languidly crossing his knees into a Cow-Face Yoga Pose *Gomukhasana*. "Sit down," he tells her. "But please put out the cigarette."

Mia looks around for a place to dispose of her cigarette. She smiles as her eyes fasten on his aquarium. She moves to get up but Sollie is too quick for her. He catches on to what he thinks she is about to do.

"Don't," he says, raising his voice. "I don't want Helen upset."

"I only meant to wet it to put it out."

"Eels are sensitive creatures and they don't like ashes or dust." Sollie accommodates her by sliding a square seafoam green glass dish across his desk. "It's really not an ashtray," he says. "But it will have to do."

The ashtray is the same shade as his banquette, perhaps a tone lighter, but the color of glass can often be deceiving.

"Do you mind if I speak frankly?"

She stubs out the cigarette, stands, and walks over to the tank. With the serpentine body of a fat snake, the creature slithers along the bottom of the tank. Its skin is the same mottled shade as an old brown leather sack. The eel's mouth is wide open baring sharp teeth. Tiny bug eyes peer at her.

Sollie comes up to her side. She detects his fragrance and knows he is wearing Aventus by Creed. "That's Helen," Sollie says. "I named her after Helen of Troy. I keep trying to find a mate for her." He stops and looks as if he means to reassure her. "Helen eats them before they can catch up to her in size."

Mia does not know which of the two creatures is more menacing: Sollie or the eel. Both are equally strange.

"In ancient Rome, eels were often kept as pets and were adorned with jewelry, earrings and necklaces." Sollie smiles and raises his eyebrows, which are extremely thin, almost transparent, like pale etching on a block of wood. His lack of eyebrows makes his eyes appear to be more alert and as if he is in possession of extraordinary power. "Eels were treated quite well, in ancient Rome, in some cases better than humans. Unruly slaves were known to have been fed to eels."

Mia thinks all of his talk about eels is utter nonsense and feels as though he is intentionally trying to intimidate her. She stares at him, noting his face is remarkably unlined. For a man of a certain age and far from attractive, he is in amazing shape.

"Don't worry, Helen does not have a taste for human flesh. But she could give you a nasty bite."

Mia grimaces just enough to let him know that she is listening. Ever since she learned Harry was intentionally trying to make her go insane, she has snapped back to reality. She sees Sollie Berg for what he is—a small man who needs props to make himself appear to be more powerful.

"Do you mind if we sit?" She doesn't wait for him and finds her way back to the orange chair. He takes her lead and returns to his banquette, where he reclines.

She speaks without apology or hesitation. "I am sorry about the way we met. Harry told me that you were a therapist. Not just any therapist but someone who is particularly good at helping women, guiding them to come into their own."

She stops talking for a moment to see if he is tracking what she is saying, but he is not looking at her. He uses the palm of his hand to lightly massage the back of his bald head.

"I thought there was something wrong with me. I thought I was going crazy. Harry told me to call you. He said you would be able to help me."

"Harry told you that?" Sollie's face lacks expression but inwardly he is stunned that Harry would pull such a stunt. "I don't know what to say."

Through French glass doors she sees the rooftop deck and a garden that has gone dormant. Jumbo ceramic urns hold miniature Japanese maple trees that have lost their leaves. Grey trunks, as thin as wire, sag under the crush of rain and wind. Perennials in planters, packed in waterlogged soil, lie dormant in thick gnarled clusters of brown vine. Black tarp covers most of the deck that is collapsing in its center from the weight of so much water.

"I bet it's beautiful here in the summer." She undoes the sash of her coat. As she unzips the coat to her waist, she watches his eyes trailing her torso and widening once they reach her neck.

Sollie does not trust her and is intentionally solicitous. "I grow roses, carnations, jasmine, wisteria, French lavender and many herbs. You can get drunk on the fragrance as I frequently do."

Mia eyes him carefully. "It's good to have a garden. It helps to keep one grounded."

"I don't drink alcohol, so I need to get drunk on something." He unlocks his arms from behind his back, allowing his legs to loosen—his release of his *Gomukhasana* pose. He doesn't tell her that he refrains from alcohol because it affects his sexual performance. Waving his arm toward the window, he says, "It doesn't look so good out there now, but in the summer, we have so much sun and hardly any rain. Anything can grow. You'll have to come back and visit me then, so you can see it for yourself."

"Essentially I came to apologize," Mia says. "You are not who I thought you were."

"After all of these years, Harry never mentioned me in conjunction with his business?" Sollie cannot squelch his suspicion. "I find that hard to believe. Unbelievable." He shakes his finger at her. "Why are you really here?"

Shrugging, Mia turns away from him. "Harry makes a big point of keeping me out of his business. I know very little."

"Okay. I've heard it all." He rises from the banquette in a fluid Eagle pose *Garudasana,* which he holds for a few seconds before settling his two legs squarely onto the ground. "This helps my back. I used to have a bad back.

No more." He smiles and moves toward her in an effort to dismiss her. "Apology accepted. Now you can go."

Mia stays in her seat. "There is something else I want to talk about."

Sollie smiles because he knew all along that she had a real reason to see him. Her apology is a smokescreen. He leans against the front of his desk, puts both hands in his pockets as if he means to restrain himself and smiles. "Okay, what is it?"

The crystal paperweight on his desk throws small shimmers of grey light against the dark walls streaked with charcoal shapes resembling daggers. The window behind him is thickly coated with strings and beads of water. He presses a switch on his desk that turns the lights on and off again. "It's getting time to go home."

"It's only around two." Mia isn't afraid of the darkness or Sollie Berg. "I'd like to work for you," she tells him.

Of all of the things Sollie could anticipate, this is odd, so very odd, and is completely out of the question. "I make it a policy to never hire couples. From my standpoint, it is too complicated and too risky. They always end up having problems and break up on my time. When they break up, it somehow always costs me money."

Mia stands, freezing in place, her voice is firm, unforgiving, tinged with a sharp edge of sarcasm. "You have many companies, the radio stations, production, post-production, agencies, magazines. I know you can create a position for me."

Sollie shakes his head. "I know so little about you. I don't even know what your capabilities are. It's not a good idea."

"I'll send you my resume."

"Go on and send it," he says, dismissively. He walks over to her and lightly traces his fingers along the side of her neck. "The only problem is every time I see you, I keep thinking about sex."

His fingers are pasty white with nails that are politely trim, manicured. Mia lifts her head and walks away from him. "That is a problem."

"And violence." He laughs. "I think of being violent with you too. It's perfectly normal for eels to bite one another when they're mating."

Mia didn't laugh. "There is something very wrong with you. And to think I was going to you to get help."

Sollie looks offended. "I don't think we have anything left to talk about."

"Oh, but we do."

She reaches into a slim pocket inside of her coat. "I keep my cell phone here to protect it from the rain." She pulls the phone out of a clear plastic pouch. "I don't know if you want to see my home video. Something tells me you don't." The phone recognizes her face and turns on, throwing forth the only light in the room. She presses a video to play. Sollie's voice can barely be detected, but it is his image lighting up the phone, massaging her feet, looking maniacally focused and still pained. There isn't anyone in the world who would view this video and not think of him as a pervert. He knows he can spin it any way he wants, but she has the video—and that is a complication.

Mia turns off her phone and slips it back into its plastic pouch. "Harry has a thing for cameras. In our house, he installed cameras everywhere." "He used to like to watch me from remote locations." She returns the phone to her inside pocket and zips her coat clear up to her throat.

Tying her sash into a knot, she smiles at Sollie. "I used to be very good at my job. I had a good reputation. I want to start again, a chance to reboot. I won't be staying too long before I get something better."

"Ultimately, I want to direct." She looks at Sollie and gives him a broad smile. "Doesn't everybody?"

He might feel grim, but he's always been wise about certain things, and realistic. He knows he is outmatched. And he thinks this one small complication can easily be resolved so long as he gives her what she wants. There is no malice in that—giving a smart woman what she wants.

Throwing up his hands, he asks, "What about Harry?"

"I'll deal with Harry." Then she admonishes him with a warning. "Just stay out of it."

Twitching his lips is a habit Sollie is trying to break. He puts his hands back into his pockets, jangling spare change, feeling around for his pocketknife. He hates conversations like this when he has to give up something for so little in return. But what choice does he have? His attention drifts to his sodden deck where rain pounds against the glass. A quiet gash of grey recedes in the horizon over the Puget Sound. The sky had looked exactly the same earlier in the morning. Only then the source of light had come from the east. East or west, morning or night, Sollie feels a loss of control over time. He is no longer operating in real time. The walls wrapping around the deck are too high. No one can climb in and no one can climb out. He has built himself a concrete bunker. At the height of summer, mineral water and espresso flows freely but that was months ago. Paradise has come and gone, and he wonders if his garden will ever again bloom.

THIRTY-THREE

SMPTE TIME CODE 20:43:14:<u>33</u> Wendy Wachter kicks open the door to her condo at 8:43 on Thursday night and drops her keys into a Cristal d'Arques Lunel bowl that is supposed to be a candy dish. Blood worries her. She thinks she has picked up blood on her shoes or splashed splotches onto her legs. Even though she has long changed into her spare pair of stockings, she could be carrying traces of Harry's blood on her flesh. Even pin pricks of blood would tie her to murder.

Petrified, she runs room to room, turning on most of the lights. Her final stop in the kitchen brings her to the trash bin where she dumps her coat, shoes and torn stockings. Frantically changing her mind, she pulls out the trash bag, ties it, and throws open the door to her deck, where cold wet air blasts her face. A violent storm is raging outside like no other she has ever seen. The wind vents fury, raging through power lines and mangling trees. She flings the trash bag from her fourth-floor balcony and knows without looking that the trash bag has landed behind overgrown hedges of conifer and heather.

Come morning, she'll retrieve the bag and dispose of her things in a way that can never be traced. Her first priority is survival, and this means staying away from the police.

She hears two men talking inside and thinks the police are already here, lurking in the shadows. Her first reaction is to throw herself over the balcony, but even in her disoriented state, she knows she will never survive the fall. It is impossible to know where the men have come from. She is sure no one is there. Cold tiles beneath her bare feet make her shiver. Frazzled beyond the exhausted edge of fear, she has lost touch with reality and is scared to death.

She longs to take a hot bath but is afraid of being trapped in the tub. It is within these moments of terror that she realizes the men's voices are intensified by the marvelous garble of airtime. The TV is on.

She walks straight down the hall, where all lights are on except one. Although she knows she had turned on the light in Ray's den, now it is mostly dark. The only light comes from the TV. Electronic blue chills her Syrie Maugham soft white sofa. Even in the dim light, the outline of Ray's craggy face appears like an apparition. She does not know how she could not have seen him in her earlier sweep through the condo.

"Where were you?"

"Dietro's." He doesn't look at her and is instead riveted by the TV.

"No, I mean just now."

"In the bathroom, throwing up."

Jarring images of light flicker from the TV and bounce across his face. As she moves toward him, so does the distention of light. The changing dimensions of TV images create shadows rebounding from the tip of his nose to the ceiling. She is witnessing the tail-end of an optical illusion and is reminded of a ghost on the video monitor—the one she had never wanted him to be.

"Then you know."

He holds up his cell phone. "Everyone knows."

"Ray," she places her hand on his shoulder. "I'm sorry, I know you liked Harry."

Ray does not move. He is so far away from her, but she needs him now. She is not going to lose her equanimity, not when she needs him more than ever.

She sits beside him and presses her face into his chest. She reaches for his phone so she can turn it off, but he pulls it away. She knows any caller will only speak about the awful shock of Harry Hill's death. From across the room, his silver and bronze trophies gleam in the outer edge of electronic light. Ray has always been proud of his awards for high school football, softball, and the Clios won for two of his television commercials.

Inwardly, she fusses. Real life can't always be planned. It would have been fairly cool to have gotten home first, to greet him at the door, fresh from a hot bath, naked under a thinly veiled wrap. She tries to get him to respond to her. "It's going to be okay," she tells him.

He strums the channel changer like a musical instrument, probing for endless commercial interruption. Most shows and movies are of little interest. He looks for the latest trends in 30-second spots. The TV is his best friend, not his wife.

"Ray, please talk to me." She feels her voice quavering.

Closing his eyes does not mask his pained expression. She tucks her tiny foot into his, curling her toes open and over the bump of his ankle bone. "Where were you last night?"

He doesn't bother to answer her.

"Honestly," she mutters. "Why do I have to ask all of the questions?"

In a swift, petite move, she throws herself into his lap. "Come on Ray talk to me, be with me."

He lifts her off of his lap. He's not mean about it, but very cold, making it clear, he is in no mood to be intimate.

"Why are you doing that? Can't you see that I'm so glad to see you, and that I want to be with you?"

"Come on, let it go. You're never like that." His one arm falls around her back but does not draw her close.

She kisses him on the face and neck, but he doesn't kiss her back. She kisses him again. This time on his mouth, which feels dry as if his lips are chapped. His breath is sour, as if he really did vomit in the bathroom.

She is nauseated but sees a vision of herself holding her nose to get the job done. Intent on connecting with him, she leans closer to him, pressing her breasts into his chest, giving him small cheeky pecks on a part of his body that is the least offensive to her. "I miss you, Ray. Really I do."

She straddles herself on his knee, allowing her body to be open and available, but no matter what she does, it isn't turning him on. She steals a glance at his crotch. Pure reflex, her nose wrinkles up in disgust. She can't bring

herself to give him a blow job. In the past, she has carefully
designed playful interludes to avoid the crudity of out and
out sex. She thinks if she unzips his pants that will get him
going, but she can't bear the idea of one more rejection. He
is in another time zone, a million miles away from her.

She drops her hand to Ray's crotch and touches him
lightly on the outside of his pants.

Offended, he pushes her hand away and glares at her.
"Okay, what do you want, Wendy?"

He looks old and tired. Maybe he always looks this
way, but she had not been paying attention.

"God, it's been a while, hasn't it?" On the couch, she
moves away from him, writhing from side to side, fluid use
of her petite limbs. Then she lets go of a long moan that is
more of a sigh as if she wants to cry but cannot. "Ray,
someone killed Harry. I'm in shock. Can't you see that?"

"Harry?" Ray's eyes wander, rolling in his head,
unable to focus. "Harry?"

"Yeah." She does not know how to get through to
him. The shadow behind his head is still. His face contorts
in confusion. "Harry," he groans.

"My director. Harry Hill." She nods. "Remember
Harry?"

Ray is keeping something from her, and she hates it
when anyone tries to keep a secret at her expense. She feels
like exploding, *Tell me where you were last night?* But she stops
herself. She has a weird feeling. What happened to Harry
Hill could happen to her.

"Harry," Ray mutters, shaking his head as though he
did not want to believe the truth. "This isn't about Harry."
He looks at Wendy as though he is making a confession.

"Did it ever occur to you that this isn't about Harry? That maybe Harry was in the wrong place at the wrong time. This is about Jewell," he says. "Jewell's been murdered."

Wracking sobs heave his body with tears streaming down his cheeks. Unable to talk, he moans, burying his face in his hands. She feels an urge to scream at him but stops herself. She cannot believe that this is happening to her. It's humiliating and scary to watch him cry. Crying is something he has never done in all of the years she has known him. His grief is powerful and unrelenting, an explosion of the deepest pain he has ever shown to her. Messy, ugly, and she does not want to see it. She does not want to see him out of control, so weak, so grief-stricken.

She eyes his cell phone in his hand, which is attached to his arm with the perpetual tenacity of an artificial limb. She grabs it from him. Roughly, he tries to get it back. But she deceives him for what will be the last time. Instead of rolling to the couch in a playful row of tug o' war, she runs out of his den, into the bathroom, and locks the door. For Ray, the amputation is painful; he hollers after her and bangs on the door. Soon his knocks against the door stop.

Before she begins scrolling through his calls and text messages, she has an inkling of the deception she will find. Finally, she can take a long hot bath. She is left to her own silence, which offers far greater comfort than her husband. Pain is always, and quickly, forgotten. Tomorrow she has the option to reshoot, redo, retake and ultimately play out a brand new scene.

THIRTY-FOUR

SMPTE TIME CODE: 12:42:12:<u>34</u> Ray Wachter's final meeting with Harry Hill is coming to closure at 12:42 p.m. on Thursday. Sollie Berg called the meeting. Ray is fraught with an unidentified but nagging anxiety. No matter how hard he tries, he cannot rid himself of the feeling that something terrible is about to happen. The feeling is so strong and so pervasive that he turns his back on the people assembled in the room and stares out the window.

His meeting is taking place in another conference room in the old brick building that faces the street and overlooks the cobblestone pavement of Pioneer Square. In this room, the windows have not been renovated and are not sealed properly. Random bursts of cold air flash against Ray's body. Wet wind blows through the street below, burying leaves, branches, and the last fragments of life that had once bloomed on earth.

Ray turns away from the window and is surprised to see Steve Olin blast into the room looking as though he has been battling gale-force winds. The Grip definitely has no place in a creative meeting. The guy is everywhere, muscling into the most unlikely places. "What are you doing here?" Ray asks him.

Steve ignores him and presses on, saying, "Harry, Harry, I've got to talk to you."

The Grip's urgency to talk to Harry Hill comes to a halt once he sees Jewell. He is young, maybe Jewell gets him all worked up, Ray thinks. Christy rushes into the conference room calling after Steve, but he doesn't answer her.

She gives Ray a helpless look. "What's wrong with this guy?"

Ray throws his hands up and smiles. "You've got me, beautiful."

Steve shakes his wet hair leaving small droplets on the floor. He's immediately intercepted by Dawn Stein who is taking an awfully long time to leave. Dawn isn't big on entrances but her exits can last for hours. Dawn and Steve hug each other in a friendly hello. And then Dawn actually leaves. Ray thinks something is bugging her. He'd like to draw it out of her and rub her face in it for a while. He hates feminists.

Steve is oblivious to the tension in the room. He drops his parka onto the floor and leaves it there. The rubber soles of his unlaced work boots squeak along the tiled floor. The guy speeds to the conference table, mumbling something about starving to death and takes his place at one end of the table as if he is in charge. "Is there anything to eat around here?"

At the other end of the table, Sollie Berg watches Steve and gives him a discreet obligatory smile. "I do have eel in my office that's been braised in beer."

Steve puts up his hand. "Think I'll pass on that." He looks around at everyone. "So, what's everyone talking about? What's this meeting about?"

"What rock did you crawl out from?" Ray snarls.

Steve refrains from looking at Ray. "Boy, your wife's sure in a foul mood. Don't you ever spend any time with her?"

Ray can't tell if Steve is stupid or being a wise ass. He looks at Jewell to see if she caught the reference to Wendy, but the blonde is lost in her phone. As much as Ray wants to intimidate the hell out of Steve, he thinks the Grip is too much of a goof to bother with and it would end up reflecting poorly on him.

Sollie leans back in his chair and folds his arms. He looks mildly perturbed and, at the same time, amused. "What brings you here today, young man?"

"Wendy asked me to be here. She wants me to be available for Harry in case he needs anything."

Harry shakes his head as if he doesn't need anything. Jewell stops looking at her phone and shrugs her shoulders. Her eyes follow Harry, then Sollie, waiting for their reaction, but not Ray. She no longer has time for Ray.

"I think I asked you a question," Ray snarls. "Mind telling me why you're here?"

Jewell comes to Steve's rescue. "Oh, leave him alone. He's made mistakes but it's not enough to be mean to him."

There is something about the goofy Grip that makes Jewell behave girlishly. He wonders why he can't elicit that side of her. As he looks around the room, he realizes everyone is watching Steve. He runs his fingers through his damp hair, locking down every stray strand, giving Jewell his best boyish smile.

Jewell feigns her own smile, trying to look innocent, as if she does not know what is going on. "Wendy's pissed because change is in the air."

Sollie gives Jewell a cautionary glance and shakes his head, but she disregards him. Not a good sign. He will have to be careful with Jewell. Her involvement with Harry Hill is a complication and he does not like problems.

"Jewell." Harry Hill shakes his head, an admonition to stop talking.

Jewell gives Steve a coy smile. "Wendy sent you here to spy, didn't she?"

Steve smirks, pointing to himself. "Who me? A spy?"

Jewell goes on. "Change is good. We're expecting a lot of change around here."

Harry's voice gets louder. "Jewell, I said that's enough."

"Please let me finish, Harry."

He sits up in his seat. Giving her a time-out sign, he glares at her. "Keep it in-house, okay?"

Sollie springs to stand but has nothing to say. He is beginning to have misgivings about Jewell replacing Wendy Wachter. She has no sense of propriety and runs at the mouth. She is playing too fast and loose, showing all of her cards before she has even played a hand. He can feel tension mounting in the room and finds it to be inconvenient, an obstacle to getting business done. "I must go, but I'll be around if you need me."

Jewell winks at Sollie and pulls her coat around her waist to create a cocoon of warmth. Sollie winks back. Hiring Jewell to replace Wendy Wachter is one thing but getting too close to her is quite another and improbable. He is already pondering the idea of replacing her, eventually, with someone else. He is seeing her true colors—this is the problem with exceptionally beautiful blondes, they always think they are infallible and irreplaceable when nothing could be further from the truth.

After Sollie leaves the room, he lingers in the hall to listen. He hears Jewell ask, "Doesn't anyone think to turn the heat on in here?" No one responds to Jewell, which is good. They know their place. It's a sign of respect. People who have been around Sollie long enough, know he is in the hall with his ears pricked up, eavesdropping. He doesn't trust anyone, except for maybe, Helen, because he can always see her teeth.

Before Ray speaks, he looks toward the hall to see if Sollie is there. Confident that he is gone, he whispers to Jewell. "Sollie suggested we meet here. He's trying to cut costs with the heat bill. Lights too," he says, turning the overhead light on and off.

Jewell's eyes widen at the notion of Sollie being so cheap. So far, he has not been that way with her. She turns her back on Harry and speaks softly to Ray. "I don't know why Wendy gets so upset. She can be very territorial. She thinks she owns Harry, but she doesn't."

"What are you talking about?" Ray asks.

Jewell's hair falls into her eyes, covering one side of her face. "I really can't say."

Dawn Stein walks into the conference room, carrying her tablet in one hand and a Starbucks container in the other. "I've been sworn to secrecy, too."

"I thought you left." Ray is amazed at the pitch of his own voice. "Will someone please tell me what the hell is going on!"

Hill flashes his hand in a long, languid movement. "Just drop it."

"This whole thing has gotten too damn incestuous," Dawn laments, looking at Hill. "Wendy working for you, me hearing stuff she's not supposed to know about. It's wrong." Then she turns to Ray. "Those two are pushing your wife out on her skinny ass, so Sollie can hire Jewell in her place."

"Thanks, Dawn," Ray says in a snotty tone. "Like I needed to hear that!"

Jewell winds her hair around her fingers, forming ringlets as tight as a rope. "It's business, Ray."

Harry's voice booms, "Your wife's paranoid."

"Even paranoids have real enemies," Ray says.

Harry smiles. "Tell me about it, Ray."

Ray smiles coldly. "The worst thing in the world is to find out your friends are really enemies."

"Where do you get that shit, Ray?" His eyes seek Jewell as he scoffs, "Give me a break."

"I don't have any enemies," Steve says. "Everybody likes me."

"That's true," Dawn burbles. "Everyone does like you."

Dawn gives Ray a cautionary scowl. "I don't know what you're going to do about Wendy. A lot of the work she's produced for Harry has come from your agency. I wouldn't want to be in your position. After all, she is your wife."

Then she turns to Harry and Jewell. "After this shoot, I'm done. I can find plenty of work elsewhere."

Harry begins to clap and stands. His black leather coat unfolds, dropping with the heaviness of a tarp down his long torso. "Let's give a standing ovation for the hardest working woman in show business."

Dawn looks to Ray; it is a plea for support, but he too betrays her and begins to clap. He hears someone saying his wife is on the phone. He turns and sees Christy standing in the doorway. "Your wife," she mouths. "She keeps trying your cell, but you don't answer. Would you pick up the phone?"

Ray looks at Jewell and smiles. "Tell her I'm in a meeting, Sweetie."

Christy's voice is out of breath. "She says it's urgent."

Ray winks at Jewell and grins, shaking his head, intimating how annoyed he is by his wife. "Tell Wendy I'm in a long meeting," he says to Christy.

"Please pick up the phone," Christy implores him. "She's called six times."

"Then unplug the phone." Ray turns his back on her.

"I'm so lucky to work with such fabulous people." Dawn drops her Starbucks cup into a trash can and walks out the door.

Jewell tosses her hair abruptly over her shoulder and turns serious. For the first time since Ray has known her, he sees her face pinch in tension. "I have a lot of good ideas about how we will work together in the future."

She gives Ray a look of disdain and it hurts him. It is at this point that Jewell latches onto Harry's arm. Looking at Ray, she smiles. "Say hello to Wendy for me."

Ray is put off by Jewell mentioning his wife. He wonders if she had any feeling for him at all, or whether she was using him to take a stab at Wendy. Jewell's affection for Harry Hill is obvious. No matter how much he had wanted to deny it, it is true. They are an item.

For a long time, Jewell has been the only person to make him smile. But now, he knows what he has been feeling is a lie that he has been telling himself. Jewell is a younger, more attractive, version of the woman he has married. Cold, rejecting, a thin secret smile hardly conceals every selfish thing they do. He runs his fingers through his hair, which is getting thin, and feels the paunch around his waist that thickens with each passing year. The walls are closing in on him.

At the far end of the room, he sees a flash of blond. Hope ricochets in his heart. He thinks Jewell is coming back to him.

The hope initially piercing his heart, explodes with the precision and cruelty of a bullet. He is disappointed the moment he realizes it is not Jewell.

Christy is trembling. "Your wife's still on the phone and I don't know what to tell her."

Her words don't immediately register. Ray is lost in anger or despair; he doesn't know the difference anymore. "Tell her..." He's befuddled. Maybe the girl can help him find the right thing to say. God how he wishes Christy could be Jewell, who is still sitting next to Harry and whispering in his ear.

"Tell Wendy to fuck off," Ray snaps.

Christy looks shocked and gives him an uneven smile. "Thanks, beautiful," she says.

Jewell stands and gives Ray a hard look. "You can rip off any of my ideas if you want. Isn't that what you Ad guys do best?"

Ray flinches. He cannot hide the sting of her words and does not understand where her vitriol is coming from.

Hill rolls his eyes and nods to Jewell. "That was unnecessary."

"That's what I felt like saying." Jewell insists. "I can say anything I want to, now that I'm in charge."

Harry can see that Jewell is rapidly becoming a loose cannon and guides her toward the door. The meeting is breaking up. Everyone is moving to leave with the dark energy of dead weight.

Ray puts his arm around Harry. "Tell me, Harry, wouldn't you just die for a chance to be with Jewell?"

Harry stops. His eyes meet Ray's. Everyone is quiet. Tension spreads from Steve to Jewell like a virus. Whatever strikes them is not only contagious but lethal. Steve takes this as an opportunity to bolt out of the room into the hall.

"Cut it out, Ray!" Beautiful, no most beautiful, Jewell is staring at him.

Crazy with anger, Ray grabs Harry by the sleeve. Harry jerks himself away from Ray and shirks the sleeve of his leather coat like it has been soiled. Ray keeps going after him. His voice is hoarse. "Tell me, is it true? You and Jewell?"

Ray's body tenses with rage. It takes every ounce of control he can muster to forestall bashing Harry's skull. Harry grabs him by the collar. Ray jerks his hand against Harry and wrenches free, which causes Harry to let go of him.

"Ray, you better not be telling people I'm fucking Jewell because if you are, I'll kill you."

Ray Wachter stands face to face with Harry. The powerful scent of leather rankles the inside of Ray's nose. In all of this time, Harry has never bothered to take off his coat. Leather hangs stiff on his body like the carcass of a dead steer. Contrasting sharply with his white skin and blond hair, the heavy coat makes him much taller than his actual height. In this instant, Ray experiences a weird feeling about Harry Hill. This moment transcends time and place and takes on the sensual texture of a dream. He could swear, under oath if he had to, that he knows for certain Harry Hill is about to die.

THIRTY-FIVE

SMPTE TIME CODE: 14:24:12:<u>35</u> Mia Hill relies on her cell phone to check the time, which is 2:24 p.m. She quickly slides the phone back into its plastic pouch, then into her pocket before it is destroyed by water. The grey-blue darkness of the Seattle sky can hardly be seen in the crown of rain. She approaches her own house slowly, balancing Chloe on her hip. The little girl swivels her head inside of her yellow rain jacket, puts her hand out to reach the sky so she can catch raindrops. In a split-second frame, Mia feels as though she is being watched and imagines Viv standing in front of the living room window, wringing her hands, waiting for them to walk through the front door.

The porch light is already on. Gentle yellow light wraps around the front of the house. During these short, dark days of November, it is not uncommon to leave lights on all of the time.

Once they enter the hall, Mia lowers Chloe to the floor and helps her to take off her wet raincoat, giving it a good shake before she hangs it on a Shaker peg. Her own coat comes off too. Next the boots. It feels as though it is a wasted effort to remove these things when she knows soon, she will be heading right back out the door to pick up Max. The children have different schedules at school.

Chloe scampers into the living room, buzzing around in a circle, making the whirring noise of a toy engine. From the living room, Mia kneels before the hearth and adds another log to the fire. Aside from Chloe's patter and the crackle of dry wood, no other sound stirs in the old house. Outside, though, is different. The wind and the rain roar with the strange temporal timbre of a violent storm. Chloe jumps and jumps, landing on her bottom. Giggling softly, she tumbles forward and rolls along the outer edge of the rug, pulling it along with her. Mia sees shadowy forms in the windows and knows it is all an illusion being caused by the fierce wind blowing through the branches of trees.

Good old Viv, Mia thinks and calls out her name. But Viv is nowhere to be found.

Mia's house is ten minutes east of Steve Olin's houseboat, twelve minutes north from Wendy Wachter's condo, eight minutes from downtown and twenty-three minutes away from where her husband will be murdered in thirty minutes.

Her home is one of the oldest in Seattle. Built in 1868, the house had been granted landmark status by the national registry. At one time, the house had been listed on the historical tour of older homes. Once in a while at some ungodly hour on a Saturday morning, Mia intercepted wayward stragglers, usually a trio of older women, who knocked at her front door and politely asked to take a look around. The unexpected visitors moved slowly through the house, nuzzling together coat to coat like wooly old sheep. They never stayed long and apologized for the impromptu invasion.

That is how Mia first found Viv Reinking, touring her home with a group of older women. Taller than the rest of the women with a doughy waist and stout arms, Viv stood out. Viv stayed in touch with Mia. One thing led to another. Mia soon discovered Viv sought part-time work. Being her live-in housekeeper is more than Viv bargained for, but she's good natured, adores the children and does not seem to mind. Even though Viv is in her sixties, she's big and sturdy, an old farm girl worth her weight in gold.

In the living room, Chloe discovers her *bah bah* bear and pulls a small blanket around her tiny body before settling on the couch where she finally sits still. Mia walks around the room, eyeing the dark, unnaturally box-shaped big room with its high ceiling, wondering if she will keep the house after Harry is gone. The house is full of his ghosts. The echoes of shouting, protests in anger, cries of sorrow and ordinary banter are buried in the boards and beams like old bugs stuck in amber.

The ghosts are also the things that are distinctly his: baseball caps, old footballs, two sets of golf clubs, a crawlspace crammed full of tools that had never been used and his collection of guns, rifles and knives. His other possessions, fine suits tailored in black, scores of Nikes, matching socks, coordinated cashmere sweaters, leather jackets, ass-grabbing briefs and trophies from awards won for his television commercials, could easily be stuffed into the back of a car and moved. The house has his robe, his toothbrush, his favorite cups, his toenail clippers, his ashtrays, his collection of matchbooks from every restaurant he had ever been to (all of them containing only one match—to be struck in the face of extremely good luck), his old coke spoons, his condoms, and of course, his hair products. The house is full of all these things, belonging to a man who no longer exists in her life.

And she wants everything gone.

"Chloe," Mia calls. "Stay here while I find Viv."

She feels something sticky under her feet and remembers it is the spot on the floor where Chloe had spilled her milk the night before. "Oh, Chloe," she sighs. The TV is on, tuned in to the low squawk of a cartoon. The child is quiet, nestling into the warmth of her blanket. Her head slides to the arm of the couch as she drifts into her afternoon nap.

Mia tucks the blanket around Chloe, moves her head to rest on a small pale yellow ruffled pillow and brushes her hand across her cheek before giving her a kiss. "Viv and Max will be home soon."

Chloe opens her mouth in a small pant on the way to becoming a yawn and closes her eyes. Mia finds comfort watching her daughter sleep, seeing her bare bud of a chest rise and fall. She listens to the low hum of the TV, the gentle hiss of the fire, and the steady lash of rain against the roof. The wind is far from calm but has stopped violently shaking the house.

There is an ache in her heart for her loss, the loss of her marriage and the loss of her old self before she met Harry. She is traveling from one span of time to another, not knowing for sure why she no longer feels broken. Viv made her snap out of it. Once she knew Harry was trying to drive her stark raving mad, she became whole—a bird who has flown into a car and is thrown to the pavement, startled. Once the bird gets over the shock, it is still quite able to fly.

The dream of Harry's death comes back to her. Even in this moment of quiet reflection, the dream still haunts her.

She bumps into the dining room table. Her eyes cannot seem to adjust to the afternoon gloom or maybe she is simply moving too fast. "Viv," she calls, as is she expects the woman to answer her.

In the kitchen, she sees the telephone and its cord, which has been unplugged. It is the only landline in the house, and she does not understand who would unplug it. The door leading to the basement is slightly ajar. The basement is old, unfinished and lacks proper lighting. Mia uses her phone's flashlight to help her navigate the steps. Peering into the dark crevasse leading into the basement, she descends the steps, bumping her knees against the walls and the banister. As she comes to the end of her descent, she stands on a concrete landing. A faint but distinct trickle of light seeps from beneath a crawlspace. Tears come to her eyes because this is the way it had been in her dream.

The flimsy door to the crawlspace is the perfect height for a child but not the perfect place for a child to be. Mia crouches, squirming into the space that is as large as a grave and reeks of mildew. Mold climbs the walls depositing a rust color stain that is not rust at all. *Wood rot*, she says to herself. She detects the odor of old metal, axle grease, 10w-40 oil and fresh shavings of wood. The trickle of light she has been seeing comes from a plastic plasma night light. The crawlspace is not wired with electricity. The plastic night light is a temporary solution meant to stick on a wall. Someone turned on the orb of light and then left.

Mia holds her phone, beaming its flashlight on the expanse of the concrete floor. Rain has risen in the saturated soil beneath the foundation to form small pools of water in the corners. She sets her flashlight on top of a two by four plywood shelf. A large black wolf spider darts through the thin passage of light and into the shadows where it can no longer be seen. She feels the sensation of cobwebs touching her face and hands, causing her to shiver in fear.

Cold grey metal catches glint from the flashlight, guiding Mia in the right direction. She unhitches the safety snap locks on Harry's gun locker and turns the combination lock, but nothing happens. She tries again, still nothing. It's not possible that Harry has changed the combination. He had not been in the basement for months. She thinks she hears footsteps descending into the basement, of that she is certain because the crawl space is built under the basement's staircase. Worrying that the battery in her phone is running down, she turns off its flashlight.

The lull in the storm is brief. The wind is picking up again. Even from inside of the dark crawlspace, she hears surges of wind wreaking havoc against the old house. Near the exterior basement door, nasty blasts of bickering wind battle against the downspouts and gutters, shaking the house from its roof down to its core. The glass in the basement windows rattle in old wood frames that should have been replaced long ago. Shedding sheaths of wood and sharp splinters, the flimsy door to the crawlspace shudders as if it will blow apart.

She no longer hears footsteps and thinks all along it was probably the sound of the weather taking a turn for the worse. No one could be there except Viv.

"Viv," she calls out, expecting an answer, thinking she might be outside by the door to the crawlspace.

For an instant, she thinks of Harry, but the knowledge and surety of the dream returns. He has hardly come home in years, why would he come home now? She remembers the dream. His murder. The blood. His head blown off, a mangled body, the explosion of entrails. Alive or dead, unfinished business remains between them like the stab of a fresh wound. She holds her breath, knowing in a few moments, the images from the dream will pass as surely as the wind will eventually die down and go away.

The keen of rain and wind is louder, snaking a wet whistle across the concrete floor. Without the flashlight on, the dull light of her phone provides enough light to see the gun safe. She tries the combination lock again. This time it clicks open. In the waning light of her cell phone, she takes stock of his collection. The names of his guns are etched in her memory with as much clarity as she is able to recall the ad slogans in his last director's reel. Small, collectible Derringers good for one shot; Colt commemoratives: *John Wayne*, *Kit Carson*, *Ned Buntline*, the *Panama Canal* and the *Texas Ranger*, a whole set from World War I, a whole host of Winchester rifles: German Crown and Crown Custom, a plastic Glock that could pass through airport security, a .44 Magnum, the kind used by Clint Eastwood in *Dirty Harry*, and a gun called *Snake Eyes* that held meaning for her as potent as the nape piercing on the back of her neck.

THIRTY-SIX

SMPTE TIME CODE 14:51:15:<u>36</u> At 2:51 p.m., the earth beneath the window is sodden and has turned into the thick offal of dead leaves, twigs, twine and mud. Old brown ivy vines border the window and cover the sill curling like fingers that are stiff and unyielding. Short eves overhead provide some protection from the rain but not from the wind that has returned with the majesty of brute strength. There might be a better time to be here, but, for now, there is no turning back.

The stodgy brown rambler dots the grey air and water like a smudge of wet sand. Curtains do not adorn the windows. In one window, a silvery mesh shade has been rolled all the way up, presumably to allow the muted November light into the home. Every important detail can be seen through the glass. The window looks into the dining room, exposing a partial view into the living room, where the gas fireplace is on and a small bonsai tree that sits on the hearth has shed its leaves.

Jewell is sitting on Harry with her legs cast astride as if she's riding a mechanical bull. Only her bare back and hair is visible. His face and torso are blocked by the rhythmic motion of her body. She throws back her head, whipping her body into a frenzy.

Her hand moves to his face. She presses her fingers against his lips, then thrusts them into his mouth. Her other hand holds shears that catch intermittent glow from the fire. In between her thrusts, the top of Harry's head can be seen, revealing stiff blond spikes. His long messy mane is gone. The floor is littered with crushed Starbucks cups, shorn blond locks and a pair of black underpants cut open at the crotch. His hands cradle her rotund bottom, driving her down hard, and harder, driving her wild. All of this is happening without sound. Their voices and cries cannot be heard.

Nor will they ever be heard again.

The shears look very sharp and this could be a problem. It's a judgment call who to take out first. One of Harry's hands runs down the middle of her back, trailing the outline of her recessed spine. It would be fun to kill Jewell with her shears, somehow that would be an appropriate end, but this is no time to be creative. Harry is stronger and the larger threat. He will be the first to go. Jewell will run. She will be second.

Jewell holds the shears against the side of her face as if she is doing her best to look dangerous and alluring, a femme fatale. It would be fun to whack off her hair, but it's too messy and there is not enough time.

Strangely enough, it would be possible to scalp her while shooting the scene for a movie, but this is real time.

Time, time, time. Timing is everything. Using the element of surprise buys more time. Shock is often underrated as being an integral part of any murder strategy. People in shock take too long to respond and are unable to save their own lives.

The bodies of Jewell and Harry look red and shiny in front of the fire. Jewell thinks this is her game—that she is in charge. But whenever women use sex as a weapon or as a tool to get what they want, they become spoiled and do not realize that sex is never enough to sustain one's ambition over the long haul.

Sex like beauty fades.

Harry does not believe he is capable of doing anything wrong. He also thinks he is in charge, and to some extent he is, but he is too blinded by his lack of conscience—that will ultimately cause him to make foolish mistakes, like the very one he is making now. He has been getting away with everything his entire life, but now he is in the wrong place at the wrong time.

The time has come to reveal what is about to occur. There is no traffic on the street. Jewell's and Harry's cars are parked in the driveway which makes it easy to walk around the front of the house undetected by anyone inside.

Water rushes down the driveway. It is best to move the recycling bin to the bottom of the steps, so it is in the way of anyone who tries to get away. The fierce rain and wind mask the possibility of eyewitnesses and the sound of footsteps coming up the front steps. The key to the front door is easily retrieved from the black metal mailbox. Easily slipping into the lock, unlocking the door, then the key drops to the ground and the door is left open.

Moving quickly through the hall, everything is peripheral, a passing blur that does not distract from the core intention. The only glitch is stepping on a black cowboy boot that makes a soft thud. No comfort is found in the sound of breath, or a pounding heartbeat. There is comfort, though, knowing that these sounds cannot be heard by them.

The shotgun has been prepared. The tube takes four rounds. The pump has been pulled back, placing one round in the chamber, leaving three in the tube. This allows adding one extra round into the tube. There are really five shots, three-inch, brutal shells. At a distance of fifteen to twenty feet, missing the target is impossible.

The shotgun is pulled up from under the raincoat and takes aim. Harry Hill does not see it coming, but Jewell does. She shifts her body to the side exposing a full frontal view of Harry. The first blast takes off Harry's head in an explosion of blood, tissue and bone. Pulling back the pump loads the next shell into the chamber. Jewell is running toward the kitchen. The second blast takes off one side of the back of her head. She immediately falls down in the spray of her own blood. The head wounds are so lethal there is no chance of survival. It only took two shots. The shotgun swiftly disappears under the raincoat.

There is no quieter time than the stasis that exists immediately after people have been murdered. The aftermath of violence is a reality that offers a panacea, a respite, a cease fire, a quiet moment of tribute for the newly deceased. As a parting shot, the TV is turned on. It is only fitting that the TV is tuned into nothing, filling the vacuum of quiet with white noise. The back door opens to a backyard and leads to a small gravel path into a neighboring yard where the lights are off. It's nearly 3pm. Long shadows float through the slim alley full of garbage cans that are toppled on their sides, having been blown to the ground by the wind.

THIRTY-SEVEN

SMPTE TIME CODE 21:30:14:<u>37</u> Steve Olin dances in front of the TV in a succession of shuffles and drunken axle turns, all poorly executed. Even sober he's a lousy dancer. The numbing effect of too many warm Coronas has taken its toll. His manic fear has overridden the effect of Ambien and he is unable to drift into sleep. High end fidelity scatters his thoughts like the repeated squeak of chalk across a blackboard. Low end dissonance shakes the walls of his small houseboat. The TV is cranked to its full volume and is too loud to hear the words of the actors. The TV is too loud for him to think—this is the way he wants it loud and annoying, an overwhelming distraction, a legitimate break from reality. It is the only way for him to truly escape. He thinks the ear-piercing blare of the TV will blow him away and remind him of anything else in the world aside from murder.

Then the switch flips. He shoves his hands to his head and covers his ears. He cannot stand the loudness. He is increasingly convinced that the noise coming from his own TV will crush his skull. Instead of turning down the volume, he yanks the cord from the outlet, but forgets about the cables that do not easily wrench free. Groaning a maddening howl, he rips the cords, and ends up abrading his fingers, stripping skin. He unhinges metal prongs, bolts and a hunk of plaster from the wall. A faint spritz of blood stains his hand. Shaking, he is shaking all over. Even though it is only a light wound, he knows the next thing he rips in half will be human.

Silence disturbs him to the point of paralysis. He stares at the TV cord he holds in his hand. "How the fuck did that happen?"

He honestly does not remember. He tries to say something and cannot speak. Approximately thirty seconds have passed. Even in a state of total obsession he knows enough time has passed for fifty-six words of copy to be spoken on screen. He expects the sounds of reality—life on the water—to rise and greet him like a great swelter of music marking the transition of one dramatic scene to another.

But it isn't happening for him.

He waits, adjusting to the quiet, but his rage persists, belting him across both ears, behind his neck, across his forehead and in between his eyes. One blow after the other lands with startling accuracy in a concerted attack. He cannot move his head without suffering the peak rush of a knock-out punch.

Steve Olin buckles his tool belt around his waist. He pats the cowhide pockets holding three Phillips head screwdrivers, a vise-grip, a hammer, a file, a small skill saw, two wrenches, a straight edge razor, a Swiss army knife, and last but not least... he is missing one thing. He turns on his Machida to check the battery and slides it into the widest pocket on his belt.

With the right size bit, the Machida could screw a hole into just about anything. He pats the leather ring of his waist until his hand came to rest on a small buttoned-down pouch that hold his bits. All of his bits are intact. He feels pleased; a five-bit could bore through flesh or even bone.

For now, TV is a distant reality.

Putting on his heavy rain parka, lugging himself through his door, he does his best not to stagger on the narrow gangplank. He knows he has had too much to drink and has taken several tabs of Ambien, but convinces himself that his real problem is with his head. His damn head is so heavy it could take down his entire body.

The dock is extremely narrow and flanked on both sides by deep black water. The heavy rain makes little impression on its surface. The scent in the air is brackish, hinting of saltwater from the Puget Sound. His houseboat is on the western portion of Lake Union, close to the beginning of a long channel that leads to the Ballard Locks.

Water laps against the wharf on both sides of his houseboat. The surface of Lake Union is dark as loam, violently churning against the wharf. Rain and wind slam against his face, but he is too drunk to sober up, and it is too dark to see. The one lamp illuminating the dock is out. The only other source of light is two hundred yards to the street, where there is a parking lot and the distant beams from cars traveling in both directions on Eastlake Avenue.

He breathes hard, worrying about the weight of his head, misshapen and heavy, a concrete boulder that will drag him into the water—a hard black plate, glass-like, catching distant fragments of light. Close to the edge of the dock, black water laps over the surface of wood. One false step on the slick wood would send him slipping off the planks and into the water.

Rain slaughters Steve Olin's pier. Wood squishes under his feet. Three floating homes abut his own. He scans the houseboats, all dark and divided from his pier by a quarter-end dock. No lights, no sound, no action, it is as if he is on a shoot ready to hear *roll sound, lights, camera,* and *Action.*

A peculiar thought occurs to him. What if someone has a video camera and is taping him? Dark silhouettes of windows, portholes, buoys on the bay, appear vitrified in layers by the slim slant of light beaming across the black water.

Even he, Steve Olin, could not shoot in the total absence of light.

A great director covers a scene from every angle.

As always, the opportunity to direct is everywhere.

An exhilarating high shoots through his body and lightens his limbs. The story doesn't matter. All that matters are the images—that is the essence of good filmmaking.

Actors get into character and become someone else, but it is the director who is God. It is the director who pours animus into flesh and blood and breathes life onto the transparency of the screen. Actors become the characters who did not have a soul on their own recognizance. It is the director who possesses the sole power to create and extinguish life. Steve inhales deeply and sees his breath rise in the dark, cold air. He knows he is experiencing an epiphany. He is beginning to see the scene unfold from behind the eye of the TV.

He is aware of a distant hum, the gentle purr of machinery, which brings him a rush of immense satisfaction. He is the director and the shoot is happening right now. The location is outside, night on the water. Away from a standard electrical outlet or power source, the mechanical purr is from generators. *Gennies* are needed to juice the lights.

Night, water, rain—Steve has ordered an assortment of powerful lights to illuminate the set. The mechanical purr of the gennies is coming from the sidelines and hidden from the camera.

His confidence is bolstered by the sight of barricades. Wooden sawhorses, each one has a sign *No parking*. Ordinary people are not allowed to park their cars too close to a film shoot. Onlookers and other hangers-on must stand way in the background in the dark, behind the action.

In his sweep of delirium, Steve finds redemption in one other cardinal law of film: Only the director calls *Action*.

The intensity of hot lights makes his face burn. Sweat and rain pours down his neck, sopping the collar of his jacket. He shivers from exposure to the damp air. He wonders how he could be cold when the lights are so hot, like blue gel cooling the lens of a hot camera.

No one needs to tell him how to capture the night on film. The time has come to make his mark. He is going to take it from the top. He moves backward into the shadows.

The pier pitches down at a slight decline. He treads
carefully, marking every slick plank of wood. Light follows
him but blackness hems him in on both sides. Stray beams
of light catch swells of waves and render them to mist. He
is surrounded by water. How easy it is to forget that his feet
are wading through water. He rolls down the pier on the
momentum of running water. A fresh dam of rain cuts
loose, wrapping around his body like a tarp of tears. Water
is as maddening as light and the night. There is too much
water, too much light, too much madness. He could easily
drown in the water and the night.

Steve Olin's route to escape is searching for the black
hole hidden in the night sky. He likes dark things, dark
thoughts, dark moods, and, often, dark women.

He thinks of light as a mirage, a tool to use expressing
fun and fantasy before the almighty lens of the camera. Too
much light bleeds the clarity of images.

Too little light creates shadows in the background, or
ghosts in the foreground circling the perimeter of heads,
faces and bodies.

He is in the dark now and it does not bother him. Not
being able to see does not raise a shred of fear.

Blackness comes to him like a companion and stays
by his side. For the first time in weeks or months he feels
strangely wonderful, renewed and full of the burn to
succeed. He has no sense of guilt, shame, or remorse. For
the first time, he is able to acknowledge the dark part of
himself that he has kept hidden from all the rest.

He throws off his hood and looks up to the black
ceiling of sky. The rain has stopped. Throwing his hands
over his eyes, he crouches down onto the wet wood. The

weight of his own head propels him into blackness as vast as a winding mountain road in a car commercial.

Steve finds redemption in another cardinal law of film: Only the director calls *Cut*.

His legs feel truncated from his body and the tips of his boots touch the edge of the wharf, gripping the last shred of creosote. Churning black water laps against the bulkhead. He hears the tread of tires hitting wood, voices, lots of footsteps running, pounding down the pier.

He feels the hard smack of his body hitting concrete. A strobe light sears his eyes. His head swims in light. He sees double rainbows. His eyes feel like they are dissolving into the light. He does not know who is trying to hold him to the ground. He fights to save his life. On his back, he cannot see. Clenching his arms to protect his face, he kicks with his legs. They flip him on the ground where he lies, floundering on his stomach like a big fat fish.

No matter how hard he kicks, his legs are being pried apart. His arms are pinned to the ground and spread open above his head. His knees are pressed together, pushing upward.

Forced to sprawl spread eagle, pinned to the wet wood, he feels like a drunken bum who has been set on fire on a cold night. There are voices and the slight whir of a motor. Handcuffs lock tight and hard around his wrists. He opens his eyes and looks around. The strobe light is gone. What remains is a soft blue glow from the fluorescent streetlamp in the parking lot. He sees the cops; there are five of them, wearing face masks and surgical gloves.

They turn him over onto his back but keep him on the ground. He does not know who they are or what they are doing to him, yet they call him by name. He visualizes the narrow dock penciling a line to his houseboat and the watery blackness on either side. He thinks about making a break for it. He knows he did not do anything wrong. He hears another voice telling him he is under arrest. He feels his tool belt roughly yanked away from his body. Someone reads him his rights. And he is amazed to see a very large, square-shaped head zoom in. Even though the cop is wearing a face mask, Steve remembers him. Earlier in the police car, Steve could not make out the color of his eyes. This time, however, Mulcahy's eyes are washed out by the light.

"Just stay calm, son, and you won't get hurt," the cop tells him.

Steve pleads with him. "Just let me get the shot. Please just let me get one more shot. I'll do anything. You won't be sorry, I promise."

One of the cops hands his tool belt to Joanna Keating.

"Even if I smeared the lens of the camera with Vaseline, I couldn't work with you. You don't have the look! Got it!"

A sloppy grin spreads across her stern white face. The heightened tension between Steve and Joanna Keating manifests itself in unnatural calm. She plays with his Machida, bouncing it around, pointing it upward as if she is going to nail clouds to the sky.

Weakly, he mumbles an apology. "I didn't mean to say that to you. What I meant to say is... I shouldn't have attempted a night shoot in the rain."

Joanna Keating lowers the Machida to her side. "It's a wrap," she says.

THIRTY-EIGHT

SMPTE TIME CODE 20:51:19:38 Close to nine on Thursday night, the kitchen in Dietro's is about to stop serving. Dawn Stein peers into the restaurant through fogged-up glass and drizzle blisters bleeding water. She knows bar food is still available and has the menu memorized: potato skins, jumbo shrimp, deep fried calamari, steamed mussels, pan fried baby oysters, roasted garlic, goat cheese rolled in coarse ground black pepper, and Susan Kauffman's fabulous French bread. Dawn's stomach rumbles as she nudges Koji through the door into the restaurant.

Susan Kauffman welcomes them with outstretched arms and holds Dawn's head close to her shoulder. "I know how terrible this must be for you. What a shock."

For once Susan didn't mind Koji Matsuno and bid him to sit. "Find a place and I'll get you both something to eat."

Susan's passion for food extends beyond the restaurant to include a catering business primarily serving film crews shooting on location. In lieu of her fabulous appreciation for the real movie-making-business-down-south, it is the local filmmakers who she holds closest to her heart. She knows all of them. She always feels someone is on the verge of making the big time, so then she can say, *Remember when you were nobody and I believed in you.*

Dawn feels warmth rise in her body and nods to the open bottle of wine that Susan sets in front of them with two glasses and a plate of her French bread. Dawn dives for the bread while Susan pours wine, which Koji declines, prompting Susan to give him a disgusted look. "Don't look a gift horse in the mouth," she tells him, pouring wine into his glass. His eyes drift to the TV above the bar.

"I'm famished." Dawn takes a thick slab and bastes it with sweet butter and eats the bread in three bites before raising her glass. "Here's to Susan's bread."

Susan looks pleased. "Stay as long as you like. I'm going to close early tonight, but you don't have to leave. I may even close tomorrow...because of what's happened. I'll have to think about it," she says, walking away. "I'll fix you something special if you like and the wine is on the house."

Dawn glances toward Susan Kauffman's kitchen. Framed photographs cover the back wall of the restaurant with the faces of the famous, soon to be famous, and the dead—with his blond hair cascading down his back, Harry Hill is on a sound stage, kneeling in front of a 35mm camera as if he is paying tribute to a pagan god.

Susan returns, balancing a plate of jumbo shrimp and pan seared oysters along with her own wine glass, and some dried snacks: Thai lime cashews and wasabi coated soybeans. The spikey-green-haired waitress rushes over with small plates, napkins and forks.

Susan maneuvers her large body in between Dawn and Koji and sits with them side by side.

"Ever notice how much men get distracted by the television?" Susan waves her hand in front of Koji's eyes. He does not blink.

Dawn also fans her hands before Koji's eyes. "It's in their genes."

This time Koji blinks and moves his chair a few inches away.

Susan leans forward and lowers her head onto her elbows, resting her fleshy face in her hands. In the amber light, she tilts her face toward Dawn, slightly lopsided. "From day to day, I never know how long I'm going to be in business. I can close my restaurant down with no warning. The only notice I have to post is a closed sign in the front window. The courts and the lawyers can do the rest. The restaurant business is like that."

Dawn pats her hand. "Most businesses are like that." She taps her glass gently against each of their glasses. "To Harry Hill. Wherever he is now, may he rest in peace."

"Or Hell!" Susan chortles, making everyone laugh. "Give them hell, Harry!"

Their glasses come together, clinking a final sequence of notes. "To Harry Hill," Koji says solemnly.

One by one in different tones they say his name again and toast. "Harry Hill."

Susan stares into a small white votive candle on the table. The light flickers on her nose and chin, leaving dark shadows under her eyes and along the sides of her flabby cheeks. She takes a large gulp of wine. "I usually don't drink, but tonight's an exception. If you work in this business and drink, it's murder."

She strokes Dawn's hair, pushing a frizzy lock off her cheek, gives her hand a squeeze and whispers. "So, who do you think did it?"

"Without a doubt, the wife."

"Huh, is that so?" Susan intones to herself, "Mmm, yeah, I can see that," and nods.

"Koji?" Dawn asks. "I'm listening."

Koji is so drawn and shaken that Dawn wants to hug him. "I hear everything."

"Well?"

Koji looks grim and nods his head. He waves his vape like a magic wand and lifts it to his mouth. "The wife."

Susan raises her glass. "Amen to that."

THIRTY-NINE

SMPTE TIME CODE 23:56:01:<u>39</u> At four minutes to midnight, Mia Hill sits in front of the fire and presses her hand against the windowpane, leaving fingerprints. She takes a small blue cloth to wipe away condensation from the glass so that she can look out into the night. The wind serves little purpose other than to summon a keener force of rain. The rain did not come from the north or south like wind. Under the dome of the street lamp, rain cuts across a weary sky, moving forward with the wind, then backward and on the diagonal. Wheeling downward like an axle with a faceless head, water penetrates the heart of all matter and rebounds from the earth like a constant splash from a violent sea.

Fire illuminates the room on this night and is kept burning by Viv. All lights have been turned off except for a small table lamp next to a wingback chair. Some of the creaks inside are familiar, other creaks outside groan like wood splintering from the force of the wind gyring around the house.

The children have been put to bed but they are unsettled. She hears Viv upstairs talking to them with a soothing lilt. Mia has been with them most of the night and is exhausted.

There is no way to fool a child. A child always knows when something is wrong. A child does not have to hear or see or touch first hand. Children can feel bad tidings in the very core of their hearts. It is as if their souls are so full of light, any darkness at all leaves a shadow that cannot be rationally explained away. Monsters, bogeyman and demons had paid Mia's children a visit, covering them in their dark beds in the disguise of a bad dream. They would not sleep soundly, not this night, not on the night of their father's murder.

Mia is afraid to sleep. She does not know what she will dream. Yet it is happening, the spiraling descent between the conscious and the unknown. She dissolves into the couch, not quite laying down her body, but slumping slightly to the side. If she had to pick a dream, it would be one where she could see herself doing things—the star— and yet at the same time a part of her is held in reserve and objective, watching the action her active persona, the star, cannot see.

In the dream, she would not sleep in the bed she shared with Harry. She knew she would not sleep there ever again.

She hears feet coming down the steps. It reminds her of the time earlier in the day when she was in the crawlspace and thought she heard steps, but it turned out to be nothing.

"Viv," she calls. "Are you there?"

Viv walks into the room and nods. "They're finally asleep." She sits in the wingback chair across from Mia. "Did you feel the temblor this morning?"

Mia nods slowly. "Just before four."

"Yes," Viv says, pushing back her hair as if she means to fluff the grey tresses that curl in soft ringlets behind her ears. "There is something I've been meaning to tell you. The police have a suspect in custody. The Grip."

Mia sits straight and looks at her. "How do you know?"

"They called me." She looks embarrassed and goes on. "They had phoned me earlier to ask if you were here this afternoon, around three." She gives Mia a hard knowing glance. "I told them you were here all afternoon."

"But you weren't here," Mia shot back. "How could you say I was here if you did not know?"

The only light from the small table lamp lit one side of Viv's face. Mia had never seen Viv look quite so harsh, almost cruel. Her eyes are troubled and dark. It is not that she is weary, something else is wrong. Mia is aware that her own body is trembling. She feels clammy and yet she is cold. She remembers the phone in the kitchen being disconnected and wonders how anyone could have called

Viv—that phone did not ring. They must have called her cell.

"I'm confused," Mia says.

"Don't be. What was happening to you, happened to me once. But it was a long time ago and I never got over it."

An enormous rush of feeling washes over Mia like violent rain. The old woman exudes grief so intense and so profound that it cuts off Mia's breath. Mia doesn't look at Viv or need to say anything to her. She can feel the depth of her pain.

Mia gets up from the couch, taking a plush throw blanket with her. She shivers as she walks over to the window. She looks toward the street lamp. The rain is coming down in large cold drops. It is the same blistering rain that is so cold it often burns her face. The wind is missing in action, a temporary cease fire. Her car is parked close to the front of the house, the same place where she had last left it.

She turns around and looks at Viv whose head is bowed, almost as if she is in the midst of prayer. "Where were you this afternoon around three?"

Viv's eyes greet Mia's eyes with the resolve of steel so well tempered that it cuts through the damp air between them. "You have to take people the way you find them. Sometimes we have wounds so deep that the slightest trigger can send us reeling."

"Will the police be coming back?"

Viv shakes her head. "No. Of that, I am certain."

Mia cannot believe that the police would not return. She knew she had to be a prime murder suspect. She had reason to kill Harry. Abuse. Adultery. Jewell Cleary had not been the first. There had been many others.

"What about the Grip?"

"Eventually they will let him go. The police have nothing to go on." Viv's eyes travel upward to the ceiling, where she knows there is a camera placed in its far corner. Smiling stiffly, she turns her attention to the fireplace and speaks into the hearth, away from camera. "This morning Harry asked me to change the combination on his gun safe to keep you from hurting someone or yourself. He said you were mentally ill." Using a poker from an ornately carved brass stand, she tends the fire, beating shards of wood, sending sparks flying, breaking apart embers. "But I didn't change the lock. The only type of firearm Harry did not own was a shotgun."

Mia remembers Viv telling her she grew up using a shotgun. Hunting.

"Harry made you forget who you are. He tried to destroy you. As women we come to marriage pure of heart. We never expect that the greatest enemy of our lives will lie in bed beside us."

She turns to Mia and smiles contritely. "I am so very tired and must go home to my own bed. It's been a very long day."

Mia looks over her shoulder, watching Viv gathering her things in the hall, putting on her raincoat and a small plastic rain bonnet. Even though the woman usually stays overnight on Thursday, Mia does not try to convince her to stay. She follows her into the hall. Feeling weak in the knees, she grabs onto the banister, quickly pulling her hand back before it has a chance to wobble. Then she realizes it is stable and no longer shakes.

"I fixed it." Viv smiles. "Long ago, I lived in an old house like this." She nods to the living room. "Make sure the fire is out before you go to bed. The chimney is old and needs to be cleaned. And the bricks need to be mortared." She gives Mia a knowing glance. "I checked."

Viv lets herself out, quietly closing the door. Mia hears Viv's footsteps going away and the start of her old blue Camry. The car has over 200,000 miles. She keeps her car in fine shape. Viv does her own tune-ups. She's mechanically inclined.

Viv had reason to kill Harry, but Mia might never know why, and maybe it didn't matter. The dream foretelling Harry's death stood on its own merits, an isolated moment in time that had somehow come true. Now the time had come for the dream to end.

Although the fire has turned into a fine bed of coals, the floor of the hearth is coated with larger chunks of charred wood that still have yet to burn. The silence of the house comforts her. It has never been this quiet. There is always the yelp of a child wanting affection, demanding to be picked up, put down. The clink and bang of old radiators. The mad scramble of children wrestling on the floor above her head. Footsteps up and down the front porch. Oven doors, refrigerator doors, cabinet doors, outside doors, car doors; doors are always slamming shut. The bark of dogs from neighboring homes. Cars driving too fast down the street in front of her house and the crash of the newspaper against the front storm door. There is always something. But tonight, on the night of Harry Hill's murder, there is nothing except silence, barely perceptible, above the persistent whisper of the rain.

FORTY

SMPTE TIME CODE 03:22:22:<u>40</u> Kenny studies the image on screen. The young dude's knuckles rap against a brass knocker on an oak door. Freezing the frame, he considers it and gets ready to insert a shot from the slave deck. His fingers strain to tap the switch on the master deck. The master monitor scatters picture moving fast forward, flaring flashes of red and blue, gunning rapid syllabic distortion of dialog running faster than it was ever intended to go. Kenny picks up a chipped mug from off of the ECB and takes a sip; the coffee is cold, but he drinks it anyway.

Andy speaks rapidly as if she is out of breath. "Scene 104, roll one. The director circled take six."

Kenny's eyes never leave the monitor. His voice is melodramatic and falls flat in the soundproof room. "Remember where you were and lock the position."

Kenny reaches for her, grabs her hand and looks intensely into her eyes. "Most directors don't know what the fuck they're doing. They think they do and that's the fucking problem. All directors are good for is their name."

He touches her cheek. "Eye candy," he says. "You're too pretty to die young. But you might have to."

Andy shirks from his touch, but still wants to appear cool about it.

"Relax." He laughs. "Only the good die young and you're not good enough."

Kenny's laugh erupts into a scratchy cough. He's made a crude joke at her expense. Turning his eyes to the monitor, his hands are steady as he prods his thumb against the master deck, entering the edit of a woman's hand, wrapped around the butt of a shotgun. "Get me a smoke."

Andy doesn't say anything. She slouches into the side of the ECB, rummaging for Camels and his Bic. She pulls a Camel out of the pack and puts it into Kenny's mouth for him. He holds it in between his lips, letting it dangle until she lights it.

Kenny swivels forward to the master deck. Gazing at the monitor, he runs the same snippets of tape through the machine again. Close-up on a man's booted foot slamming a door shut with the force of a hard club.

Exhaling a long plume of smoke, Kenny rambles. "The bit is meant to be powerful," Kenny says. "Kicking the door shut is rooted in his primitive urge to be brutal. He's just being a man. Man in all of his heroic majesty is nothing less than a conqueror, an animal, a barbarian. Even when it comes to carnal feats and affairs of the heart, there isn't a dude in this whole world who doesn't want to take a woman by force."

Andy swallows hard and bows her head in a humble show of resignation. It's obvious that she has been broken. She's won the battle against Ensley, but what has she really won? Now she will have to bear the full brunt of his psychotic ranting without having a relief pitcher to take some of the heat. Her eyes scan the edit log affixed to a clipboard and skip upward to the monitors. She turns to Kenny and smiles. "Scene 109, circle take four."

"You see that foot there." He points to the one big foot on the screen.

"That foot there does not, I repeat, does not belong to the young dude." He elbows her in the ribs. "As a matter of fact, that dude probably wore a size eight shoe."

Kenny points to the screen. "That foot belongs to one of them parts models. The young dude's feet were not powerful enough to fit the agency's expectations. A man's gotta have big feet. Big feet means he's got a big dick."

Kenny is aware of several things happening all at once. Aside from the Andy looking green, the door to the editing suite is thrown open from the outside. Kenny is so charged, he immediately lights another cigarette without noticing that he has one burning in the ashtray.

A lanky figure clad in black leather blows into the room along with a rush of electronic-scented air. To Kenny, the dude is extremely tall and smells like a director.

"How's it going?" Harry Hill asks.

Kenny and Andy smile, tight and biting. The director's eyes are bloodshot and he reeks of alcohol.

Kenny holds his hands over his heart and says, "I'm so blown away." He nudges Andy. "She's blown away too. Aren't you, doll?"

Andy bobbles her head. The white light from the hall casts a blue sheen on her curly blond hair. Kenny slouches in his swivel seat, slipping, about to fall off. Before he even has time to think about it, he is bullshitting up a storm.

"I'm like really touched," Kenny goes on. "I'm too moved to speak. It's like really real. The lighting is like perfect. The blonde is just gorgeous, so is the dark girl. The guy is like a guy. The old lady is a great character! This spot is a fucking mystery unraveled before our very eyes! This is the greatest work I've seen in a long time—from any director. It's so well covered, I don't even have to think about cutting it. Seriously, it cuts like butter."

Harry rocks back on his heels, unsteady on his feet as he helps himself to one of Kenny's cigarettes. "Let me see what you've cut."

"This may be like the fucking greatest spot you've ever made." Kenny assures him, and nods to Andy. She jogs the dial to preview, rolling frames forward in sequential order, showing the rough cut in progress. The young dude walking up to the house, ringing the doorbell. The door swings open. Beautiful girl throws herself into the young dude's arms. Young dude's booted foot slams the door shut behind them. The grey-haired old lady lurks outside of the house, watching, waiting—a cameo role.

"Let me see that again," Harry says.

Kenny nods to Andy. "Take it from the top."

"No," Harry says, spewing smoke. "I just want the last shot."

This time Kenny works the deck himself. He reverses the last few frames, then jogs forward. The young dude's foot slams against the inside of an oak door.

"Beautiful boots," Harry says. "Jewell got them for me. She had them custom made. Those are fifteen-hundred-dollar boots. Look, I'm wearing them. See." He lifts one of his feet to show Kenny. "That's my foot in the spot."

Kenny nods, admiring them. "Snakeskin. Cool."

Andy's eyes glow. "Where'd she get those boots?"

Harry looks at her and smiles. "Calgary." He looks down at his boots. "If you want great western boots, go to Calgary."

"Calgary." Kenny nods *uh-huh* like the boots are the most important thing in his life.

Harry abruptly turns to Kenny and yells, "Let me see the cut again!"

Kenny snaps his wrists against the deck. Again, they watch a close-up shot of the boot kicking the door. Except for the squeak of videotape, the room is silent. Kenny and Andy bow their heads, waiting for the director's approval.

Harry takes his own sweet time assessing the frame. He knows they are waiting on him. No one else says a word. He walks behind where Andy is sitting, so he can look at the frame from different angles. Finally, Harry speaks. "I'm not sure I like it. It cuts but I don't know if it's the best take."

"It's the one you wanted," Kenny says. "It's your circle take."

"I still want to see what we've got."

Kenny is pissed but he does not show it. He hits the control on the slave deck to preview all the other takes of the boot kick. As the footage spins by, warbling the sound of dying honeybees, Kenny intones. "Great boots you got on, sir."

The stop on the first take shows too much cuff on the young dude's leg. "Great fucking boots," Kenny mutters.

The next take looks exactly the same, but Kenny gets excited. "Check out that stitching on the side of them boots. I mean, I didn't notice that before!"

The third take misses the full range of motion in the kick. Harry looks down at his feet.

Kenny nods as if this was the most important thing in his life. "Uh-huh. You're right," he says. "Those are great fucking boots."

The fourth take is the director's circle take. Kenny makes a jump cut of his own. "Who shot this? This is like fucking great shit. Who'd you say shot it?"

"I did."

"No shit. You're the director, I can't believe you shot your own feet." Kenny is in awe. Not only did the director have big feet but he somehow finagled the ability to shoot his own dang foot. "No shit!" He can't figure how anyone could shoot his own foot kicking against a door from a reverse POV. What happened to your DP?"

"I sidelined my DP." Harry shrugs and smiles. "I'm trying a new technique."

"Hell, shooting your own feet is like walking on water." Kenny holds his fingers up to his lips so Andy will get him a cigarette. It pisses him off that she did not anticipate his urgent need.

"Let me see the rough cut again." Harry stubs his cigarette in the ashtray and leaves it smoldering. "How can you smoke these things?"

Kenny runs through each take again. He looks at the screen in awe, as if he is seeing the footage for the first time. "Great technique. I'm like impressed. This is a truly bonafide fucking fine piece of filmmaking."

Harry's voice dips lower and is well-modulated, casting a spellbound effect. "All day, I worked on this one shot. The close-up had to be a match. It was a very important set-up; the camera was locked-off. I knew later in post, they'd have to match in a special effect. The set was hot. The camera was hot. Everything is in position. If anyone were to touch that camera, the shot would be blown. A whole morning's work down the tubes. We're not talking overtime. We're talking an extra shoot day. Money. Heads would roll."

Harry closes his eyes, pretending to be blind, wading his arms though the smoky air as though he is swimming in water. "This dumbshit Grip wanders onto the set. The Grip walks right up near the camera. Now the rest of the crew is watching this happen, but they don't really believe the worst can come true."

"I'll wager the producer didn't see any of this happening?" Andy squeaks.

"That's right," Harry shouts. "That's why I had to get rid of her! It's not the first time Wendy Wachter screwed up!"

"That sucks," Andy says.

Kenny does not appreciate Andy butting in, sucking up. "Do you want to tell the story!"

"No." She looks like her teeth are chattering.

"Then shut up." Kenny stubs out his cigarette into a clean ashtray.

Harry laughs, shaking his head. "This *dumbshit* Grip walks right up next to this locked-off camera and bumps it, like this…." Harry bumps his hip against Andy's shoulder.

He can feel the girl's small body shudder, but she is too afraid to move.

Kenny swings around and claps excitedly for Harry to continue. "And the director? What did the director do?"

"Do you want to know what the director did?"

Andy giggles. "I bet that Grip will never work again."

"Right." For Harry it's a moment of triumph. He has them eating out of his hand, hanging on to every word. In the sharp flood of video light, their eyes are huge and hungry. Kenny brushes his hair away from his face, streaming it into a messy ponytail.

"I walked over to the camera and knocked it on purpose." Harry shines a smile that is meant to be a blatant act of seduction.

Kenny looks at Andy and doesn't like what he sees. Tears are coming to her tiny eyes.

Harry leans into Andy and takes one of her cigarettes. "I saved that Grip's ass!"

Andy gives him a look of total adoration. It does not go unnoticed by Kenny and causes him at first to get pissed, then he laughs maniacally. He shakes out his hair from his mock ponytail and fires off his words. "Bet you still fired that Grip's ass!"

Harry gives him a condescending smile. "I'm going to fire him tomorrow right after he drives me to the airport. By then, no one will remember why."

Andy giggles again. Harry gives her a curt smile because she's cute; he wouldn't mind banging her. Maybe some other time. Then he turns around to leave.

Kenny could feel the air shift; the weight of his leather coat has a fan effect. Kenny is tempted to ask what happened to Jewell Cleary and why she had left with Ray Wachter, but he knows his place. He hears the door close, which automatically dims the lights. The scent of Harry's leather lingers in the room. The girl hands Kenny a burning cigarette. He takes one long drag before he opens up.

Kenny stands, flailing his arms, pointing to the door and screaming, "He is not a filmmaker! How could he claim he shot his own fucking feet! He is a fucking insult to my intelligence!"

Manning his position between the two monitors as if he has taken possession of a machine gun, he taps furiously into the source deck and starts pulling shots—all circle takes. Editing feverishly, he purposefully does not ask for Andy's assistance.

"He doesn't know a goddamn thing about making films!"

On the monitor, the young dude is carrying the blonde. Kenny screams, "Fucking primadonna," as he enters the shot into the master deck.

Next cut, the young dude sets down the girl in the living room. Next cut, closeup to the blonde's face. Next cut, the blonde twirls around the dude with shiny sharp scissors in her hand. "Look how her scissors catch the light. You just know she's going to give this dude a mighty fine haircut!"

As Kenny enters the edit into the master, he hits the deck so hard, the image on the monitor bounces. "This dude's hair looks on fire. They lit it too hot. See that *bleed out* behind his ear. Hill doesn't know what the fuck he's doing. He doesn't know what the fuck he's saying. And he calls himself a director!"

Kenny pounds his fists on the ECB. "Who the fuck does Harry Hill think he is? He thinks a fucking pair of boots is going to make him look like a director!"

The next take is a sweep. The girl is on top of the dude in a final embrace. Her shirt falls off her shoulder. They are hugging, kissing, melding into one. The camera is pulling back, holding on the embrace. "Just wait and see how fucking hard Harry Hill will fight me over this cut. All jump cuts! He'll hate it, I guarantee it, but I could give a fuck…because he'll go for it. Deep down inside he knows he's not any good."

Kenny's hands are jittery, the same as those days when he was on toot. He's talking fast too. "One of these days, I'd like to kill the fucker, blow his fucking head off and leave it on the floor between his snakeskin boots!"

The room rocks and pitches. Kenny feels like he is in a small boat, adrift on the Puget Sound. There is no noise except for and eerie rattle coming from five crushed coke cans and three pens on top of the ECB. An empty Starbucks container falls on its side. His pack of Camels has not moved, but his Bic trembles as though it has a mind of its own. The rolling sensation only lasts for seconds then stops in a mild lurch. Kenny feels wobbly in his seat, a delayed reaction. Too many hours in the cutting room makes the ceiling look like a dark sky raining with small hailstones of fire.

"Did you feel that?" Andy asks. She felt something too.

"What?" Kenny looks around, dazed. "Not sure what I felt."

The video tape has run to the end. The screen turns prickly haze. Kenny relaxes. He had his cut. He would get paid. "What a piece of shit!" He sighs.

Andy scrolls through messages on her phone. "There's been a small temblor," she tells him. "That's what we were feeling. It's mild." She reads from her phone. "A magnitude 3.2 earthquake struck near Snoqualmie at 3:38 a.m."

The blank monitor buzzes. The room has absorbed an infinite amount of high energy but does not return comfort. Kenny's job is done. Cutting is hard work. He's sweating, dripping under his arms, but his palms are dry. Sweaty palms are a sure sign of being of a pussy. The Master would agree.

"Film keeps its own time." Kenny jogs the dial, making his points as they occur to him. "Film is circuitous in nature, moving fast forward and in reverse, in slow motion and rapid pace editing, jump cuts and close ups, two shots and over the shoulder, point of view. The long shot, wider, opening-up, the moving shot, ambiance and the sweep."

Andy nods. She is really hearing him. "Your spot's looking good. This is really where the film gets made."

Kenny moves the dial as if he is molding clay. "Film throws out extraneous words—dialog, copy—having everything or nothing to do with the imagery it is projecting. Television commercials are the short form. Movies are journeys for the long haul. Film is the essence of rhythm constantly transcending life's experiences in a cathartic patois of perfect, unspoken, images. Film possesses its own measure, its own momentum and its own reality."

Kenny holds his own thoughts, taking a thoughtful beat. He is totally in awe of what he has just said. He catches his own reflection in the glass of the monitor and thinks it's ugly, but nonetheless awesome. No edits, no playbacks, he knows he is the meanest cutter alive.

"What's this commercial for?"

Kenny can't believe that after all of this time that she has asked such a dumb question. "Lady, who gives a shit? Who cares what it's for? It's all the same shit."

Trying to recharge, he takes a deep breath. His chest hurts from smoking. The room is sealed in the dark. The only light comes from the two video monitors. The master screen rolls a slow sweep of everything he has cut. Cutting red-eye late into the night, anything can happen. After a while a man's eyes are no longer the same. He stops being able to see things or begins to see things that are not here. A part of him thinks he can see Harry Hill, but he knows he is not there.

He turns to Andy and smiles. "Let's call it a night. It's a wrap."

Andy Andrisevic feels confident. She thinks she has passed the test with flying colors. "Just text me my new hours," she sweetly says.

Andy is too self-conscious for Kenny's liking. He talks directly into her face. His warm spittle tickles her nose. He tells her he hasn't made up his mind yet, but the truth is he has. He's already made the call, requesting two new interns. Fresh meat. He isn't going to keep Andy as his assistant. She isn't quite right. His hand sweeps through the air with the majesty of what he perceives to be the flair of a great orator, and he is loving it. "No matter what, you've got to believe in the magic of film."

Fade
to
Black

About Patricia Vaccarino

Patricia Vaccarino is an American writer. She has written award-winning film scripts, press materials, content, books, essays and articles. She has published four novels, and five nonfiction books. She founded the P.R. firm Xanthus Communications LLC, and the internet media company, PR for People®, where people share their news. She has an audience of 40,000+ followers on social media. She divides her time between homes in downtown Seattle and the north coast of Oregon.

Made in the USA
Coppell, TX
08 November 2021